The
Unworthy
Blood Knight

The Unworthy Blood Knight

A Tale of Vampires, Clerics, and Aristocrats
Tome One

Negus Lamont

ISBN Print: 978-0-920583-12-8
IBSN E-Book: 978-0-920583-16-6
Masani Press
Toronto, Ontario

*I dedicate this novel to all those
who seek wisdom, may you find the
hidden meaning within.*

CONTENTS

BLOOD AND COIN

Zurie watched as the hooded figure slowly approached with a blood-stained sack over one shoulder. Upon seeing the visage of a hook, she placed her palm underneath the counter. *I really hope there isn't any trouble. This new location has served me well so far but why is this person brandishing a hook? Every time I request assistance, I get chastised.* By the time she snapped back to the present moment, the figure was already through the door of the small wooden shop and in the patron's seat. *Hopefully, this patron will be similar to the last handful.*

Faking a massive smile, she spoke. "Greetings, great patron. Welcome to the Merchant's Corner, a vampire den which services humans and vamps alike. The only true neutral trading den in the entire city. Our motto is: You want it, we have it. You got it, we buy it." She shuffled in the wooden chair easing the pain on her buttocks.

The figure raised its head and took off the hood that covered his face. With a sneer he revealed a row of sharp iron teeth. "We will see about that."

Upon closer inspection he has iron fingernails as well as iron teeth. That, in conjunction with his silver hair, tells me he must be one of the rare and often aggressive Sasabonsam from the Dark Continent. I'll have to tread carefully. She licked her lips. *I wonder what great treasures he has brought from the Dark Continent. Perhaps something of legendary status. I have never had a legendary artifact in my humble shop before. That fat slob Rufus will be so jealous of me when I walk in with something like that.* The sound of an iron fingernail scratching against the brass counter summoned her attention. The Sasabonsam squinted as he observed the contents of the quaint shop. His eyes darted from the glowing black candles to the empty shelves.

With a low chuckle, he said, "Are you sure you're from the Merchant's Corner? I heard they always had full stock of valuables."

Zurie lowered her head. As she shrunk her body, she said, "They don't trust me anymore with the valuables. I must order everything on demand." Pausing to rub the back of her neck, she continued, "One could say I was taken advantage of and deserve to be wallowing in The Order's fighting pits. Members of my den tell me a weak vamp is a useless vamp."

The Sasabonsam burst out into laughter. One didn't need the supreme hearing of a vampire to know that he could be heard from a long distance. He reached into his large bloodstained sack to pull out an object that was odd yet familiar to her. Zurie peered closer as she poked it with her quill. The sapphire in the middle was of the highest quality, while the gold lining along the frame was valuable as well. She placed her quill against the parchment, "One deformed cross without engraved incantation. I can't give any pinyooks for a useless cross such as this. The sapphire could be worth a pretty pinyook, but it's not enchanted."

He tilted his head to the side as he placed three more deformed crosses on the counter, "What are you daft? I thought you merchants were supposed to be experts. This isn't a deformed cross." His eyes quivered as he placed one sharpened fingernail back upon the counter.

Her sweaty palms gripped the summoning orb that had saved her life on many occasions. The warmth of the orb tingled her fingertips. "Please calm down. It's just that... crosses are not supposed to have loops at the top. They are meant to be enchanted and then have incantations placed on them. Everyone knows this. The best I can do is make you a trade for your deformed crosses. Perhaps a Merchant's Corner enchanted map? It's a one-time use map that will guide you to the nearest Merchant's Corner. Then when you have something of real value, you will know where to find us." Zurie shrugged as she finished.

The Sasabonsam's eyes turned a mint green. "This is of real value... twenty-five thousand pinyooks, and I won't remove your vocal chords."

Sweat dripped down Zurie's forehead onto her exposed neck, "N... now... now... there is no need for any of that. What if you head back to the Dark Continent and we just go our separate ways?"

He slammed his iron nails against the counter. "The Dark Continent? So it is true, that is what you people call my beloved home. You will pay for your ignorance on this night." The Sasabonsam slashed at Zurie's chest with his claws—but she was prepared for it. The iron claw of the foreign vampire bounced off the auric shield of her protective amulet, causing an explosion. both her shop and her assailant were rebounded into opposite directions. With great force, both the Sasabonsam and the shop crashed into nearby buildings, leaving two massive craters in their wake.

She rushed over to the pile of wood and merchandise in search of the summoning orb. Picking up the orb, she rubbed it and read out the incantation. "A dead merchant is bad for business." The foreign vampire screeched as the iron fingernails at the end of his hands and feet glowed bright green. *Marvelous, he enchants his iron fingers and feet by circulating his own energy. He must be a blood knight.*

Now is not the time to admire him. Where is he? The foreign vampire rushed forward at blistering speeds, almost twice the speed of an average vamp. An imbued talon came within inches of its mark, only to be redirected at the last moment. The Sansabonsam was launched into a stone statue of the Duke. Zurie let out a sigh of relief. Her legs quivered as she approached her savior. "H... hello... Rufus."

Rufus made no effort to respond. The putrid stench of Rufus' existence penetrated her nostrils as they both scanned the area looking for the aggressive patron. Several moments passed by in silence before Rufus wobbled over to Zurie's Merchant Corner.

Pointing at the deformed crosses, he asked, "Dispute over ankh?" She had heard the word before but had never placed the word to the image. *Ankh... ankh? Could this be the fabled item that those witch doctors use over there in the South? How could I have been so foolish?* Zurie ran out a few meters in the direction the Sasabonsam was thrown. She analyzed her ransacked location. The wooden planks lay on the floor in a pile at her feet. *My first night at this location and it's already a mess. What good am I?* The scratching of the stone rubble alerted her to the survival of her patron.

Sluggishly she approached the Sasabonsam, who held what she could now identify as an ankh in his hand. He looked at her with furrowed brows. "This is not a deformed cross. It is an ankh. A common-level artifact from my continent. The *Wisi Men* use them to exorcise the very essence of vamp kind. It is similar to your cross, yet different in a few ways. It is challenging for most to eliminate even a common level *Wisi Man*. As you will come to see, I have rid this world of ninety-seven. I counteroffer with sixteen thousand Pinyooks for an artifact that you will not get your hands on otherwise."

Zurie's eyes zeroed in on the common-level artifact that could not be obtained anywhere else in Europia. *A rare find indeed. At the very least the high-level clerics will pay just for its novelty aspect.* Her palms became moist as she bit her bottom lip. Caressing her long curly hair, she leaned in closer. *Curses, here comes that bulbous whale on his way to inspect my negotiations. Probably just wants to calculate his cut for adding a show of force to my hand.* Zurie crossed her arms, "I don't know... it's a risk taking on a product that most haven't even heard of. Besides, what use would foreign exorcist artifacts be against local vamps?" The look that came next was exactly what she was expecting.

He scrunched his face into a twisted expression. "That's the whole point. They will have the artifact, but not the necessary scroll that accompanies it. Why would you wish to further arm your enemy?"

Zurie raised an eyebrow. "The clerics are no enemy of mine. We live in peace for as long as we keep it."

The stench of Rufus' oily fluids entered her lungs once again. Zurie outstretched her pale hand to shake the sharpened weapon that was this Sasabonsam's hand. He smiled, gleaming his sharpened iron teeth. "My common name is Zurie. I am unaware of my lineage name, so I go by the surname of Valentine."

The dark-skinned vamp with long silver locks smirked. "Of course... a toxin vamp wouldn't know her lineage name. Abandoned right as you were turned, I suspect. You will refer to me as Oakes of the Night Wood clan."

Finally closing the distance, Rufus responded, "I am Rufus of the Worm Foot clan. It's a pleasure to do business with you. We at the Merchant's Corner always believe that a happy customer is a returning customer, and we love to make returning customers." He struggled to smile between breaths.

The silence of the broken-down cathedral always caused bumps to rise upon her arms. Every few paces she glanced back to see if Rufus was still there. As they approached the location of their hidden den, her steps seemed to weigh a ton. *Would be nice if he fell off a cliff somewhere. Fell? More like rolled. But what would I do without my fat, stinky savior? What is this... thirteen times this month? It is certain that I am to be reprimanded, ridiculed, and perhaps even lashed.*

Her thoughts droned on as she descended towards the basement of the cathedral. Slumping her shoulders, she peered at the large wooden door of her den. This was the only place she truly felt safe. She gazed at it for a few moments longer. Allowing herself a low sigh, she lowered her head before initiating the ritual. Tracing the sigil that represented her den sent her into a trancelike state. She placed her hand upon the sigil, copying it with her finger.

First a medium-sized circle, then two dashes below it, followed by a line straight down the middle of the circle. Finally, she traced the two smaller outer circles at each side of the larger one. The sigil oozed a bright purple glimmer, causing her gaze to switch swiftly. The door creaked as it cracked an inch or two. A familiar voice erupted into the air, causing her knees to buckle.

"Well, if it isn't the all-glorious and great Zurie the toxin vamp? How many pinyooks are you contributing to the clan fund on this night?" Before she could muster a response, the voice continued. "Tis a poetic night, is it not? The blue hue of the full moon somehow looks down upon us mockingly. I suspect another day of zero from the illustrious hero of our tale. I suppose your sly toxin brain has concocted a brew of an excuse for the madam. But I'll have you know: She is in an extra blood-thirsty mood on this full moon."

Zurie sighed once again. "Yes... he took all my pinyooks from the deal. This time was urgent, there was this Sansa..." A glove-covered hand poked its way out through the small crack between the door. With a whooshing sound, the door slammed before fully opening.

Before Zurie stood a tall white skeleton wearing a leather cavalier atop his head. A red feather poked out from inside the curled brim. The skeleton had gaping holes where eyes should have been, along with a distinct crack in the middle of the forehead. The Graveyard Vamp, as it's kind liked to be called, glistened bright white underneath the full moon. It snapped its fingers repeatedly and did a quick jig as its bones clinked together like two bells signaling a poor man's demise. It was at this point in time that Rufus bumped Zurie with his belly, nudging her forward towards the bony figure.

"Move, weakling." Led by their skeletal den mate, Rufus squeezed his way through the narrow passage, carrying the large sack of ankhs. *Ankhs... ankhs... why couldn't everything have clicked earlier? Why did I have to be sired by a toxin vamp?* Instead of entering the den, she jumped as high as she could, grabbing onto her favorite thinking ledge. With effort, she pulled herself onto its flat marble surface. *The ridicule that awaits me will have to be suspended for a few moments.* With her back against the cracked marble tiles of the cathedral's second floor, she gazed above. The ceiling was made of painted glass portraying the great Vamp Lord. *Now, what if I was sired by the great count himself? I bet we would have won the Cleric Vamp War. Back when we were adversaries, the clerics would have bowed down to my supremacy. I'd walk towards them and their crosses would melt.*

Her thoughts turned into vivid images of her swishing and whooshing through the sky in a tirade of power, grace, and above all grandiosity. She summoned one of her serpents to keep her company. As she lay there, caressing her spotted boa constrictor, her thoughts wandered upon feats of greatness. After about an hour of this display of her great power, she sighed. *Is this all I'm good for? Summoning snakes and creating toxic gases? What kind of ill-infested ability is this?* No answers came as she sat there in her puddle of self-pity. Her strained eyes ached for reprieve. It was an unfortunate thing that vamps couldn't cry.

She pulled out her lucky pinyook and examined the markings on the triangular piece of lightweight metal. Her hand caressed the etched engraving of the circle and square that indicated its value. She smiled to herself. "To any other merchant you're barely worth your weight, but to me, you're the beginning of my vast fortune." She lowered her head before taking another fleeting look. *Who am I kidding? A toxin vamp with a vast fortune? An oxymoron if there ever was one.*

A powerful aura entered her field. She wrinkled her ears before closing her eyes to activate her serpent sight. Taking three deep icy breaths, she focused on the area surrounding her. The cool breeze cut through her skin. A faint image appeared to illuminate the black of her eyelids. Just when the image became clearer, clouds of darkness rushed in to shroud it in further mystery. *Death is around the corner*, she thought. As she glanced down to the bottom of the cathedral, her eyes widened. A giant purple bat entered the cathedral grounds with glowing blades beneath its claw-like hands. Its eyes were glowing a menacing green as it grinned, revealing two rows of sharp teeth. Its lengthy ears twitched at the slightest sound. With purple fur covering the vast majority of its body, it looked as if it had climbed right out of death's coffin.

Shivers ran down her spine as the entity slinked its way towards their den gate. Its aura was a putrid teal that made Zurie gag. *The stench of death weighs heavy with this one. I must warn them. I could... I could jump down, open the door, and shut it before it gets there.* She glanced at the creature's powerful muscular legs. Swallowing deeply, she continued her train of thought. *Yes... that's what I will do. I mean, it is said that one must lose a life to have a life. I could be a hero.* She moved her hand an inch to get a better launching grip when the entity paused its long stalk to the gate.

Zurie froze. The acid in her stomach turned and sloshed as she felt her gut wrench and twist. The entity leaned back and let loose a wad of green colored phlegm two meters to Zurie's left. With great effort, she turned her head to see an owl washed in the acidic phlegm. It flapped and hooted in despair as if calling out to Zurie for help. *Better you than me*, she thought. She returned her attention to the large glowing intruder in time to see it descend into the steps of her precious den.

I must do something; I have to do something. Perhaps repeating it would give her more courage she thought. Zurie was about to yell out when her throat seized up, causing her to let out a low whoosh of a breath. The entity kicked the enchanted gate down with a mere nudge of its foot. Zurie clutched her lucky coin, waiting for the carnage. *Now what I'll do is help them fight. Now that I think about it... I'm probably overthinking. He is probably a customer. One who kicks down the door to the den... where no customers are allowed.*

There was a blinding flash of teal light, then a loud screeching sound, followed by silence.

Within mere moments the entity slinked out of the doorway with two large sacks over its shoulder. Its body was drenched in the blue vamp blood that often filled Zurie with unease. Each step it took left a blue trail along the cathedral grounds. "Maybe... maybe... they're alright?" With a flick of her wrist, she flung herself towards the open entrance to the den. The repugnant scent of her clan's innards filled her nose. She upheaved her last two blood rations. Her stomach only tossed and turned further as she traversed through the den. Blood covered the stone walls; their wooden tables and chairs were all deformed acidic heaps. Pieces of Rufus were stuck to the ceiling while the rest of the clan was heaped into piles divided by body parts: the arms here, the legs there. The torsos lay stacked together, divided by gender. Finally, the heads were lined up on top of the bar counter, all staring back at her with their eyes wide open. Zurie closed her eyes but still saw the carnage. Shaking her head and opening her eyes, she gave words to her rampant thoughts.

"How can this be?" She sat there for a few moments with her head in her hands. Her thoughts swirled about as daybreak was now upon her. She did the only thing she could do: She curled herself into a ball and attempted to sleep.

— 2 —

A CLERIC'S OATH

The clanging of the morning bell echoed throughout the city. The sun's scorching rays fell upon the aged yet vibrant skin of Althalos. Despite waking up with a nagging feeling, he managed to beam his usual smile. *Another successful morning bell. Glad to hear the putrid vamps have scurried back to their rotten dens.* Stretching his back and shoulders he sang a tune that angels often joined in harmony. He picked up his enchanted mace and watched as it sparkled under the sunlight. The iron-tipped bludgeoning tool served him well during the Vamp Cleric War, but had plummeted its way upon very few heads since he became the resident mentor. Wiping a spider's web off the cross at the front, he placed his chainmail upon his body. He removed his favorite pendant from its gold case, then brought the cross to his lips and kissed it.

"Lord protector of all that is holy, may you bless my hand on this day. There are students that must learn their lessons." Althalos guided the twenty-two-karat necklace to its lofty perch around his neck. Humming to himself, he snapped his fingers in synch with the sweet melody. Walking towards the golden barricade of his door, he had a peculiar thought. *What if vamps and clerics went to war again? I know I have kept up with my conditioning, but the rest of these clerics are too lackadaisical with their own. Not to mention the weak nerves of these scrubs.* He clenched his fists, placing them across his chest in an x formation. *It matters not, the vamps know better. As long as we have the other two Cleric Commanders, they wouldn't dream of engaging us.* That nagging voice tugged upon the thought strings of his mind. *But what if?*

Shaking his head furiously he opened the door to the Hallway of Triumph. It was a brightly lit hallway with red carpeting, paintings of the three commanders, and the golden armor of their deceased Bishop. He glanced at the armor for several long moments, as he

— 16 —

always did. *Maybe if I had parried instead of blocked, I could have reached him sooner.* Each time he stared at that armor he came up with a different scenario where the Bishop survived. Across the hall he could hear the snoring of one commander and the squeaking bedsprings of another. Fists clenched again, Althalos stampeded downstairs towards the feeding quarters. That nagging feeling he woke up with intensified. *I already had words with those two about their behavior. Yet the next month they only serve to intensify their impious nature? If we were at war, the Bishop would...*

His eyes trailed across the room as one fresh-faced cleric took his sword and pointed it at another, who giggled hysterically. A cool breeze swirled around Althalos' feet, rising up to his head. He approached the bench where the scrubs were horsing around. His cold, luminous blue eyes peered down on the now-shivering youth. With one hand on his mace, he spoke. "So you think weapons are a game?"

There was no response.

Althalos clenched his teeth. "Silence will not bring fortune now. What is your excuse for horseplay with your sacred weapon?" The blonde-haired cleric raised his head slowly. His pitiful eyes turned the stomach of the seasoned war veteran. *If only he was bold and commanding, I could let him off with a warning.* He mentally flipped through the Cleric's Code for any reasons not to do what had to be done. *If I don't hold up the standards and stipulations... then who will?*

The young cleric said something that could only have come from a nitwit the size of the Dark Continent: "I wa... wa... was demonstrating how I would kill a vamp the size of their Vamp Lord. Commander Althalos."

Althalos closed his eyes at the mere mention of the Vamp Lord. *This boy is going to need a level three repentance,* he thought. Calmly, he said, "Show us. Demonstrate to your peers your wondrous vamp-killing abilities."

By this time, the rest of those in the food hall had paused their meals to watch the exhibition. The weight of the sword slowed the boy down as he swung left, then right. Althalos deflected each blow with his pinky finger. Finally, the boy attempted a lunging motion towards the commander. *So desperate that he would attempt a forbidden move to appease the audience? What scrubs we have for clerics. If we were at war...*

The seasoned veteran sidestepped the lunge to grab a fistful of blonde hair. With a twist of his wrist, he raised the boy into the air and slammed him into the table, headfirst. Blood spurted out. Althalos closed his eyes once again. It must be done, or else they would continue to disrespect the Cleric's Oath. Tense, he glanced over to the tables where his pupils sat, "Lief," he bellowed.

His most prestigious pupil approached with his arms folded and head tilted. "Yes, Commander Althalos?" said the pupil, one hand on his Cleric's Code. He knew where this was going.

Althalos turned and pointed towards the boy who murmured and squirmed under the weight of his hand. "What is the punishment for horseplay with a weapon, cowardice, and visual insubordination? Read it out loud for all to bear witness to."

Lief flipped through the pages to the very last section where each punishment for every transgression was highlighted. His jaw dropped, "Well... it says the punishment is excommunication, expulsion, and permanent injury."

Horrified looks filled the large stone room. Some quivered, others shivered, but the gravity of the situation was clear. Althalos raised his head as his hand tightened around his mace. "To be a cleric is to be of the highest discipline. For too long there has been a great disturbance in the balance between the various sections. This will end from here on out. I expect everyone to follow the Cleric's Code to the letter." He turned to the blonde boy. Pity filled his heart, but his eyes stayed cool, blue, and callous. "Hold out your hand. If you do not do it of your own will, it will be worse for you." The enchanted mace cooled within his hand, almost as if it knew it was about to be used. Althalos gripped the boy's wrist with one hand, raising the mace in the other. The crashing blow caused the boy to screech out in a high pitch cry. Tears flowed down the boy's face as he looked down at his now-useless lump of a hand.

He gazed across the large enclosed field. The hands at his side quivered while the blood rushed to the tip of his feet. Althalos' sharp, hawk-like eyes scanned the courtyard area for anyone else near his prey. He swooped in, scattering the leaves surrounding his sleeping mare and causing her to jerk to the side, tugging at her reins. Letting loose a low whine, she jumped up and down to see her rider. With a smile that could blind a sparrow, he beamed at the elegant white creature. "Swan, look at you. All shiny and glistening in your nap. It's time for your morning ride, my precious." He untied her from the post then smoothly placed the saddle on and sat atop his beloved horse. Lightly clasping the reins, he flicked his wrists. The horse galloped down through the courtyard of the castle, blazing past the onlookers who often gathered for his morning ride. The horse dashed past the watering well where a large, stocky man had been cleaning his battle-axe. Althalos pulled hard on the reins to swerve to the right. The horse eased up on the large bulky figure. Althalos tapped him on the shoulder, "What is the meaning of this, and who are you?"

He barely shifted his head to look back. "Hmph," the man replied. He cocked back and spat in the well. With burning eyes, Althalos nudged the mysterious figure. This time he glanced back halfway and smirked. His beard was scraggly, and he had a gold tooth. The battle axe that he was cleaning contained an odd enchantment. "Leave me to my own devices, you wind-sucker," he slurred.

Althalos' eyes widened. "Windsucker? I don't know where you're from, but you must have been struck with woodness. Only a mad man would talk to Commander Althalos like this." said the Commander.

The gold-toothed figure turned around fully, his battle-axe resting on his shoulder. The veins protruded at the side of his head while his teeth ground like a brand-new mill.

That got his attention. I wonder if he will have the bollocks to strike me. My mace is crying out for more blood on this day. Althalos furrowed his brow, clasping the handle of his glorious weapon. "You do not reside here, vacate these premises." A group of scrubs entered the courtyard, followed by the drunken Commander Brom Forthwind.

The gold toothed beast nudged Althalos in the chest with two of his fingers, "What if I don't?"

Althalos withdrew his mace at lightning speeds. "Then you will be removed in a casket. Trespassing upon the grounds of the Cleric's Order is a capital offense." By the time he finished his sentence, the group of scrubs had gathered around in a circle. Their mouths watered in excitement, to see Commander Althalos in action was a rare treat. The large figure swung his battle-axe at blinding speeds, forcing Althalos to block with his mace. With a loud crack, the mace snapped in two. Althalos was thrown fifteen meters into the distance. The impact caused that section of the wall to crumble upon Althalos, adding insult to injury. With mouths ajar and hands quivering, the scrubs rushed over to the figure who had dismissed their commander with ease.

Commander Brom sloppily moseyed his way over to the broken wall, "Are you?" He paused. The face that looked back at him was furrowed.

Althalos glanced down at his beloved broken mace. With his teeth clenched, he stood up and dusted himself off. "Fine," he mumbled.

With what was left of his weapon, he marched towards the figure. "Listen, you vagabond. Now you have two problems. You will also have to pay for the repair of my weapon. This mace served me well during the Vamp Cleric War, and you will see that it is put in tip-top order."

The figure threw back his head in a fit of deep laughter. "I will pay to fix nothing. You are talking to your new High Cleric. You will learn to respect what that means."

The scrubs each bowed on one knee, holding their crosses, and said the special prayer. Althalos tightened his fists, his face turning pale. He stuttered, "N... no... you lie."

Brom eased in between the two, placing a crumpled-up piece of parchment in Commander Cleric Althalos' quivering hands. As he read the parchment, his eyes shook, causing them to burn. *The High Council of Clerics hereby authorizes the owner of this letter to obtain and hold the illustrious title of High Cleric to hold dominion over the western provinces of Europia. As the High Cleric he shall be granted autonomy, and as such, all privileges of said position. The resident cleric's order of Titania has been elected for the housing of the High Cleric. Commander Althalos has been selected by committee to be the second in command to the High Cleric.* His hand tightened around the letter before he handed it back to the new High Cleric. Sighing, he clasped the pendant that rested against his neck. With his eyes twitching and hand jittering, he dropped to one knee. The words: "Praise be to the High Cleric. May he lead us to the light within through his guiding..."

He bit his tongue. *How could they have chosen this abomination to be the High Cleric? It should be me. I have followed every rule, regulation, guideline and have done my best to uphold the standards in absence of a superior officer. Without a Bishop or even a High Cleric, I have kept this facility functioning.*

The figure revealed his jagged teeth. "Do you forget the words?"

The grinding of Althalos' teeth could be heard. "Hand upon his principles and light. I stake my life to protect the High Cleric in times of disarray, for he is closest to the light a man can become, in the absence of a Bishop."

With a loud snort the figure turned to the scrubs, holding his battle-axe in the air, "Forget everything you know about being a cleric. There are new rules and regulations that will be posted by evening's supper." He turned to Althalos with a smirk. "You have lots of work to do... Althy."

— 3 —

VAMPS CAN'T CRY

She saw the massive entity rip the head off Rufus with a mere flick of his hand as it approached her. She crawled on her knees, begging the creature to spare her miserable existence. The creature glanced at the coward with cold, vacant eyes.

The bloodstained hand of the creature reached towards the den symbol she wore around her neck. With a slight tug, the necklace snapped. "Your den is no more... you weren't even worth the effort to eliminate."

Zurie shot up, clutching her pendant. Covered in a cold sweat, she went to her room to change. *A dream... just a dream. I should be sad, but I'm not. I should feel something more than fear, but I don't. I suppose this is the gift and curse of being a vamp. Perhaps if they treated me better, I would have established that heart thing called a bond.*

She pushed thoughts of bonding and emotions out of her head. The room had been ransacked. Most of her files had been thrown across the room and torn up into pieces, while others were smeared with vampire blood. *What could it possibly want with my files? They are just historical records of vamp-cleric dealings. No vampire has ever showed any interest in such things.*

She sighed. *Except myself. I really am an oddball, as my den-mates used to say, even for a toxin vamp.* She lowered her head. *Well... look at me now. I am the owner of my own den, I wonder if my sire would be proud.* Her head pounded as her thoughts rattled on. Stooping down, she sifted through the pages that remained intact.

Zurie's eyes widened. "Everything on the Vamp Lord is gone." *The detailed account of the Vamp Lord's known existence and how it achieved such a high status in our community. All gone.*

She collapsed to the stone floor. "My most valuable treasure... gone." The walls of the already cramped room seemed to close in, and a chill passed through the door as she gazed into the common room where their remains were. It was only a matter of hours before they turned to dust. Zurie took the pieces of her den-mates and piled them in the corner of the common room. Every piece she moved weighed heavier upon her heart. She gazed across the room at the empty cases, which only alarmed her more. "It took all the most powerful artifacts we had, along with the ankhs." The glass cases that once contained the orb of manifestation and the sword of impalement were now empty cases of despair. "This cannot be undead life... without artifacts I can't open my shop. What good is a merchant's corner without artifacts? What use is a den without den-mates? The only thing I know is to be a merchant." Her stomach turned.

For the first time since the incident, she truly took stock of the gravity of her situation. "This was the only den in the entire city that would house me." Vivid memories of scrounging for blood rations through the trash at night and hiding in abandoned caves during the day came to mind. "They may not have been ideal, but at least they took me in. I can't go back to that life. I'd rather become dust." The triple bells of dusk echoed out into the distance. The streets had been cleared of all humans and vampires could now exit their dens.

I wonder if... Dazed, Zurie slithered over to the den leader's room. The room was five times the size of hers. Various animal heads were laid out evenly across the walls, and several pieces of pink silk were suspended in the air. The coffin itself was mahogany, with the den sigil carved in gold. The vibrant aroma of lilac graced her nostrils.

I'll never see her walking through those archways with her magnificent staff again. The way she used to smirk before she would yell out my name. She slammed her fist on the nearby cabinet, cracking it. "Must I be reminded at how lonesome I have become while my eyes stay blocked?" Her dry pupils itched as she strained them, to no avail. Zurie approached the illustrious coffin and opened it. Taking in a large whiff of lilac, she peered into the cushioned habitat. There it lay. She quickly grabbed the contents and clutched them towards her chest. Her heart throbbed at double time against her chest cavity. She scurried out of the room towards her closet, nearly tripping over her own feet. *Artifacts, artifacts, artifacts.* She carefully placed the artifact upon her stone bed. *I can't believe it didn't check her coffin. To think that I could hold this... in my possession.* She had always eyed the treasures of her den-mates. They weren't hard to miss, from Rufus' belt of summoning to that walking skeleton's hat of dismay.

Every time Zurie had earned an artifact one of her den-mates would steal it from her, citing some unknown den rule to her in the process. But this time was different. *This is my time; tonight is my night. I'm going to wield this artifact and be the belle of the boardwalk.* With the utmost delicacy she clasped the handle of her new staff. The handle throbbed in her hand, and the shrunken skull at the end morphed into a serpent. Energy surged through her veins, causing her body to transform. She could feel her formerly brittle ankles strengthen as bone became steel. Her mind cleared as a wave of ecstasy washed over her. With razor-sharp focus and poise, she stood upright with confidence for the first time in two lifetimes. She peered across the room.

"I feel... something different for the first time in forty years. Is this what it means to feel powerful?" asked Zurie. A rush of blood caused her veins to pulsate. As she glided towards the exit of the den, she turned back to take one last glance at a large pile of vamp dust. *Still no tears.*

Looking up at the full moon, she took a deep breath. The boardwalk was not for the faint of heart. The walkway was a long strip of wood surrounded by swamp land. Every few meters, a stand sold contraband to both vamp and human alike. At the end of the boardwalk was a twenty-four-hour port where one could wet their whistle on the newest contraband as well as the latest gossip. Her stomach turned, but her eyes blazed with ambition. The long walk to the boardwalk gave Zurie plenty of time to muster what little courage she had.

I'm going to find that creature and have words with him. I want my things. In addition to the den leader's staff, Zurie held a tidy sum the leader had stashed away. *We were supposed to pool all our pinyooks in the den bowl. She really held out on us.* Taking a deep breath, she opened her mouth to speak. There was one vamp and one human, as usual. "G... greetings. I'm here on official den business." The two guards looked at each other. Zurie's hand tightened around the staff in her left hand, "What are your concerns?" she asked, this time with more bass in her voice. The vamp guard wasn't much to look at: he was short with muscular arms and a sharp overbite. The human was another story. He was a massive brute of a man wearing spiked gloves and an enchanted helmet.

The vamp spoke. "What den are you from?"

Zurie stood up straight with her head held high. *I feel so confident. Who would have thought this staff could make me feel so good.* "I'm from the Merchant's Corner."

The human guard scratched his head while the vamp guard stepped forward. "I thought as much; I used to spot you coming down with Rufus. You smell of the withered. Something happen to your den?"

Zurie furrowed her brows, doing her best impression of the den leader, "I'm still here, thus my den lives on."

The two guards chuckled to themselves, allowing her passage in the process. Grinding her teeth as she passed by the guards, her thoughts blazed. *Just when I was beginning to feel a tiny bit better about myself someone comes and kicks me down.* As she hovered towards the port, the shopkeepers would stop what they were doing to gaze at her staff. *This staff is so rare, I bet those shopkeepers are already scheming and plotting a way to pry it from my hands. Luckily for me, the merchant's code prevents them from harming me directly. But they could send an agent in their place. I wonder how this higher version of me will hold up in a duel.*

Me, survive a duel? That'll be the night.

Quickening her pace, she passed the makeshift stands to enter the classier section of the boardwalk. The shops here were made of colorful marble and had glowing lanterns lighting the sigils on their fronts. These were shops tied to the more prominent dens. If there was any sympathy in the vamp world it certainly wouldn't be found here. In the corner of her eye, she saw the Sasabonsam known as Oakes. He was downing a pint of red liquid. "Why is the liquid red and not green like all blood rations?" she whispered.

A small voice emerged in the back of her head. *Real human blood is red.*

Before long she was standing next to Oakes, her fangs dripping saliva.

He barely turned to her, his sharp iron nails tapped against the glass mug, "Oh, if it isn't my little trade partner. It seems you have come onto a windfall. Though it also seems much bloodshed was needed to acquire it." The barkeep stopped wiping the mug to peer at the staff. Oakes leaned in closer. "You're either brave or daft. You can't defend yourself: You're a mere toxin vamp wielding useless snakes, even if you have ironed up a bit due to that staff. Sooner or later, one of those human vamp hunters will have their blade down your gut. Or worse, one of the shopkeepers will hire a vampire to do the job. Maybe it will fall on me."

Heat bubbled within Zurie as she considered Oakes' words. *Everyone thinks I'm weak just because I'm a toxin vamp. They don't know what a toxin vamp is capable of. I could... well I don't know what a toxin vamp is capable of either. Perhaps it is time that I find out.*

She got up and raised her staff to the full moon. With her other hand to her chest, she spoke in the loudest voice she could. "All you marks, listen up. I know what you say about me behind my back. I've heard the whispers. 'Oh, there goes that toxin vamp with her smelly protector. She must like eating a donkey's arse for breakfast."

The crowd erupted into a fit of laughter. Zurie clenched her fist as her heart bombarded her chest. Her blood boiled, causing her to shuffle uncomfortably. "I have a wager for the one who thinks himself the swiftest. The first one to drop 50,000 pinyooks here on this bar stool will duel me to first blood. I will put up this rare artifact I have in my hand."

The barkeep leaned forward. "To the question of whether she is brave or daft, the answer is both. But much more so the latter." Oakes nodded in agreement.

It wasn't long before a fast-footed blood knight from the Tyrant Den showed up. He smirked. "I had to borrow it from our vault, but your blood is going to pay for it three times over." All the vamps knew the blood knights were king. They could get anything for anyone, and rumor had it they even had dealings with some in the Clerics Order. To be a blood knight was to be a true vampire of the continent: the ability to harness one's own aura as an energy source and imbue weapons with it made being a blood knight a sought-after position. Not to mention the respect that accompanied it. The Tyrant Den was an up-and-coming blood knight group; and this knight was the right-hand man to their leader.

Zurie gazed at her opponent. Her eyes beamed confidence, but her stomach turned in fear. The knight had enchanted boots with wings at the sides. They glimmered a golden bright light, threatening to blind those around him. He held an enchanted curved dagger.

Oakes leaned in and whispered in her ear. "Be careful of that dagger. I've seen its enchantment before. It inflicts grievous wounds with even the slightest touch."

Zurie nodded. *I can't believe someone took the wager... what was I thinking?*

With a wave of her hand the barkeep initiated the duel. Zurie imposed her snake hole tactic, the only tactic she knew. It was quite effective: she created illusionary images with the toxic gases that escaped her mouth. After numerous instances of striking air, the knight bellowed out. Orange aura surrounded his feet, causing the crowd to shift their attention on the weaponized artifact. The knight dashed forward, striking all the illusions in one diving blow. His blade came within inches of impaling her heart as she backpedaled into a bar stool.

Is he trying to kill me? I thought first blood meant we both walk away in one piece. Am I really going to die in this circle of blood-thirsty, unscrupulous vamps? Am I going to die a nobody? Heat rose to the top of her head as she fervently gripped the staff. The eyes of the staff beamed a bright purple light, causing the knight to stumble. Clasping the base of the staff with both hands, she twirled around and slammed the head of the weapon into the skull of the knight. Purple aura engulfed the knight, and he collapsed to the floor with a loud thud.

Pardon? That was rather anti climatic. Is he withered? Please don't let him be withered. She stooped down and nudged the now-decaying blood knight.

A voice in the back of the crowd yelled out, "She granted the second death to the blood knight. I'll go and get their leader, see what he makes of this."

Another voice echoed, "Good idea, I'm going too." The shuffling and clanking of feet against the wooden boardwalk rang as they rushed to snitch.

Low down rats. What do I do? Do I run? Do I stay? I mean, how dangerous can their leader be if his right-hand man was so weak? Or maybe I am now that strong? Questions upon questions swirled in her head.

Oakes clasped her shoulder. "Listen to me carefully. Claim your spoils before those other vamps do, and meet me at the port. You'll have to leave with me if you want to save your skin. You can't possible take on an entire den of blood knights." As the sharp breeze passed by, she focused her attention on the group that laid before her. The once-cheering crowd was now a pack of leering beasts. Without taking her eyes off the crowd, she removed the enchanted boots and dagger from the corpse. A twinkle on his finger caught her eye. *Might that be an enchanted ring?* The stomping of heavy boots approached their area gave her just enough time to pry the ring off the finger. With seconds to spare, she pushed through the crowd's tortuous glares and onto the boardwalk. Walking quickly to the port, she slid the ring on her pinky finger. Emitting a subtle blue aura, it captivated her being.

Am I really going to leave everything I have ever known behind?

Do I even have a choice?

She glanced back to see a flurry of blood knights emerge from the pitch black of night. As they stampeded towards her in their enchanted armor, she glided towards the port. *There is Oakes. I wonder where we are going? Will I survive what is to come?* She had no answers.

He was dressed in odd foreign clothing that revealed much of his dark skin. She pressed her tongue against her fangs. *I haven't had a mate since being turned. I hope he isn't trying to seduce me. I have bigger things to worry about than mating.*

She approached Oakes, the blood still rushing to her head. The side of the ship read "The Cardinal's Impalement." The ship was made of beautiful oak-wood, with a giant mast in the middle and a square-rigged single sail at the stern.

"What a wonderful ship you have procured," she said.

Oakes raised his eyebrow. "You're not here for an inspection. Get on before I change my mind."

As she climbed the rope she looked back once more to see the fangs, swords, and daggers of a dozen vampire knights approaching the dock. With her staff raised high, she yelled out, "They're coming! We have to go!"

Looking at the deck, her jaw dropped. "Wh... where is the crew?" Her mouth quivered, "You've doomed us both. They will string me up and drain me of all my blood before skinning me alive. Who knows what they will do to an exotic vamp like you?"

Oakes pushed past Zurie. "You're a coward and a poor excuse for a vamp who makes rash decisions when angered. But I see something valuable deep in your core. The very same thing my brother once saw in me. To activate that staff without undertaking the ritual is quite peculiar. It is time for your horizons to broaden and your scope to fix on what's to come."

He took out a small green pouch filled with green powder. Taking a handful, he threw it in the middle of the deck. Immediately, seven figures appeared. They wore bows and arrows at their back and short swords at their side. They circled for a moment then ran towards their positions. Within moments, the boat was on its way to a position unknown.

TILTED CROSS

Althalos gazed across the room to where the High Cleric was hunched over. With a scowl across his face, Althalos ate his mushroom soup and bread. His usually empty bench was now filled with inquisitive pupils. He stopped his ruminating to look at the doe-faced Lief, who had been waiting for his response. The commander took one more bite out of his dry bread. The stale bread only increased his distaste for the High Cleric. "To answer your question, I don't bloody know how he was chosen for High Cleric over me. Now that I have given you an answer, I'd like to eat my meal in peace."

Lief raised his hand once again. "I beg your pardon for one more question, commander." Althalos let out a low grunt but nodded his head. One of the female pupils whispered in Lief's ear, he ran his hand through his hair before speaking, "Well..." Beads of sweat dripped down his forehead.

The Commander took a deep breath. "Spit it out so I can go back to my peace and quiet."

Lief shuffled around in his seat for a moment. "Well... we were all just kind of wondering... why are you eating the mushroom soup and bread like the rest of us? Normally, you'd be eating venison and potatoes." The veins on Althalos' face protruded, and his face turned red. All the pupils except Lief made their escape. *Remain calm, a holy cleric does not take out his anger on those that are innocent. I must remain calm.*

He raised his head slightly. "Because... the High Cleric said so." The distaste in his voice was evident. "That was the answer I was given and thus that's the answer I'm giving."

Lief lowered his head while mumbling something like, "That's not right." He bowed and took his leave.

Althalos placed another spoonful of mushroom soup in his mouth. The taste only served to sour his mood even further. With tension still gripping his body, he stood up and approached the table where the High Cleric and the other two commanders were laughing up a storm. *Look at them, like a dog upon a nun's arse. I bet they were talking about me.* He glanced down into their bowls and inhaled. "I see you've been enjoying venison and potatoes." One of the commanders began to speak, but Althalos shot him a glance that froze him in his tracks.

The High Cleric stood up to meet the gaze of his commander. "What of it?"

The grinding of Althalos' teeth could halt a rogue horse. Placing one hand on the table, he leaned in further, "Why? I was under the impression we were to eat like common scrubs."

The High Cleric shifted his head backwards and let out a maniacal cackle, "We? No..." He paused for a few moments looking Althalos directly in his piercing hawk-like eyes, "Just you." The temperature around the group increased significantly causing Althalos to perspire. The High Cleric smirked, "Go dip yourself in cool water and then head back to your meal, Althy."

Althalos placed a hand where his mace should have been. *The blacksmith is still looking it over. Would I dare to strike down the High Cleric? Could my jealousy and fury allow me to do such a thing? Perhaps it is best that I do not have my weapon with me.*

Althalos turned to leave when his lips seemingly moved on their own. "It's Althalos... not Althy."

The High Cleric clapped his hands together. "Oh... I know. But it's going to be Althy from now on. And speaking of corrections, soon we will be making a grand announcement. The other commanders and I have come to a crucial decision." The commander clenched his fist again, and the High Cleric took notice. Grinning, the High Cleric placed a hand on Althalos' shoulder, causing his skin to crawl. He whispered, "Unclench your bloody fists before I turn them to soup and make you eat them."

The warmth within his being became a cold sweat, causing bile to twist in his stomach. *What is this spell he has placed upon me? The only other entity to induce such fear in my person was the Vamp Lord. But he can't be such a being; he isn't even a vamp. Could another human truly induce such terror with a mere whisper and a touch? Perhaps the fallen Bishop if he were so inclined, but this beast of a man? How aged my wits have become in these trying times.*

He unclenched his fists and nodded before traversing his way back to the empty bench. While he marched back, he could feel the poisonous eyes of the High Cleric daring him to turn back. *There is something wrong with that beast. He is no High Cleric of mine. I must find out more about him. Yet I must worship the light that shines through him—for only one that is blessed by the light can achieve such a status.*

The blacksmith's sullen eyes lowered to glance at the broken mace once again, then at Althalos' necklace. He repeated himself: "Your mace is an abomination. I cannot repair it while it is in such a state." The commander's glare intensified, causing the blacksmith to shrivel into the corner.

He lowered his head and spoke unevenly, "What do you mean... cannot repair? Why not?"

The blacksmith bit his lip, holding up the two pieces of the impotent mace. "Whatever hit it was enchanted with decay magic. Causing it to diminish over time. Unfortunately, Commander sir, this mace has been removed of everything that made it an enchanted mace. Essentially, it has been poisoned beyond repair. No human can do anything close to repairing this item."

Althalos was about to turn and leave, but he snapped his head back. "What do you mean no human?"

The blacksmith leaned in, lowering his voice to a whisper, "There are rumors of a certain boardwalk that is open twenty-four hours. During the day, there are humans who operate their shops, which is nothing of note. It is the nighttime when things become interesting. 'Tis said that at night the vamps and humans intermingle to open up special shops with rare artifacts for vamps, blood knights, and vagabonds alike. Perhaps a blacksmith there could manage something with your beloved mace."

Althalos' eyes danced back and forth. The hawk within threatened to launch forth and pluck out the blacksmith's eyes. "Need I remind you that what you're saying is treason. The segregation between the vamps and the humans exists for a very good reason."

The blacksmith shuddered. "I... just was trying to help. Please don't reprimand me."

The commander nodded his head. "I suspect you will keep such bright ideas to yourself from here on out." The blacksmith nodded fervently, handing back the broken mace to the commander along with a complementary boot shine kit. *How could he suggest such a thing? That a commander of the Clerics Order break oath and enter the cesspool that is the world of the vamps? Lord only knows how repugnant this boardwalk must be. The mere thought of sharing a city with these cockroaches is enough to turn my stomach, but for me to interact with them is a whole other story.*

But what about my mace?

He passed the open door of the High Cleric on his way back to his room. A purple basket filled with fresh fruits lay atop the bed. He grumbled to himself, "Now the beast has an admirer."

Upon entering his room, he took off his boots and opened the boot shine. He removed his captain boots from the closet. After shining his boots a sense of relief washed over him, "This boot shine is of superb quality." Holding his captain boots into the light of the shy sun, he stomped his foot against the marble floor.

What about my mace?

The evening bell rang calling all humans to finish their errands for dusk was soon upon them. His fingers tapped against the feather-filled mattress. *I'm going to go and investigate this illegal activity. All humans are supposed to be in their beds by night's bell. Yes, that's it... an investigation will do very nicely. I shall bring my mace just in case.*

Althalos removed his cleric's armor, laying it down with care upon the silk coverlet. As he was rummaging through the closet, a peculiar thought dropped into his mind. *Why wasn't I included in whatever big announcement he has planned? Could he be moving to have me removed from my position?*

He took a deep breath, draping himself with his red cloak. It was adorned with rubies at the side and had a large cross at the back. He put on the newly shined captain boots he used to wear into battle. Removing his tome from its silk cover, he placed it on the bed and dropped to both knees. "With all my might I ask that you guide me upon this night. 'Tis with great fortitude that I do your bidding." Lifting his head and signing the cross, he raised to his feet.

Leaving the tome on the bed, he picked up the broken mace and his hunting dagger. Opening the door, he was met with the bright face of Lief.

He perked up upon seeing the fully dressed commander. "Commander, sir. Going for an evening's ride?"

I'd hate to lie to my most promising pupil, but it is best that he doesn't know. He grumbled, "It's none of your concern, but if you must know. Yes." Lief nodded his head, energetic as always. Althalos shuffled around in his cloak, "Why are you here?"

Lief beamed a wide grin, "I came to see if you managed to partake in the gift basket that I had left outside your door. We all came together and got you the freshest fruits we could find."

That low down... piece of... I shouldn't think about our High Cleric in such a manner. It is a cherished position. I must grip my thoughts with vigor. I am better than this. Althalos managed a rare smile as he placed his hand on the shoulder of the youthful Lief. "You lot did well." The energetic pupil saluted then bounced his way down the marble steps towards the common room.

The investigation will need to wait until tomorrow evening. More pressing matters desire my attention. The comfort of his room beckoned his person. As he rested upon the bed, the warmth in his body escaped him. *What am I to do about the High Cleric? The way he conducts himself is inappropriate. A true High Cleric would never steal from one of his commanders.* Althalos closed his eyes as the cool breeze of sundown entered the room. The crisp wind caressed his skin; a sigh of relief escaped his lips. Thoughts of his battles against the vampire scum swirled in his brain. His eyes closed as he drifted into a slumber.

Althalos catapulted his mace into the vamp's head, causing blue liquid to spurt out. The vamp crumpled to the floor in a pile of its own mess. The woman the vamp had attempted to feast on clutched to Althalos' strong, muscular thighs. He glanced down to see tears streaming down her face. As he knelt to cleanse her of her tears, the vamp snickered. Dragging itself away from him, it erupted into a fit of laughter. He walked towards the vermin. His steel boots vibrated upon the stone floors, and the blood in his veins turned to ice as his heart slowed. Even as a fresh-faced scrub he couldn't stand to be mocked by vamps.

Raising his mace high into the air to finish the job, it dawned upon him. He had forgotten the most important rule when faced with attack victims. His commander always said to make sure to check for festering wounds, lest you become a snack. By the time he turned around, she was upon him. He had never seen a female vamp before. He was captivated by her beauty: Her skin glowed, captivating his attention, while her eyes seemed to sparkle. He froze like the scrub that he was. By the time he regained his composure, he knew it was his time to be turned. All he could do was accept his fate and close his eyes. Then he heard a thump as her body dropped to the floor. He opened his eyes to see the glowing arrow of the Bishop lodged within her neck.

When his eyes opened, he ran his hand through what little hair he had left. "If only he were still alive, I need guidance."

— 5 —
SANCTUARY OF THE UNKNOWN

The waves crashed against the sides of the ship, causing its wooden beams to lurch and groan. The wind threatened to sweep Zurie away. Hands tucked into her wool garments, she relieved her hunger with what was left of her blood rations. *I need more rations... I'll meet the second death at this rate.* Stumbling towards the captain's quarters, she knocked on the door softly. She waited a few moments before cracking the door open, "Oakes?" she queried.

She slid through the now half-opened door to enter the blinding room. In the distance, she could see an odd clay sculpture beaming bright light. Covering her eyes, she approached the sculpture. *It's as if some force is pulling me in closer, and I must take a few more steps. I wonder how much it's worth.* Some brisk, unknown aroma embraced her heightened senses, causing her to lunge forward towards the sculpture, her mouth salivating.

She examined it within her grip. She tasted it. Zurie jumped back at the sour taste. Finally, she gazed at it. She said aloud, "Why would I study it in such a manner? To treat a clearly nonedible artifact as if it was a feast—how foolish of me."

Oakes emerged from the shadows as if he was made of them. "Because you are in deprivation mode. I doubt you've ever known what it was like to suffer as a vampire. Living in a city where vamps are given dyed goats' blood to drink like pets. You've probably never even feasted on a live creature, much less from a human. I want to purge myself thinking about it." he said, clawing his wrist with his iron nails.

Zurie ran her hand through her hair. "We live in peace with the humans. This continent has lived through many decades of peace and I don't see anything wrong with it. I don't know much about the Dark Continent, but I have heard stories about gruesome wars and the skinning of humans and vamps alike. I certainly hope that isn't where we're going." She stood, crossing her arms.

Oakes smirked, "You don't even know the name of our continent, let alone know what we do there. You call it dark because you are ignorant and scared of it. That is why we have traveled such a long distance to..." Oakes bit his tongue, causing a few drops of blood to drip down his chin.

Zurie perked up and furrowed her brows. "A long distance to what? What were you going to say?"

He wiped the drops of blood from his chin. "You will find out when the time is right—if you haven't met the second death by then."

The ship anchored itself at a small docking station in front of a small island compared to the Europia mainland. *This island screams contraband and illegal substances. Could this be another blood knight test?* Oakes glanced at her with one eyebrow raised. His distaste was evident in his piercing green eyes. As he stared at her, she could feel beads of sweat drip down her forehead, causing her to stir. "What... what is it?" she said.

Oakes smirked. "You're rather anxious for a vamp. I take it you were turned within the last fifty years."

Zurie scrunched her face together. "As a matter a fact... that is correct. What of it?"

Oakes burst into a fit of laughter. His sharp teeth glistened under the moonlight. "Elementary, my dear Zurie. Female vamps reborn within the last fifty years on this continent tend to be cross. The male vamps aren't much better... I won't reveal what we call them. Just know that in Africanus, we have a deep understanding of you people."

She stomped her feet. "Why do you hold us in such contempt?"

Oakes paused for a moment before speaking. "How can I not? To see an entire continent of vampires be turned into pets, bowing down to their oppressive masters. We are the superior creature, and yet you let them sleep in peace during the night. They should be cowering behind their crosses every single night. Not sleeping in silk threads and marble towers, while you what? You eat rations you hate and live in servitude to the boot on your face. Forced to live huddled together in rat-infested dens."

Zurie mumbled, "One gets used to the rats..."

Oakes gripped her by the throat, his iron nails latching onto her skin. "You are a poor excuse for a vampire, and we will have to rectify that before we pursue further."

Zurie's eyes bulged outside of their sockets. *I don't like this. To be dominated. I'm sick and tired of being intimidated. I must achieve greatness, not for my own suspicious goals such as my greed but for my noble ones of which I have none yet...* The blood rushed towards her head. As her strength left her, she tapped his wrist with what little power she had left. Releasing her, he walked towards a small cage that contained a small white-and-red creature with wings. Opening the cage, he beckoned Zurie over. It had been three days since she last consumed rations, and the effects of starvation had changed her radically. Her eyes were not their usual purple, and her fangs had extended without her will.

Oakes smiled, displaying his sharp teeth. "This here is a chicken. It's quite abundant in your city, though you wouldn't have encountered one during the night. I think you should have a taste."

Zurie picked the chicken up by the legs and opened her mouth—then paused. Her mouth was salivating at the thought of drinking from a live animal. "But... to feast on a living creature is punishable by the second death."

Oakes sighed, "Who is going to know but me? We're in the middle of nowhere. Go on... it will be ok." She could see a twinkle in his eye.

Zurie gripped the neck of the flailing bird and was about to sink in her teeth when her thoughts intruded once again. *Am I really going to break the sacred oath as a vampire? The Cleric's Order made me swear upon my second life that I would follow their rules when I was turned. Plus, I have* my former betrothed *to think about: the one who truly spared my life on that eve. Would he really come back to finish the job he should have completed that evening?*

Before she knew it she had sunk her teeth in the neck of the chicken, the warm liquid soothed her tongue, provoking a tingling sensation. Her free hand quivered, making the entire arm vibrate. As she sucked the sweet ruby liquid from the neck of the creature, her eyes rolled to the back of her head. Finally, when it was nothing more than a dry carcass, she dropped the chicken to the ground.

Her lips curled into an eerie smirk. Her body tingled in satisfaction after consuming the pure liquid. Her heart raced; the creature's life force flowed throughout her slim body, tensing her. With her eyes fixed on Oakes, she commanded his attention with two fingers, beckoning him closer.

She whispered into his ear, "You will tell me what I am doing here, and you will tell me now."

Oakes' eyes flickered between green and brown and, for a moment, he resembled a human.

He ran his hand through his gorgeous locks before pointing to the island that they had anchored near. "This island is where we will find out your true nature. It is a place where a crossed vampire becomes a blood knight or stays a mere vamp. I'm sure you feel like a real creature of the night now."

Zurie winced but kept her composure. "I have taken the test many times and failed, though never on such an island. As for the chicken, I admit… it was as if I was on the brink of the second death for the past forty years and no one told me. Those sneaky clerics. Depriving us of our natural food source weakens us. But why should I bother failing the test again? Each time only results in more ridicule and embarrassment."

Oakes rubbed his chin. "This is a special test that I think you will be aptly suited for, now that you have had your fill. A common tactic before engaging, and something your den-mates would have told you had they truly wanted you to succeed. Your distrust of me is misplaced. It is I who truly wants what is best for you. Deep in your core is something that very few vamps have. It's rare even among blood knights. It's a spark of hope that keeps on dreaming even when backed against a wall. What feats would you accomplish if you were a blood knight?"

Zurie licked her lips. "First, I'd rebuild my den. With my newfound respect, I could build a healthy den of merchants. Then…"

Oakes gripped Zurie by the collar. "You think to be a blood knight is to be a mere merchant? This continent must have gone further down the pits than I could have imagined. To be a blood knight is to be the paramount example of vampire dignity and resistance. We take aim at our oppressors and strike fear into their cold hearts."

Zurie felt small in her clothing, "I don't want to talk about this. War is bad for business. I'm a merchant, and artifacts are what lift my spirits."

But she felt something stir within her stomach as if his words had touched her heart.

He gazed at her. "Very well. We will pause such matters for now." He pointed towards a small stone structure in the distance. "Try and keep up."

With incredible speed he dashed forward and jumped off the side of the boat. Zurie followed suit, pushing her legs to their limits. *I am three times as fast, and I feel as many times as strong. All this from drinking blood straight from a living source? I wonder what human blood would do to me. Blast, I must cast such thoughts away from my skull, I'd be a fool to try such a thing. The clerics would have my head on a platter.*

As she blitzed through the water, vivid images of feasting on a human tickled her mind. *My thoughts are as intrusive as he is. I need to think of something positive. Perhaps I'd be able to unlock the true powers of a toxin vampire if I continue to follow his lead. I must exist for a valuable reason. I can't only be good for parlor tricks like some parrot. The other vamps treat me and my kind the way humans treat us all. If it wasn't for the Cleric's Order the humans wouldn't dare to be so arrogant and abusive towards us. But... how did we lose the war? Why is it that none of the books on the war go into detail about how it ended? What about the twenty-year time gap between the end of the war and the ten-year revolt?*

She had reached the island only a few seconds behind Oakes.

Breathing shallowly, she bent down to touch the grainy material beneath her feet. She took up a handful. "How can such a place remain hidden from the clerics?"

Oakes glanced down, took his own handful and threw it into the water. "The clerics are not the all-powerful collective that they appear. It is true that this mysterious light of theirs grants them the ability to stand toe to toe with most vampires. But the oppression they have placed upon this continent can be lifted."

Zurie placed a hand upon her head. The muscles of her scalp strained against her skull. She raised one eyebrow, "What is happening? It feels as if my mind is fighting off some sort of attack from within."

Oakes folded his arms and tilted his head back. "It would seem you're fighting off their programming. It's a shift of paradigm. We suspect they put something in the dye, some sort of incantation that clouds the judgement and further weakens the spirit. Drinking the diluted blood is almost like a double dose of trouble for your mind."

She gently touched her forehead, "There is so much that I don't know. I suppose I have lived my life blinded to the truth." With her hands clasped one over the other, she held her staff tight. "Where are we?"

Oakes placed both his hands on his hips. "This is a sanctuary for vampires who wish to live the way they were meant to." Zurie touched the odd-looking stone structure. It was solid with a strong base, and triangles that met in a point at the top. As she walked around the corner of the structure, her fingertips buzzed from every centimeter.

Her gaze was captured by the sparkling white pointed top of the structure, "What manner of artifact is this?"

Oakes touched it, causing it to flare bright sparkles of dust. "This is what we call *The Pyramid of Destiny*. It is a key ingredient to your success in the event. If you're lucky, this will remain your home. Essentially it is a feeding quarter that you must defend while simultaneously attacking another."

An eerie silence filled the air as a soft warm breeze cast itself between them. *Luck? I must rely on luck to survive this event? I haven't had luck since the day I won the race to procreation.* Droplets of sweat covered her palms and forehead. Rubbing her forehead with her clammy hands, she licked her lips. "Now... let's just say Lady Luck does not smile upon my face this eve. What would happen then?"

Their gazes met as he stared without blinking. His vision seemed distant, as if he was in another time or place. He took his sharp fingernail and clawed it against his wrist, causing blood to streak down. The two vamps stood there as his blood dripped onto the sand. *What the fang is wrong with him?* She shuffled in her winged boots slightly. She was about to speak, but he beat her to it. "Let's just say... one would prefer the second death to failing to meet the requirements of the event while on this island."

Zurie's knees rattled. "I see." She pulled her staff from her back and stood it on the unsteady sands. Using the staff for leverage, she walked towards the entrance. After a few steps, she had regained her composure. With one hand on the door handle she took a deep breath. *Am I really going to do this? Risk my neck for some high-stake version of the blood knight test?* Zurie cracked the door slightly to feel a gust of air rush past her. She lurched forward as if a hidden force were controlling her. Her eyes widened.

The large room inside was filled with monkshood plants: one of the most poisonous plants on the mainland. Its vibrant purple color beckoned her. The walls were painted gold and purple, with pictures of famous vampires from the past. First was the illustrious and ferocious Vamp Lord himself. Second was the sweet and ever-melodic Durriken with his violin. Third came the Duke himself, who might or might not have been a vamp. In the middle of the room lay a large golden coffin decorated with various sigils and symbols. "It would seem the vamp who lived here was well off... I wonder if he left behind any artifacts."

With one hand clutching her staff and the other open and sweaty, she approached the coffin. Her greed far surpassed any sense of caution. *It couldn't hurt to peek; Perhaps this is what I'm supposed to do.* With her free hand she attempted to lift open the coffin to no avail. *Artifacts, artifacts, artifacts.* Resting the staff against the golden object, she pried it open with both hands.

Looking down she was met with the visage of herself.

— 6 —

A NIGHT'S PROWL

*I*t had been sixty days since the High Cleric took over, and Althalos had found numerous reasons to avoid the night's investigation. This time he found himself pensive after a blowout with one of the other commanders, who had newfound gall since befriending the High Cleric. The more he tried to maintain the standards and regulations of the Order, the more the other high officials' distaste for him increased. The power and respect he had once wielded over the facility had dwindled to a mere sliver.

To think I have found myself in such a position. An outcast in the facility that I helped build with my own two hands. How could this be? The cool breeze of the night washed over him like a bath from the city's House of Ice. The average human would have gone into shock during the cold winter nights, but Althalos was no average human. His every step left large footprints in the snow. His hawk eyes dashed back and forth on high alert as he scanned the putrid scum creeping along his beloved city. The vamps watched him with rabid curiosity, but none made motion to approach. It was as he had hoped: His scent gave him away as human, but their fear of the Clerics Order kept their grimy hands at bay. While permitting himself a slight smirk, he continued his path towards the boardwalk.

Upon arrival he was met with two large guards. One held an owl on one arm and the other had a spear in one hand. *Is this supposed to be security? I find it completely preposterous that they would be this organized. These new age vamps are not intelligent enough. Must be stragglers of some kind.* He made motion for the two guards to remove themselves, "Boardwalk pass?" said one of the guards.

Althalos raised an eyebrow and placed one hand on his short sword. "I don't have one of those. I just came here to shop."

The two guards looked at each other and sighed. He recognized one of the guards as security from one of the taverns, while he suspected the other was a vamp. The human took

— 39 —

one step forward. "Sorry, friend. But ever since that blood knight met the second death during a duel, security must be airtight. Only approved merchants or buyers can enter."

Althalos weighed his options. *Must I reveal myself? Stealth was never my strong suit. Bribing them is beneath me for I am a commander of the highest order. But first I must know, how far their fear of the Order runs.*

He tightened his grip on the hilt of his short sword, "Listen here you beef-wit. If you don't let me in, I will tell the Order about this illegal operation. There will be so many clerics running down your vamp throats that this place will be nothing more than a swamp." He waited, satisfied, to be granted entrance.

After a long pause, the guards' cackling filled the ears of the Cleric Commander. Ears ringing, he switched between cold calculated rage and mild curiosity. On this night it seemed the mild curiosity would win. "What's so funny?" he grumbled.

The vamp guard paused his laughter for a slight moment to respond, "The Cleric's Order has all but been bought out. They claim it's to give the vamps something to do and promote vamp and human relationships, but we all know the higher ups in the Order just do it for the pinyooks."

Althalos took a step back, his eyes wincing at the very thought. *This lying scum will die at the tip of my sword, but I must know if they will dare sully my name in this rouse.*

Forcing his mouth open, he managed to respond, "Who?"

The human guard leaned in closer and whispered in his ear. "Two out of the three Commanders have indulged in the criminalities. They say the third is on his way... to his death bed, that is." He chuckled. "The prickly iceberg that is Commander Althalos would never bend to such a promising proposal. They say he is so cold and stupid that he defecates snowballs and eats them for breakfast."

Althalos lunged forward, his short sword aimed at the heart of the human who sullied the Order. The blade slid through into his chest into the heart. Blood spurted out in all directions. The vamp guard had time only to see the carcass drop to the floor before his throat was slit with the same weapon that downed his companion.

Wiping his blade with his cloth Althalos gazed out into the view before him. A long wooden boardwalk surrounded by swamp. He pulled the hefty bodies into the swamp and watched as they sunk under the weight of their own armor. *What little good their armor did them. I almost forgot how smooth a short sword can be.*

While traversing the boardwalk, he wiped as much blood as he could off his red cloak—not that it would matter. The vamps' uncanny sense of smell would pick up on the scent within moments. It would either help or hinder his progress. *I must know. I must find out more information on who manages this boardwalk, but I shall be discreet about it. I made a vow to myself that I would not kill in vain from the moment I picked up a weapon. I only hope I have not broken that vow on this night.*

Every step on the boardwalk was like a step into another world. The merchant shops offered rare delicacies from all over the continent, not to mention some dry goods that could have only come from the Dark Continent. *How can they have artifacts from the Dark Continent? I thought trade routes were ravaged by sea beasts and closed off to all.* On this night it would seem his curiosity would beckon his attention once more.

Althalos sat at what he recognized as a volute table. *I remember when the Bishop and I used to play before training. A young scrub like myself couldn't find a better mentor. I wonder if I can still execute that special move.* His mind wandered to days of the past where he was once the top volute player in the Order. The table had a large board on it with sixteen pieces on each side. A vamp sat across from him placing a large sack of pinyooks on the table.

He wore an eye patch on his left eye while revealing a menacing grimace as he sniffed the air surrounding them. "You've had a busy night, Commander." The Commander attempted to stand and gripped his short sword when three vamps placed their grubby hands on his shoulders, pushing him down. *How scrub of me, allowing myself to be blindsided by these creatures of blight.* His eyes shifted from vamp to vamp. *A total of ten. In my heyday I could have exterminated them like the vermin that they are, but I'm pushing sixty now. Will my age get the best of me?*

What he presumed to be a blood knight pointed to a vamp holding a small hammer, "He can fix your mace and imbue it with a suitable enchantment. That is... if I tell him to."

Althalos grumbled, "Who says I need a mace fixed?"

The blood knight's gruesome demeanor matched his face. Clouds of yellow vapor bubbled as the knight spoke. Althalos shuffled in the chair, in an effort to avoid the knight's decaying scent. *It must be a ghoul class vampire. The scent of human flesh is still upon its tongue, I had thought them to be extinct. It seems we are in the direst of situations.*

The knight curled its lips into a grotesque expression. "It seems you did not hear me. You're making me repeat myself, and I don't like repeating myself. I said, your fellow commander Brom Forthwind mentioned it in jest. He described the way your new High Cleric flipped your top with ease." The group of vamps chuckled to themselves.

Clenching the bottom of his cloak, Althalos spoke evenly. "Finish what business you have with me so I can go about my way."

The knight contorted his face into an even uglier expression, "You're as icy as they say. I'll be brief, human. I have a shipment of live goods coming in from the Northern section of what you guys call the Dark Continent. Normally I'd bring it in through the normal trade route and land it right here on the boardwalk. However, due to unforeseen circumstances, I need to use one of your trade routes. It's mostly taken care of; all I need you to do is remove the guards at the southern port. I wouldn't need to involve you if your pupils weren't unwilling to take bribes or forgo their positions. Naturally, you'd be compensated with a king's ransom."

Althalos glared at the blood knight, his eyes piercing through to its very being. *This poor daft creature thinks I'm like my comrades. I'd rather perish right here in my own filth than betray the Order. It seems I truly am underestimated. Do my forty years of service mean nothing?* Althalos glanced at the volute pieces on the table. He paused for a moment before speaking, "Do you play?"

Yellow mucous dripped from the knight's nose onto the table. His hand brushed one of the pieces, making it wobble, "I'm the best volute player in the world. I haven't even come close to being beaten since I was turned forty-nine years ago."

Althalos kept his icy stare upon the knight. "That's good to hear. I'm quite the player myself. Perhaps we could make a wager?"

The knight smiled, revealing several golden teeth and two sharp yellow fangs. "A wager? What did you have in mind?"

Althalos permitted himself a bit of relief upon hearing the response. *It's almost as if being turned unlocked a gambler's curse in the process. I have yet to hear of a vamp that could resist a healthy wager, especially if there was a life on the line.* It was at this point that he noticed there was a large crowd surrounding the pirate crew and himself. Most were vamps, but some were humans. The crowd seemed harmless, though increasingly curious.

The commander leaned in, still maintaining his glare, "If I win, you will fix my mace and allow me free passage back to the heart of the city."

The blood knight sat there for a few moments. "When I win, I'll take your arm for a nice snack, and you will arrange for free port of my live goods." A crisp breeze blew by, causing a few pieces to topple over.

I wonder if that is meant as a good omen or a bad one. I shall have to take my chances; my volute is a bit rusty, but how good can a vampire be? Althalos glanced at the purple piece that had fallen over at; it was the cleric piece that he was so fond of. *Not the best of starts.*

After fixing the pieces, they started their match of volute. *I'll have to refresh my memory as I go along. I can't trust the crowd to aid me,* thought the commander. He glanced over as the curiosity turned to interest in the eyes of the crowd and shook his head. The blood knight aligned his peasant pieces in a series of squares, a common setup for those wishing to end the match in short order. The commander, taking heed from his days in training, placed the peasant pieces in triangle formation: a defensive tactic used to prolong the match against superior opponents.

With a chuckle, the blood knight clutched his stomach. "I haven't seen such a childish tactic used since I was a mere human."

These vermin believe the vamps are the superior race. Yet look how they live, in squalor with trash laid about. Skulking in the night feeding off our good will. I think not. My defensive formation will last; I just need to procure enough time until daylight.

There was a loud groan as one of the vampire buffoons stumbled towards the table. He brought what smelled like unsanctioned human blood in a mug for the blood knight and a beer for the commander. *Probably mixed in with his urine as added flavor.* He nodded and continued to play.

The peasant pieces dropped back and forth as the knight attempted to trump the defenses of the commander. After losing most of his peasant pieces to the commander's cleric pieces, the knight flipped the board and withdrew his curved sword, "For fang's sake, let's just eat and kill him. We still have to find that rogue toxin vamp."

Before the pirates standing behind Althalos could move, he grabbed his short sword and slit their throats. The rest encircled him with their fangs protruding, their eyes vibrant as the moon's glow.

He said a small prayer to the light before activating the enchantment upon his weapon. "In the name of the light, I seek reprieve from the wicked; I shall cleanse them in your honor. I activate Frost Touch." The commander's muscular figure assumed this battle form for the first time in twenty years. His muscles stretched and ached, but they remained steadfast like their owner. "Let's go, I don't have all night."

He could hear the chatter among the vamps whispering about the legendary Frost Touch enchantment. "Oh, I have heard the commander could use it, but I didn't believe it." said one vamp.

"I wouldn't want to be those vamps right about now. That's the legendary Althalos Frost Touch. Feared amongst vamps and humans alike." said another.

The knight joined the fray with his weapon unleashed. He snapped his boots together and activated his own enchantment. "Winged flight upon winged blight. I activate Blight Foot." The boots hurled the blood knight into the sky, raining down sticky liquid upon the crowd. The stench made several of the vamps gag. Boils emerged on the skins of the unlucky victims. The blood knight whizzed over Althalos, launching the boil-inducing rain towards his body.

The commander grabbed a nearby vampire by the collar and raised him in the air as a shield. The putrid liquid washed over the vamp, making him bellow out in agony. Another vampire pulled out a pistol and fired it at the commander's head. While dodging the bullet, he dived upon the vamp with his short sword in the air. The weapon came crashing down on the vamp, causing severe ice damage. The ice spread from the tip of the sword throughout the body of the vamp, freezing him completely.

The remaining knights stood there with their weapons drawn and jaws agape. Their blood knight leader landed with a gentle touch, his energy running low. Althalos gazed at them while breathing heavily. "What are you waiting for, you scum? Engage so I can send you to your frozen destiny."

The blood knight sheathed his weapon. "You've done well. I was never fond of them. Daybreak will soon be upon us; allow me to reconsider my position. Let it be a gesture of good will that we fix and enchant your mace. It is my hope that you will reconsider your position on future shipments. Business is good, and as such it is only fair that we share such fortune with our future partner."

His slimy grin made Althalos want to gag, but he maintained his cool expression. The blood knight directed his crewmate to fix the commander's mace. Within a few moments the mace was enchanted and in proper working order. All that was left was to personalize the weapon making it more in synch with its wielder. The commander stepped beside the mace, wrapping his pendant around the weapon. The vamp blacksmith said a few words in the vamp tongue, a language punishable by castration. *The vamps no longer fear the Clerics Order. An insurgency can break out at any moment.*

7

REFLECTIONS OF ME

How many nights has it been? Ten, twenty, thirty? I've lost track. The corpse before me has yet to decay; it lays there in the coffin calling me forth. I touch it and it stirs ever so slightly. For umpteen days I have sat here, watching my reflection lay there decorated in foreign clothing. The difference does not stop with my garments, for my reflection holds a white and gold pistol. The scent of monkshood brings me back to childhood, when the older kids would stuff it down my pants. Why would this reflection of me be surrounded by such a flower? Where did she come from? Is she my future self or the best features of myself? I mean she seems well-off...

The slot cracked open, breaking her concentration, but before she could turn around it was closed shut again. Another chicken had been thrown in for her consumption. She looked at the pile of dry chicken carcasses. Feasting had made her mind clear; she could focus her intentions and had gained access to many different types of serpents. Yet she was stuck on the bigger questions, like what was the purpose of the facility? How could she get out? And what should she do with her more well-off reflection laying in the coffin? Zurie paced back and forth, her staff held by her beloved boa constrictor twirling under the dim lighting.

With both her hands free, she talked through her train of thought again. "My premise is quite simple. This must be for my highest good. I have grown stronger, smarter, and more powerful since meeting him. Additionally, me being here will aid in his future endeavors. I don't know how I know, but I sense it. Could it be that I am unlocking even more powers?" She flicked her wrist, causing her boa constrictor to toss the staff in the air. With her brows furrowed, she continued to pace. The frustration swarmed her like a tornado as she bellowed out. She clasped her throbbing temples and stooped down to gather her bearings.

It was then that a small voice, something akin to a whisper, called out to her. "Come."

Zurie hurled her body towards the coffin. "Yes? Yes? Did you call me?" There was no response. Zurie looked up to the ceiling for the umpteenth time, gazing at the image of two vamps bowing to each other, "Those purple lines of energy weren't there before."

Using all her might, she lifted the slender figure out of the coffin and placed it against the base. The figure was more royal than merchant with her foreign purple and gold garments. While focusing all her energy towards her doppelganger, she managed to establish a mental link. Visions of great battles on the sea, land, and air against vampires, humans, and countless other creatures swarmed her consciousness. Feeling the heat of the link increase, she pulled away instinctively, causing it to close. Zurie stood up with her jaw clenched.

"I will not be a poor excuse for a vamp my entire second life. It is better to perish a great blood knight than to live a coward." She switched clothing with the doppelganger and took the pistol from its body. Armed with staff, pistol, and dagger, she felt like a true knight. Upon reaching the exit of the structure, she knelt and focused her energy upon the door. The door swung open to reveal a full moon. Zurie peered out onto the open sands to see that the pyramid had moved somewhere else on the island. There was a group standing in a crowd in the distance.

Could this be the beginning of the event? She closed the distance quickly and joined the crowd, who paid her no mind. *There are vamps of all kinds, some said to be extinct. It's clear there is more to vamp culture than even I know. I'll have to be careful lest anyone try to steal my artifacts.* Above the crowd was a stage with three full-fledged blood knights dressed in jewel-encrusted silk garments. She recognized one of them as Oakes.

One of the knights stood up from his seat and placed his fingers atop the head of a rattlesnake. "Welcome to the sacred ten-year event where one can taste the power of the Vamp Lord." Everyone in the crowd lowered their head at the mere mention of the prominent figure.

Zurie raised an eyebrow. "Could he be a toxin vamp? He must be a toxin vamp, for only my kind can communicate with serpents—yet he is communicating to a massive crowd via a mental link. That would require a tremendous amount of focus. I would love to learn from him. I can sense his power."

A short furry creature with pointed ears kicked her on the shin. "Quiet, you. You're making it difficult to hear what the Sansabonsam is saying. That toxin vamp is just a distraction."

Zurie focused all her attention on Oakes, who was explaining the value of the pouches that would be handed out. With one red, one green, and one blue pouch in hand, he finished his demonstration. Beads of sweat dripped down Zurie's face.

"I failed to catch the beginning, what did my ears miss?"

The furry vamp gazed at her through squinted eyes. "I'll tell you the beginning if you tell me the end. If you lie to me... you'll be the first one I hunt."

Zurie covered her mouth to keep from chuckling and managed to pull off a nod instead. The furry vamp crossed his arms before speaking, "He said if you have a red pouch you must bring back red and green pouches, if you have a green pouch you must bring back green and blue pouches, and if you have a blue pouch you must bring back blue and red pouches. Now you're turn, what did he say after that?"

Zurie nodded again. "If you have the same colored pouch as another vamp you can work together, but know that you will be expected to bring back two each of the required pouches, not one. He also mentioned something about a terror being set free on the event grounds."

The furry vamp's eyes grew wide. "How unfortunate. This year they are looking to cull the herd in the most gruesome of ways. I suppose I must introduce myself now that we have been acquainted. You will refer to me as Dr. Asher. Nothing more and absolutely nothing less."

Zurie placed both her hands on her hips as she peered down at the supposed doctor. He wore a monocle over one of his vacant black eyes. The lack of irises sent shivers down her spine. The red fur of the "doctor" was raggedy at best, while the large pointed ears had a small golden ring at the tip of each ear. He wore a squirrel skull as a hat. The toxin vamp covered her mouth once again but to no avail. She burst out in a fit of laughter.

The doctor withdrew a razor thin blue dagger and a blue iron ball. "Didn't your sire teach you not to laugh at other vamps? You never know who you may offend. Lucky for you I am used to other vamps ridiculing me due to my stature. One day I will be known as the greatest doctor among humans and vampires alike save for the legendary Dr. Caspian. My name will ring out over the rooftops and through the heavens." He let out a guttural cackle, making the vamps surrounding them scowl.

Something about this vamp draws me in. If only I could exude even half the confidence that he possesses. I constantly flip flop and it irks my spirit, but what am I to do besides push forward into what is my destiny? I must win this event and become a full-fledged blood knight or die trying.

With her red pouch in hand, Zurie turned to glance at Oakes one last time before taking her position in front of the pyramid Oakes had procured for her. The rules were simple. Any vamp that still drew breath and had the correct colored pouches by the third night would drink the blood of the Vamp Lord. If one lived but failed to obtain the correct pouches, one was free to leave in shame but could never try again. She took a handful of sand and threw it in the air, the sand sparkled in tandem with the moon. Before the beginning of the challenge, she revealed a final smile.

A semicircular horn went off blasting a high-pitched sound across the island. Upon hearing the horn, she drew her staff and assumed her battle stance. *I'm fortunate he rented a pyramid that was close to the safe zone. I can lay here for three nights, and when the time comes, I'll just make my way outside. Unless... that means more vamps will want to attack me for the spot? Perhaps I have been placed upon a double-edged sword? Lord of the Night I ask that you watch over me on this eve.*

As she paid quick homage to the Vamp Lord her hand shivered, causing the staff to rattle. *I will stick to my strategy and utilize the high ground. It would be improper for me to meet my second death when I have just been given hope for greatness.* As Zurie bent down to scratch her knee an arrow whizzed by her head lodging itself into the door of her pyramid.

With her mind clear and body fierce, she aimed her pistol at the vamp's chest. Her finger caressed the destructive weapon. With a slight pull of the trigger she sent a silver projectile into the chest of her adversary.

Another vamp descended from the heavens, its fangs glistening under the moonlight. Zurie ducked, and the vamp slammed into the door with a loud cracking sound. She whipped around with her staff and threw the full weight of her might onto the back of the creature's head. The skull cracked upon impact bringing a slightly pleasant sensation in the toxin vamp.

With her mind and body abuzz from the battle she had a peculiar thought. *If drinking the life force of the Lord of the Night would make me stronger permanently, what would happen if I drain the life force of these lesser vamps?*

Fangs in place, Zurie was about to pierce skin when a portal opened, allowing Dr. Asher to walk through. With a pipe between his lips he said, "Now why would a toxin vamp break taboo like that? Very odd indeed; this will make for quite the experiment. Carry on then."

With her pupils dilated Zurie turned to the doctor. She swung her staff at the vamp's head, but upon impact the staff broke in two.

Dr. Asher let out a cruel shrill of a laugh as Zurie clawed at the shattered pieces of wood. "Look what disaster you have caused! Begone with you, foul rodent."

The black soulless eyes of Dr. Asher darkened in their depth. His paw tapped against the hilt of his dagger as if he was teetering upon the edge of death itself.

He licked his lips and sniffed the cool damp air with fervor. "Do you taste that toxin vamp with minor toxic powers?"

Zurie placed one hand on her pistol. She could feel herself weakening by the minute, "I'll know the... the... taste of your blood when I'm done with you."

Dr. Asher grinned, revealing several sharp teeth and two golden fangs, "I taste the air of confusion, fear, and above all... death. The Terror has been set loose and over half the contestants have met the second death by its hand already." Zurie's knees buckled, and she dropped to the floor.

After a few moments her energy was cut in half. "Wh... what... do you want me to do about it?"

Dr. Asher clapped his paws together. "My tent was destroyed; in fact most tents have been destroyed. One could imagine my luck when I picked up your scent at one of the more sturdy locations. We will team up and defend this position with our lives. I assure you... this beast is something I have never seen before." He jammed his left paw into his mouth, making thirteen pouches of varying colors to purge themselves from his insides, spilling to the floor covered in a pink liquid.

The toxin vamp glanced at the pouches and plucked out a green pouch with a piece of her shattered staff. "It seems to me that I don't have much of a choice." She piled up the pieces of her broken staff and threw them down the hill. With her other hand she took out the enchanted dagger.

Dr. Asher analyzed the dagger with his monocle, "Where did you get that dagger?"

Zurie pulled it out of the good doctor's range of vision. "I won it in a duel against a blood knight's right hand." There were a few moments of silence before the Doctor took out several pieces of parchment.

He held them up one by one under the moonlight, letting out a few grumblings here and there. "It seems they have placed you on the hunted list. There is a bounty of one hundred pinyooks to capture you alive, probably so they can torture and flay you themselves."

Zurie gasped, "I've seen lost horses garner higher bounties. Is my head only worth a hundred pinyooks?" The furry creature looked up to the scrawny figure before him.

He took out a piece of chalk and scribbled on the bounty sheet, "Lucky for you, I'm not interested in betraying an ally for a measly hundred pinyooks. But one would think there are plenty of vamps who would wish to find themselves in good favor with a blood knight. You ought to settle your debt with them or you will be on the run for as long as you draw breath." He took off his squirrel skull and did a bow with his ears touching the ground, "Fear not, Dr. Asher will..."

The giant bat creature emerged from the shadows.

Zurie trembled, "That's the creature that wiped out my den and put me in this position to begin with."

"You've encountered The Terror and lived? Perhaps you will serve a greater purpose."

Its wings swayed, causing tornadoes to form out of thin air. The towering tornadoes swooped up a few of her competitors, shredding them apart in mere seconds. With its green blades, it severed the heads of two other vamps. Covered in blood, it opened its orifice and let out a high pitch screeching sound. Zurie felt tingles all over her body as the echolocation bounced off her and back to The Terror. Her head buzzed with thoughts while the screaming words of Dr. Asher rang in her ears. Zurie snapped back to her senses to hear one word: "Run."

8

KINK IN THE ARMOR

Althalos had scoured every single portion of the Cleric's Order's grounds in search of the High Cleric. The large, bulky figure was a mere mist following the days of his investigation. Althalos had turned to the streets, where his search had led him to the pubs. *I must find the High Cleric. He has been gone too long. The High Cleric is a holy person who must be protected and tracked at all costs.* Before he entered the last pub at the edge of the city, he thought to himself, Could *it be that the man is so repulsive he would day-drink in public? A High Cleric is one position under Bishop. It is a position of unimaginable influence and reverence, yet he day-drinks daily—but to do it in public...*

When he entered the pub, the bartender widened her eyes. She bowed halfway and poured a mug of ale while sliding it towards the commander. The commander raised both his eyebrows and clenched his teeth. *How presumptuous of this bar maiden, that I came here to... well it is a pub.* He retained his cool expression. He looked around to see that it was empty. It was a dingy place, with boarded-up windows and blood stains on the floor. Clearly it housed vamps during the night. He could barely hear her soft-spoken voice above the grinding of his teeth. She bowed again and repeated herself. "It's on the house, milord. Would you wish to have company or be left alone? I'm sorry to ask but I never know, with you cleric types."

Althalos tapped his fingers against his belt. His white day cloak was already being stained by his surroundings, "Company would please me on this occasion. Perhaps you can tell me more about my comrades."

She shook like a mighty storm. "I'm not sure... I do not wish to get anyone in trouble." She placed her open hand on the table.

Althalos adjusted his belt. *Once again it shows its ugly face—the weight and power of humanity's one true sovereign, greed.* He pulled out a large pouch of pinyooks all made of the highest grade of material. He removed two pinyooks with the Cleric's symbol on them and tossed them on the counter. They bounced off and landed in her grubby palms.

With a smile and nod she gave him the story that was not hers to tell. "We don't get too many of your people, but we do have a few regulars who come this far for privacy." She covered her face with her hands. "I can't believe I'm doing this. Perhaps it would be best I reconsider milord."

Althalos remained cool as ice. *The common folk have become depraved just like the vamps. Naturally she has her price. What happened to human decency? Honor? Sense of duty? For the second time I am made aware of my age.*

He took out three more pinyooks, spat on them and placed them on the counter, "Better the pinyooks than your face, one would suppose. You have tried my patience; it is time you tell me what you know."

Without hesitation she scooped up the three wet pinyooks and placed them in her apron pocket, "There is a group of pupils who come by twice a week. I don't know all of their names, but there is this one handsome one—I think his name is Lief." Althalos' heart sank to his stomach as he felt a twisting sensation fill his innards. He bit his lip to prevent from speaking in an ill manner.

She continued, "Brom comes by frequently as well. Though I haven't seen him in a while. Perhaps he found himself a drinking buddy. He said he missed drinking with you and hadn't had a drinking buddy since you know what…"

Althalos' eyes turned frigid as he gazed into her soul. "No… I don't know what. Tell me."

Frozen stiff, she bit her tongue before she spoke. "Si… since… the death of the Bishop."

Althalos drew a sigh of relief. *Good, he has kept his mouth shut about… her. The past mistakes must stay there.*

The great commander placed a hand on her hand. "Continue. You will not be reprimanded over what you speak of. You have my word as a cleric."

She nodded, although she backed up against the counter that stood behind her, "We had this one peculiar patron. He was a large, bulky fellow and he carried a large axe. But the odd thing was that he dawned the markings of a High Cleric. He drank up a storm before cackling and boasting of how he had a feast to go to. Paid me one quarter of a pinyook to keep quiet. I honestly didn't know pinyooks could come that small."

Althalos dropped two more pinyooks and was about to leave when she spoke up once again, "One more thing milord... he said he was going to the brothel outside of town. It's been a while or so but I'm sure the maidens there will have remembered such an odd fellow."

Althalos nodded as he rushed out the door.

With a swing of his leg he mounted his purebred horse. The visage of white and red blurred past the iron gates of the city limits. *It's been over a week since I've last seen the High Cleric. Could it be that he would stay at a brothel for that long? To think: a High Cleric being entertained by maidens of low status. What would the council think?*

The horse galloped several miles out before they arrived at a large building dawning pink and purple drapes. He dismounted his horse with ease to gaze at the large sign that said Pilgrim's Inn. "I was the one who banned this filth out of my beloved city; now I must enter for the good of the city. This city was supposed to be the epitome of human vamp relations, a new frontier." He curled his hand into a ball and slammed it against the door.

A latch unlocked, and the door swung open to reveal a maiden less than half his age with glowing features. She wore blue mascara and glitter on her face. She smiled with beaming pearly white teeth. Althalos shuffled around in his cloak. "What... manner of angel has the underworld sent forth to persuade me into depravity?"

The maiden raised an eyebrow. "I beg your pardon milord?"

Althalos removed his crest and pointed it in the maiden's direction. "I am Althalos Clarke of the Cleric's Order. You will grant me passage into your domain. I'm looking for a member of my Order."

The maiden smiled once again. "Oh milord you are so formal... I'm sure we can find someone worthy of your attention, if I am not suited as such." He squinted his eyes. *I'm not sure if she is toying or flirting with me. It has been so long since I have been with a woman.* His ravenous appetite threatened to return while he traversed the insides of the brothel. He was led down a pink hallway filled with the scent of lilacs. The walls had paintings of naked women in various positions. Althalos' member stood to attention as they continued down the hall and into a private dining room.

The madam was a woman of middle age with a scar down her left eye that did little to diminish her beauty. She eyed Althalos from top to bottom and pulled out a writing utensil and a letter. In a smooth raspy voice, she spoke. "He said someone of your like would arrive within due time."

Althalos' eyes intensified. "Speak in quick succession; I'd rather not spend more time..." he looked around, "here than I have to."

The madam of the brothel gave him a lustful gaze. "I like a man who knows how to take control. Are you the one they call Commander Frozen Touch, sometimes poked at as being a stern finger?"

His demeanor remained cool while the frigid storm of his temper twisted and turned. "I am Althalos, commander of The Clerics Order in this city, the experimental garrison of the entire continent. Now, if you please," he said through gritted teeth.

The madam stood up before lowering her body into a curtsy that revealed a large portion of her bosom, "This is the number that we are owed from the Cleric's Order. A bill accrued by your High Cleric. Additionally, this is the bill for the damages that we have incurred, including my prized merchandise."

Althalos scanned the madam up and down. "You mean to tell me he incurred the cost of 17,940 pinyooks in the span of seven days? You must take me for a fool. How can a wench cost so much? I cannot agree to pay such an invoice."

The young maiden crossed her arms, "Could the kind sir refrain from referring to me and my kind as wenches? We are maidens of the highest order." Althalos' stomach did back flips.

He covered his mouth with the back of his hand, "This farce will carry on no longer. You wenches will close down your business and tell me where the High Cleric went." The madam pulled out a throwing knife and pointed it at the commander.

His icy demeanor softened. "Madam, put that thing away before you hurt yourself. I will not lay hands on a woman; that would be unseemly."

She pulled out a second dagger from underneath her skirt, "You have offended past your position, and you will be taught a lesson in how to talk to a lady." The commander turned to the young maiden, who brandished a metallic whip with blades on the end.

He gripped the hilt of his mace but remained steadfast in his vow never to injure a civilian woman. *I will not draw on these women lest they get hurt. I will have to use my hands to defend myself. If I can just get in close and subdue them, I can diffuse the situation.*

He placed his arms out in front and widened his stance, assuming the defensive position of the Order. The maiden twirled and danced about using the whip to keep him in position, while the Madam launched forth several daggers, each aimed at his heart. He dodged the first, then the second, but the third he was forced to deflect with his hand. The dagger sliced his hand.

I must take the offensive or I will fall on this day.

He launched forward, causing ice to form beneath his feet. Gliding quickly, he was about to grab ahold of the maiden when her whip latched onto his leg, pulling him to the ground. The Madam did several front flips until she landed her boot into his face. His face stung as blood gushed out, dripping down his face as he laid tangled in the young maiden's whip.

She swiftly tied his arms with wire, leaving him at their mercy. The one known as Commander Frozen Touch sighed as he prepared to change his destiny. *I truly underestimated these... women. It seems there are places where chivalry need not tread.*

With what little maneuvering room he had, he gripped the hilt of his mace and focused his intention upon freezing the whip. When the whip shattered, he rose to his feet, facing the two women. In his most commanding voice he spoke, "This ends here. Although I do not take back my words, I will apologize for having said them out loud. For some things should not be said, and even ladies of the night such as yourselves deserve to be treated better than I have demonstrated."

The madam of the house smirked and bowed. "Perhaps we can come to a mutually beneficial arrangement."

9

NOT A SPRINT

Zurie ducked another echo wave, the pulsating force nearly bounced off the back of her head. Her sensitive nature had paid off, as she was able to sense when the wave was coming. The Terror rampaged in their direction, ravaging every vamp it met along its path. The screams of the damned filled her ears. The woods were filled with destroyed huts and tents.

She ran towards a place that she hoped would bring salvation. *I don't know how much longer I can last; this body isn't meant for long distance running.* When the two misfits arrived at a cave reeking of blood and death, Zurie collapsed to her knees. The Terror could be seen further out in the distance, but it had stopped to drink the blood of a large vamp who had attempted to fight it off. Dr. Asher watched with his mouth agape. "What a fool that oaf was, nobody tries to fight The Terror. To resist is to endure the most gruesome of torture. Better to run and hope that some other poor schlub takes the blow for you."

Zurie's stomach bubbled. "Maybe he had the right idea? I'm sick and tired of being a coward. This is the creature that put me in this mess to begin with. If it wasn't for this beast, I would still have my den." Dr. Asher took a few puffs of his pipe and smirked.

The harsh aroma filled Zurie's lungs, sending her into a coughing fit. "What, do you have a death wish? What if The Terror smells us?"

Dr. Asher gazed up at the toxin vamp with vacant eyes. He took one big puff of his pipe and blew into her face, "I'm sick of not having a puff of my pipe. Besides, if you take a look at where it is patrolling, you'll see it has pigeonholed everyone this way." He pointed into the distance to a group of vamps hiding in the bush, then to a few other groups scattered behind the trees. "Very few have attempted to fight The Terror. Perhaps the two of us can make a name for ourselves in such a deed."

With her hand over her mouth, Zurie's brain functioned at its maximum limit. "There is no need for it to meet the second death during our encounter. We only need to do enough damage to convince the other vamps to assist us. If we all engaged in battle, there is no reason why we cannot emerge victorious. I have once heard it whispered that fear stands for false evidence appearing real. This is something that we can do. We will avenge my den-mates and make a name for ourselves in the process."

With a paw caressing his iron ball, Dr. Asher gazed out at The Terror, who could be seen dismembering the limbs of the carcasses. "Do you know how The Terror came to be so?" asked Dr. Asher.

Zurie shrugged and shook her head.

Dr. Asher looked up to the sky as raindrops fell. "No one knows when or why, but the only vampire ever to be sired by the Lord of the Night is the one we call The Terror. All that is known is that The Terror followed the event coordinators to this continent from Africanus. Some say it is here to reclaim its birthright, while others say it is here to start a war. I say... it's here for the sheer pleasure of fresh blood, both human and vamp alike. But lately I've been thinking, maybe it's here for all three. My point is this. That out there is not some false reason to be scared. That is a very valid reason to hesitate. If I stick my furry neck out there, I need to know your arse isn't going to turn tail and leave me holding my hat at the last second."

She stared at the one that vampires called The Terror. Her eyes glazed over while her chest threatened to explode. "There comes a time in every vamp's life when she must stand for something. I will no longer run like the coward many take me for. On this night I stand for the pride of my den." She gripped the pendant that represented the Merchant's Corner.

With her other hand on her pistol, she slinked through the bushes towards The Terror. The distinct scent of vamp blood entered her nostrils. The Terror grabbed a bulbous vamp cowering behind a tree. Within moments, the snapping of bones and crushing of flesh could be heard. Zurie circled through the bushes, entering the range of her pistol. Her mind took a turn of its own. *We could make a run for it from here. The Terror isn't as fast as it looks.* She turned to Dr. Asher. *But what about my grand speech?*

A pox on grand speeches. Glory and pride are overrated.

Zurie was about to speak when Dr. Asher launched his iron ball towards the purple monstrosity. A shrill cackle erupted from the doctor as he launched forth with his dagger in hand. The ball struck The Terror on its head, exploding upon impact. A disorienting gas released, causing The Terror to kick and cough. Dr. Asher danced around the swipes and slashes that came in all directions while dealing damage of his own.

Zurie looked up to the full moon in an attempt to summon some unknown assistance, of which none came. She took a deep breath and pushed forward, pistol aimed at The Terror's chest. Sweat poured down her face as she took aim. She flicked the latch and pulled the trigger.

A large silver bullet shot forth and lodged itself into the chest of The Terror, causing it to bellow in agony. With the gas wearing off, The Terror grabbed Dr. Asher by his tail. It let loose a maniacal laugh before opening its jaw. *I suppose that's the end of that experiment. 'Tis a sad day for vamps everywhere, I had never heard of a vamp doctor before.*

Zurie was considering leaving when a wave of energy washed over her. One of her serpents whispered in her ear. *Cowards die miserable deaths.* She turned to see the doctor had gotten loose and was still engaged in battle. She screamed and slapped herself in the face as hard as she could. "I'm not going to die a coward!"

She rushed in with her dagger drawn and pistol loaded, this time within eyeshot of The Terror, who paid her no mind, "You will respect me," said Zurie, letting off another bullet into The Terror's body. She took her knife and slashed the stomach of The Terror, who glanced down at her with its eyes wide open.

Letting loose a low guttural growl, it gripped the necks of both Zurie and Dr. Asher. "Death comes slow for those that think they can resist." said The Terror.

Zurie's body cried out for oxygen. As her eyes closed, her brain activity raised several notches.

Two constrictors launched forth from her hands, wrapping around The Terror's neck. The beast gasped for air. *What is this sensation? I feel part of his essence flowing towards me. What am I gaining? Better yet... what is it losing?*

The toxin vamp felt power surge through her veins as her serpents drained energy from The Terror. A pool of acid gathered around The Terror's feet, causing it to sink in the toxic soup. Zurie and Dr. Asher both broke free. She took her dagger and jammed it into the abdomen of The Terror. It looked at her and curled its lips into a grotesque smile. Green liquid oozed from its mouth, coating the dagger and causing it to dissolve. Dashing backwards, both Dr. Asher and Zurie managed to get some distance.

The Terror glanced down at the wounds it had suffered and placed its hand over them. Within moments the wounds were sealed shut. It stretched its arms, then released the blades hiding beneath them.

"My turn," it said.

The voice sent shivers down Zurie's spine. The Terror catapulted itself towards Zurie with its blades drawn and slashed her stomach. She looked down to see her innards spill out onto the floor. As she glanced at the full moon one last time, she felt a wave of lunar energy rain down upon her body. Her mind drifted away as she collapsed to the ground.

The last thing she heard was a hiss.

The noise of the crowd filled her ears, causing her head to throb. She lifted her head, only to lay back down. Pressure was being applied to her shoulder. "Where am I?" were all the words she could muster. She wasn't so foolish to believe that there was an afterlife for her kind, nor was she wise enough to think what had occurred was possible.

A familiar voice said to her, "You're safe now. You did well." While she was unconscious certain events had occurred that would alter her life permanently. With her eyelids heavy, she took note of her surroundings. She was on an open stage in the middle of the night. The moon was waning, and she was parched, frail, and in pain. Underneath her body, many hands held her in the air. Zurie could hear a familiar voice tell them to place her body on a tablet. With her hands flailing up into the sky, she kicked and squirmed with the little strength she had. A gentle hand caressed her pale white face.

With great effort she spoke, "Where am I and what happened?" Through blurry vision, she recognized the faint image of Oakes. He lifted his hand from her face as they placed her body on a stone tablet.

Oakes opened a small vial and poured some type of liquid in Zurie's open mouth. A stinging sensation flowed into her as the liquid seeped through her body. She screamed in agony as the burning sensation spread throughout her body. *It hurts so much. I have never felt pain this great. Could they be killing me? No, I trust Oakes. I must endure and stop thinking the worst all the time. What do I remember last? I was fighting The Terror and then my guts were all over the ground. There was a hissing sound.* As her mind struggled to recall all the details, the burning sensation slowed and became a soft tingle.

The booming voice of the toxin vampire she saw earlier crept into her mind. "Rise, our sister in blood. You are no longer what you once were. You have passed the right of passage and are now a blood knight. The blood that runs through your veins is the same as many of the legendary vampires, and we expect great things from you. I now give you blood knight Zurie, the leader of our thirteenth division."

Cheers thundered from the crowd.

Other vampires plucked Zurie from the stone tablet, raising her to stand on her own feet. Her legs wobbled and her stomach hurt. Before the crowd, the others placed upon her the oversized armor of a blood knight. She looked down to see the flamboyant colors that expressed her new armor. *I look rather elegant for a blood knight. I thought blood knights were supposed to instill fear. Who fears an elegant knight?* She caressed the teal pauldrons that covered her shoulders. *However, I can get used to their function. I feel safer already.*

Oakes tapped her on the shoulder, refocusing her mind on the situation before her. "Come with me," he said. Dr. Asher and Zurie followed Oakes down a small opening in the middle of the stage. As they descended the stairs it became notably warmer. At the bottom, they were met with a large room and odd markings on the walls. Oakes walked over to the middle of the room, picked up a large, still-beating heart, and brought it over the two newly appointed blood knights.

Zurie crossed her arms. "What is going on? I will not take part in anything more until you explain to me what happened."

Oakes glared at her with those piercing green eyes. "Dr. Asher, it is best if you would explain; I'm not one to repeat myself," Oakes stated.

Dr. Asher bounced up and down with an iron ball in his hand, "Well, it's very simple. When you passed out, you managed to summon this massive serpent creature that dealt all sorts of corrosive damage, most of which was directed at The Terror. This carried forth until the bell rang, and The Terror retreated. I had never seen such a destructive creature before."

Oakes nodded. "After hearing the story the other knights decided that we would have to impart special changes for this year's event. It was decided that you will be promoted to blood knight of your own division, and as such you will partake in the vampire ritual to become a full-fledged blood knight. The last step is for you to enchant your weapons so you can embark on your mission with full confidence. To keep it in terms even you can understand, you're heading back to the Europia mainland."

Zurie dropped to her knees. "Why would that change anything? I'm still at a loss."

Oakes sighed. "Don't you see? The fact that you managed to summon such a high-level creature as your final attempt to survive shows great grit, focus, and above all cunning. All valued traits in the blood knights. It's a sign of hope for things to come. It means that there is something inside of you that lays dormant, something greater than the sum of what you are."

Zurie swallowed. Her hands shook, but she remained steady in her gaze. "So I am to achieve blood knight status for something I did unconsciously?"

Oakes and Dr. Asher both nodded with gleaming eyes.

With her fists tight, she lowered her head. *To finally become the one thing I sought after for so long through what? Sheer luck? I truly am unworthy.*

— 10 —
TRICK OF THE LIGHT

The night was crisp and cool, just the way he liked it. While the older scrubs were in the dining hall playing a game of volute, Althalos was in the stables brushing his beloved horse. With each stroke of his brush the mare cooed, causing him to flash a bright smile. "You're the only one I can trust in this place. Everyone else is either a liar or a scoundrel. What am I to do? Shall I write a letter to the council?" He continued to brush with gentle vigor. "On one hand, the council may view my letter as written insubordination due to my inability to get along with the High Cleric. Worse yet, they may see it as me simply being jealous and in fact, demote me." He paused brushing for a moment. "But on the other hand, they may send someone to investigate. However, an investigation would cause these unscrupulous characters to band together like a pack of dogs.

"They would lie, cheat, and rob their way into the good graces of the investigator and blame any discrepancies on me." He clasped the hilt of his mace. The cool steel calmed his spirit.

A shadow careened across the large yard, diverting his attention. With his weapon drawn he yelled, "Who goes there?"

He was met with silence.

Following his training, he stood still and waited for the figure to move again. *Most likely a scrub sneaking in from a night at the brothel.* His mind drifted slightly towards his time spent with the two maidens. Shaking his head, he cleared thoughts of women and focused his mind on the matter at hand.

The shadowy figure moved once again, and Althalos was ready for him. He dropped down to one knee and placed the palms of his hands on the grass. With his mind focused, he said the words that would activate the spell. "With a heavy heart, I aim to stop yours."

A layer of ice careened from his fingertips towards the figure, who had been dashing towards the entrance. Althalos smirked at the thought of another scrub stuck in his ice trap. As he moved closer, his jaw dropped at the sight of two giant purple wings.

Just when he was about to deal another blow to the creature, a familiar voice called out, "What are you daft? I'm the High Cleric. You will unfreeze my legs this instant."

Althalos shook his head and closed his eyes. When he opened them, the bulky figure stood before him with his battle-axe in hand, vainly attempting to break the ice attached to his legs. Althalos pointed as he staggered towards the High Cleric, "Bu... but... you had wings."

The High Cleric grimaced, "Your mind must be running mad in your old age. Perhaps that's why they wanted me to be High Cleric instead of you. No need for you and your ancient ways. Times have changed old man; you ought to put on spectacles to see that. I will not repeat myself again: Release me."

Althalos crossed his arms. "What were you doing sneaking in, and where were you?"

The High Cleric spat on the grass between them, nearly striking Althalos' boots, "You forget yourself; I do not answer to you."

Althalos stepped a little closer to see the High Cleric in his full plumage. He was wearing odd purple and green attire and had a large gash on his right arm that seemed to be infected. Althalos knew little of the healing arts, but anyone could see that the arm would need to be amputated. They locked eyes for several moments. Eventually Althalos smirked. *Knowing him, he aims to treat it himself; he may very well die from his wounds. Best to leave him to his own demise.* He weaved several hand signals causing the ice to melt into a puddle of water.

The High Cleric trudged into the building, his blood dripping onto the grass. The commander sat beside his mare for a few more moments, contemplating. *That letter needs to be written... but who says it must be me that writes it?*

Althalos entered the common room area to see Lief at his desk, whittling away at his wooden sculptures. *What sloppy craftsmanship! It seems he isn't gifted in everything as I had thought. Though he is a talented actor. Here I thought I had a prized pupil that would follow in my footsteps, when all I'm left with is an oath breaker.* For a quick moment Althalos' eyes looked down. When Althalos arrived at Lief's desk, he placed a piece of parchment and quill on the desk.

Lief smiled widely. "Hello Commander Althalos. It's great to see you, although I apologize for not being dressed in my uniform. I was not expecting company. May I know what brings you to the common quarters? I would have gladly come up to see you somewhere more fitting for one of your station."

Althalos winced. *This scrub must take me for a joke. I specifically instructed all under my care to stay away from the pubs. The brothel is acceptable only on birthdays, and if I don't find out about it, then there is no harm in it. Every single one of them swore an oath to me, yet my supposed star pupil brings down the light upon my head, only to spit in my face with these sweet words.*

Althalos glared at his pupil, his cold piercing eyes made Lief squirm in his chair. "Is... something the matter commander?"

Maintaining his glare, Althalos spoke. "Plenty, but tonight there is only one thing you need worry about. I need you to write a letter for the good of yourself and the other pupils."

Lief raised an eyebrow. "What kind of letter... I mean, I'm confused, sir. But I will do my best."

He felt a sudden urge to stick a foot into the face of this letdown, making a mockery of his tutelage, "You will write a report on the depravity going on in our beloved Titania. You will take down the number of pupils and officials who go to the brothel, the number who go to the pubs, the number who engage in unsanctioned gambling, and the officials who fraternize with the pupils and vice versa. It is to be known how many have disgraced this order and our great oath. I will then add in my own letter, and we will send it to The Council."

With shaking hands, Lief picked up the parchment and quill. "Please sir, please do not make me do this. I will be viewed as a rodent, and the other pupils will..."

Althalos placed a hand on one of the crummy sculptures laid upon the desk. While transforming it to ice, he said, "Who should you fear more? The friends that have pushed you down the wrong road, or the mentor who stands before you with full knowledge of your transgressions?"

Lief sniffled. His hand trembled, causing him to drop the quill and parchment. A few moments of silence passed by as Lief sat there, hunched over with his hands on his head, "I'll do what you command. I just ask that..."

Althalos cut him off. "The Order does not appease cowards and oath-breakers. You have failed me, Lief, but above all, you have failed yourself. I wasn't going to dive into this with you, but it seems I must put to words your ill-conceived actions. Frequent trips to the brothel, pub, and even an underground pupil fighting ring." Althalos looked up to the ceiling with his hands raised. "Each pupil is a direct reflection of their mentor and each mentor is a direct reflection of the Order. It would seem my reflection is nothing more than a dry and decaying image of its former glory, for the carcass that lays before me has withered."

Lief dropped to his knees with his shoulders hunched over and tears streaming down his face.

—11—
A TERROR IN CLERIC'S ROBES

The morning rays shone down upon the High Cleric. It hadn't gotten an ounce of sleep through the night, nor any reprieve. The extravagant room served it well. The High Cleric sat on the edge of its bed with a hand gripping its right arm, which oozed green pus. Wincing at the sting, it dabbed at the wound.

In a guttural voice, it said, "That accursed toxin vampire has access to a corrosive gas that even I am not immune to. She will have to die, and her secrets along with her." The High Cleric stumbled towards its black dresser painted with silver stars. It yanked the top drawer open, nearly pulling it off its hinges. Inside the drawer laid several vials of colorful liquids. Its right claw clasped a bright yellow bottle. Drinking the entire contents, its eyes rolled to the back of its head.

The claw transformed into a copper toned hand. A tingling sensation flowed through his stomach as his eyes transformed back to their usual menacing green, the only tell of his unusual nature. The High Cleric touched his features and rubbed his arms, confirming that the transformation had born fruit, "To think that there is a concoction that could disrupt my transformation and my healing. It is to my benefit that I have one that can fix such a disruption. I wonder what the relation is of that toxin vampire and the she-witch? Could she be her sire?" He snorted as he furrowed his brows. The High Cleric took his battle axe and placed it in its holster behind his back. "Matters of the whim are not of import. Now is the time for me to see the streets run blue, red, and all the colors of the rainbow. I will see heads decapitated, arms laid about, and bodies piled as high as buildings. I will see my purpose come true."

The High Cleric trotted downstairs, the heavy weight of his armor clinking together. The heavy plate armor revealed the High Cleric's presence with every footstep. He wore a belt containing several small throwing axes, each with a different color hilt. He scanned the room to see that all members of the Titania Clerics Order were present for the breaking of their fast.

With his arms folded, he cleared his throat. "Who can tell me the number one priority of the Clerics Order?" Several hands shot up. *Naturally, the prefect of each commander looks to score bread points with their High Cleric. What a load of piss pot suck-ups these humans are. Soon both the humans and the vamps will bow down to me. A superior race, greater than both combined. But will I turn them?* The High Cleric approached his seat, where he was served a large helping of lamb, potatoes, and ale. Pushing the meal aside, he downed a mug of ale.

Following his drink, he turned to the two lap dog commanders who had patiently been waiting for his arrival. In the distance he could see Althy eating alone. The High Cleric chuckled when their gaze locked. The servant brought a double serving of ale to appease the ferocious thirst of their High Cleric. After downing the second and third mug, he felt a slight buzz within his being. *It is quite humorous for me to dine with my food. Soon all will fall into place as it was written on the stone tablets. They suspect nothing, as they are nothing, but they will not remain as such. With me leading they will pose useful.*

The High Cleric stood up, slamming his empty mug repeatedly. He scanned the silent room again: fresh-faced clerics, with a few veterans sprinkled in. A true sacrifice if he had ever seen one. "I know some of you have been curious about some of the changes that have been made since my arrival. Changes such as allowing meals to go past sundown, and volute games going further into the night. As High Cleric of Titania, I am not obligated to explain myself to anyone save for the light that shines through me, but I will commit to this. There is a storm brewing, my comrades-in-arms. The vamps are gearing up for what they call a revolution. We must prepare before it is too late. Training will extend full on into the night, conducted by Commander Althy Stern Finger."

Many of the scrubs erupted into laughter. The High Cleric glanced at Althalos' clenched fists and a menacing scowl. He continued, "Now I know some of you are scared, some are anxious, and some are excited. But know that your training will serve you well in the coming months. Are there any questions?" For a few moments none dared to raise their hands.

Finally, at the nudging of her table, a young woman raised her hand. "Why don't we ask for assistance from the other more experienced facilities? Based on our estimations the vamps outnumber us 2 to 1. Perhaps we could ask the High Council..."

The High Cleric stomped his feet, crushing a roach in the process, "Titania is the newest of all the facilities, that is true. But keep in mind you have legendary Commanders to balance out the experience. With your increase in time spent on battle preparations, you will see vast improvements. The vamps may be numerous, but they are weak of will and hurt of heart. Besides... I have a plan," said the High Cleric, as he smiled the most mischievous of smiles.

— 12 —
A PINYOOK OR MORE

Zurie's ship had docked at the boardwalk. She glanced up at the giant number thirteen on its flag. She had yet to give the ship a name. Her quarters were not as large as Oakes', but neither was she as important. It had come to her attention that he was a grand vampire who was held in high prestige. When it was time for Zurie to choose the members of her vampire guild, she was left with the bottom of the barrel. The difference in class between the vampires, blood knights, and the tiers of blood knights was fresh in her mind. However, that information was of little use when left with a rag-tag group of vampires. To think that there was a whole slew of ancient information that only a select few knew was enough to fill her stomach with nerves. She turned to Dr. Asher, whose very nature confused her. The good doctor had only drunk half the vial of the Vamp Lord's blood, making him something less than a blood knight presently, while he kept the remaining for later. He did, however, indulge in a premium grade enchantment that was unlike anything she had ever seen.

Zurie crossed her arms. "I suppose we will have to encounter that blood knight den I've been avoiding."

Dr. Asher threw one of his chaos balls in the air, "One would suppose," he said. The two distinguished vampires were accompanied by eleven ruffians, each of which seemed more bloodthirsty than the last.

Oakes had said, "You have the unruliest group of all the vamps. Training them will do well for your leadership skills." He had sneered as he said it.

"Or end my career in quick succession," she had muttered in return. Oakes was on her mind quite often, causing her great anxiety. *I didn't know a vampire could worry this much. Here I thought I'd feel things less. But I'm vigilant of everything that could go both right and wrong. What does it mean to be a vampire that feels human emotions on a heightened scale? An anxious vampire is one thing... but to be an anxious blood knight with eleven blood thirsty usurpers hiding in the shadows is another.*

Feeling a kick to her greaves from Dr. Asher, she descended the gangway towards the boardwalk, where she saw a familiar group of vampires approach her ship.

The rival blood knight walked up to Zurie and placed his hands across his chest, "Oh, look here boys... the toxin vamp has received herself a promotion. I'm surprised with flimsy armor like that you didn't blow away with the wind. Why are your stomach and elbows exposed anyway?"

Zurie clenched her jaws and gripped the handle of her pistol. The rest of her crew jeered him while screaming profanities. The unwritten blood knight code was clear. To insult one's den and blood knight status was one thing, but to insult one's armor was something else. This Tyrant blood knight was itching for a bloodbath.

The blood knight had his hand on his golden blunderbuss, a short-barreled weapon that caused a destructive amount of damage within its limited range. The two blood knights sized each other up as they circled, each preparing to dodge the other's shot. A direct hit at this range would certainly mean the second death for Zurie.

Will my new enchantment hold up against his? I mean, it still contains a silver projectile so that must count for something. But his blunderbuss is made for close quarters... that counts for something more. The Tyrant Blood Knight spat on Zurie's brand new armor causing her to look down momentarily. In seconds, he had his blunderbuss removed from its holster and aimed at her chest. With a flick of the trigger, several projectiles launched themselves in Zurie's direction. She ran towards the fire, ducking at the last second with her pistol drawn and cocked at his forehead.

The tyrant knight handed over his blunderbuss and blood knight's necklace. "I beg your mercy, oh great knight." The sarcasm was evident in his voice.

Zurie could hear her crew calling for blood, but in the end the decision was hers to make. She paused to contemplate her next action. *At least I don't have to kill another on this day. Killing his right hand still haunts me to this night. Besides sparing him will give us more...* Zurie felt a sharp stinging sensation explode in the middle of her stomach. She looked down to see the hilt of a blade sticking out. "That's what mercy will get you in times to come. Lucky for you, I have lost my lust for blood on this eve. You can keep the buss, dagger and necklace; something tells me you're gonna need em." said the knight.

Mouth agape, Zurie watched as the blood knight of the Tyrant Den strutted off as if he was the victor. His crewmates cheered on their way to the bar. Zurie turned to her crew, who all had solemn looks upon their faces—none more pressing then Dr. Asher. He was slow to remove the silver dagger from her body and get out the healing blood ointment that he was so famous for.

As he applied the ointment, he said, "I'm not sure if you know already, so I'll say it anyways. The key to keeping together any group of men, especially vamps, is mutual respect. Something you just lost a lot of. Mercy on the battlefield gets the crew killed. You'll be sure to remember that."

Dr. Asher turned to the crew and raised up the necklace. "I move that we sell the necklace and the dagger to buy our way into a drunken stupor, considering that we're a rag-tag group with no pinyooks." The crewmates cheered and stampeded past Zurie who was sluggish to follow.

It's true we are broke. The decision to only serve her crew live creatures was one that kept them from mutiny, but the cost of such action was rearing its ugly head. *Perhaps I should have taken Oakes' offer on that loan. Then again, I couldn't very well accept 40% interest. That is high pocket robbery. What kind of merchant would I be if I were to accept that?* She let out a loud sigh as she moved towards the bar. *Perhaps it's time I stop thinking of myself as a merchant and start thinking like a blood knight. All this time I have sought after this position, yet I do not even know what it means to have it.*

Zurie sipped her blood rations. The putrid taste was highlighted now that she had something to compare it to. The ointment served to improve her healing, but did little to stop the pain. Her crewmates indulged in the blood of a fresh goat. More for them, she told herself.

I don't feel like a blood knight.

Why am I even thinking about feelings?

She thought about how far she had come: from a measly merchant in a medium sized den to a blood knight in a massive division of vampires. *I thought status would make me happier. But it is only a burden that has been placed on my shoulder. I have the weight of twelve beings upon my back, all of whom would be better suited to my position. But the rules are clear:*

The only way to lose a blood knight position is through the second death. For fang's sake, why does everything have to be so severe with us? She took another sip of her blood rations, nearly gagging. The cool liquid slimed its way down her throat and left a sour taste in her mouth. *Once you've tasted real animal blood, nothing compares—save for maybe human. I wonder what human blood tastes like?*

She focused on more pressing matters. *How am I going to feed and maintain my den? We don't even have a specialized profession.* Zurie beckoned the bartender, a dark-skinned vamp with several markings across his arms. She raised an eyebrow. "Those are interesting markings... what do they represent?"

The bartender leaned in close enough to whisper, "They represent my tribe from Africanus."

Zurie nodded her head. The word "Africanus" sent shivers down her spine. "There seem to be a lot of your kind walking around here lately. We don't usually have such exotic vamps here. Why the sudden migration?"

This time it was the bartender's turn to raise an eyebrow, "I thought they would have told you. The other blood knights have been prepping for it. There is going to be a revolution, and we're here to bolster your ranks." He scrunched his face into an odd expression then went back to cleaning the mugs. A gentle hand grasped Zurie's shoulder, causing her to jerk to attention. She donned a pensive expression upon being met with the sight of Oakes. As always, his attire was as exceptional as his demeanor was regal. His blood knight's armor was extravagant yet sturdy.

If there was ever a time that he was equipped for battle, now would be it. "We have a meeting to attend," he said. "It's time for you to be alerted to the current situation."

The two blood knights walked the boardwalk within eyesight of the entrance. He then turned to the swamp and jumped into the water. Zurie glanced down at the green liquid in time to see him lift his arms and pull her in with him. They swam for a few moments before reaching an underwater cavern. Rising up from the deep, she looked at her brand-new armor. It remained dry. The cave had a massive round wooden table with thirty vampires around it. She recognized each vampire as a blood knight due to their knight's badge or necklace. Out of the thirty blood knight leaders there, she only recognized a handful: the Tyrant knight and the leaders who were promoted during the event. All others were blood knight leaders that either had eluded her vision during her time on the boardwalk or were foreign.

She nodded her head to every single one in an effort to keep things civil. From her short time being a blood knight, she realized how much more volatile they were in comparison to lesser vamps. "Greetings, all. I'm Zurie of the Unruly Thirteen."

A large bulbous fellow with short arms bellowed, "We know who you are. Sit down and keep quiet. You're late."

Oakes and Zurie took the only remaining available seats. The toxin vampire from the event placed a large ball in the middle of the table. The ball glowed a bright orange as it let loose an extreme amount of energy. The cave lit up, and the attendees covered their eyes.

When the light subsided, an image of The Terror walking into the Cleric's Order facility during the night appeared, "For those of you who don't know, The Terror has the ability to morph into his pre-vampire form—essentially coming across as human. With this ability, it is suspected that he has spilled word to the Clerics that we plan a revolution."

The attendees dropped their jaws and raised their fists into the air. One called out, "I thought he was one of us. Why would he betray our cause?"

The toxin vampire tapped his fingers upon the table. "The only thing I can think of is too gruesome for words."

Oakes stood with his hand raised. "The Terror would never side with the humans unless he wished to obtain the red topaz."

While he visibly gathered himself, the toxin vampire continued. "This goes against everything we believe in, but the tablets do say the Lord of the Night may be reawakened with the red topaz."

The air became heavy. Zurie's heart skipped several beats. *A sin so great that no punishment had been thought of. This Terror truly is a menace that must be stopped. I do believe vampire law needs to be changed, but some rules are not meant to be broken. To reawaken a vampire who has met the second death is said to wither any entity that shared comradery with him, including all who have shared in its blood. But on the other hand... no. I mustn't think like that.*

The toxin vamp gave Zurie a menacing scowl. Then he turned his attention to the rest of the group. "Many of us have shared a battlefield with the Lord of the Night during the Great War. Some of us were there the night that he fell to the Bishop's blade. Not to mention that all of us have drunk the sacred elixir that is his blood. The point is not that we don't want the Lord of the Night back: It is that we do not want to lose our existence in the process. The ancient tablets are clear in what they say. We must stop The Terror and it must be done now. We outnumber those humans by at least two to one. If we storm the Cleric's facility during the night, we can submerge them in a bath of their own blood. This is not the time for discussion or debate. It is the time for battle."

The crowd of Blood Knights erupted into cheers and screams. A young child raised his hand. The crowd of vampires immediately went silent. The child had short curly hair and was fair of skin. With two ear piercings and a tilted crown, he had an air of regality. The toxin vamp bowed deeply before addressing him, "What is it that you have to add, Lord Salem?" He was clearly more than just a child, based on the level of respect he garnered.

The child addressed as Lord Salem tapped his crown before speaking. With a voice to match his visage, he said, "What about their commanders?" The group of Blood Knights spoke amongst themselves as he continued. "The Terror is one thing... we all know what he is capable of. But the Commanders only make things worse. There are three commanders and each one more formidable than the other. We tested a commander recently and as many of you know, he showed face. Not to mention the mystery of what the mini clerics have been up to. Who knows what star pupils they have trained in the time that we have grown fat and lazy? Yes, I admit we have bolstered our numbers, but I still urge us to use caution now that The Terror has betrayed us. Remember, we fight a foe that has defeated us before, the sting of which still rings true."

The group sat there considering the gravity of their situation. Heat rose from Zurie's feet all the way to her head. Her eye twitched and her hands shook. *I cannot believe what has befallen my ears, I thought these blood knights would be more resolute than this. Someone needs to say something.* One of her serpents whispered into her mind. *Why not you? It could be just what you're looking for to prove yourself. Feelings of inadequacy and such.*

With her hand still shaking, she pulled out her pistol and placed it on the table. For the first time in two lifetimes, Zurie was able to muster the ability to speak in a group setting. She stood up despite the tugging on her arm from Oakes. Freeing herself from his grasp, she scowled. "I may be new here, but my hair has more luster and vigor than you lot. To think a group of thirty blood knights would fear a bunch of mini clerics and old commanders. The commanders have aged well? Then so be it. We are knights of the highest order: the position held at the highest of esteem. We are like a fine wine. We become better, stronger, and smarter with age. Some of you are four times the age of the oldest commander and thus four times as experienced. We have nothing to fear save fear itself. Remember comrades, fear stands for false evidence appearing real."

The group remained silent, looking severely bewildered.

Oakes broke the silence with a round of applause. The other knights joined in save for Lord Salem and the other toxin vampire, both of whom could be seen scowling. The toxin vamp coughed a few times, then slammed his hands against the table, "It is customary to raise one's hand when one would like to speak. We are not knighting without class. In any case, I suppose that was a rousing speech and whatnot. You may sit down now."

He shot Zurie an errant glance. The toxin vampire smirked as he glanced down at the five rings in his hands, "If we will be going to war, I have procured one of the rarest artifacts to ever exist in our underworld. I sought forth with my guild for decades in anticipation of this very moment." One by one he placed the rings on the table. The rings had varying stones in the middle, each surrounded by the Eye of Horus. He clapped, and a colorfully glowing serpent raised the rings into the air. "I present to the blood knight divisions five day strong rings: rings that allows their wearers to bask in the light of the accursed sun that has plagued every one of us since being turned. With your blessing, I will hand out the rings to those that I feel will best carry out our divine plan."

A cloaked figure with a mask covering his face shot up. "I challenge that notion. The new knights are just as capable as the old ones. I see where this is going already. You're going to grant the coveted positions to your allies, granting them the bulk of the spoils once the Cleric's Order has been taken. You're not as sly as you think you are, Ragna."

Ragna raised his hand, and three serpents appeared wrapped around his arm. "You dare to challenge me in my own meeting?"

The masked vampire withdrew his dagger and held it to his own nose. "Who died and made you lead knight of all the knights?"

An errant vampire shouted, "Knight duel!"

Both the masked figure and Ragna jumped atop the table. The two dashed and ducked, neither wanting to be struck with the first blow. Zurie peered in awe as Ragna exhibited a great confidence in his every step, dodging the strikes of the masked vampire, while using the serpents to defend the attacks he could not dodge.

Ragna launched an attack with the three serpents, which zigzagged towards the masked vampire. He dodged the first two, but the third swung around his neck, immediately piercing his exposed flesh. The body dropped to the floor in a lifeless heap, awaiting the withering of its nature.

Zurie's jaw dropped. *blood knight duels are short because our enchantments are powerful, and our defenses are weak. We are so used to being the predator that we fail when we become the prey. My den will need to specialize in defensive tactics if we are to survive this war. I don't even know what I seek through this revolution. Is it fame, fortune, respect? Or something more?*

From the corner of her eye she glimpsed Oakes receiving one of the day strong rings from Ragna. On the surface it appeared to be a regular ruby ring, but she could feel the energy pulsating from it. *This ring possessed the power to counteract a vampire's most glaring weakness. If only there was a ring to cure me of my cowardice. This courage in spurts is serving me as well as that dagger served the masked figure.*

— 13 —

POWER DYNAMIC

The dueling sanctuary was the largest room in the facility, containing a stadium where citizens could watch duels between full-fledged clerics. Before the death of the Bishop, the townsfolk were invited to watch daily matches fought by their protectors. There hadn't been a viewing session since his brutal passing. Althalos's eyes were glued to the sharp flaming daggers in each of one cleric's hand. She was short for a cleric in the battle division, with a body that would lead many men to their demise. She'd take their hearts in her hands, one way or another. Her opponent was a large cleric with a massive mace. He was slow and powerful, the type of lead hand that Brom would find appealing. He watched as her breasts protruded with every step that she took. She swiftly dodged the hefty blows, but failed to do anything else of note. Her attacks seemed to be nothing more than pin pricks to her opponent. *What kind of farce is this? She is more suited for the brothel than my elite unit. If only Lief hadn't failed me.* He turned to leave when Brom came waddling by with two large buckets of enchanted water in his hands. The sweet scent of the water was a dead giveaway.

Brom placed the buckets on the floor and beamed a peculiar scowl as he gazed at the two combatants, "I take it you're bored of watching her practice her dagger skills. I never liked watching it. Somehow it lacks grace. I keep telling her that the dagger isn't for her. Stick to what you're good at is what I always say, but does she listen? My words go in one ear and out the other. There was once a time when a commander spoke, and the clerics listened. But now these young sprouts each think they're the king of the castle with their young energy and newfangled artifacts."

Althalos took a deep breath. "There was once a time when you weren't drunk as well."

Brom sighed. "These idle days have been tough. The three commanders are nothing more than figureheads. At least with the new High Cleric, I felt some resemblance of the old days. But that's over and done with."

Althalos raised an eyebrow. "Spit it out. I could never stand your vague comments."

With his hands clasped firmly together, Brom looked at Althalos. "Please tell me it wasn't you that sent that letter."

Althalos hated lying more than he hated cheating or stealing. It was one of those things that always irked him. Perhaps it was fate that he would have to lie on this evening. He placed a hand on his comrade's shoulder and gave him a wink. "I wish I knew what letter you're talking about, so I wouldn't be caught with my pants down."

Brom lowered his head for a brief moment but replied with a groan. "Someone wrote a letter to the High Council about the state of affairs of this facility. It doesn't name names, but it essentially makes all of us look like bumbling oafs who can't take care of our own waste. It is especially damaging of the High Cleric. It paints him as some kind of... monster."

Althalos widened his eyes, raising his voice as he spoke, "I see. What else?"

Brom grabbed Althalos by both shoulders and looked him dead in the eyes. "You were never a good actor. Please, this is serious. Tell me the truth. What do you know about the letter?"

Am I truly so easy to read? Though we were once the closest of friends, perhaps I am as transparent to him as he is to me. It is not time yet to demonstrate my hand. Should I bring up the boardwalk? No, that would only serve to tie my hands further into it. "One of my mentees wrote the letter without my knowledge and sent it by night carrier when no one was looking. That's all I know."

Brom clutched his chest as if he was having a heart attack. "Thank the glorious light. I was worried sick. The High Council is sending The Dark Horse, and he hates leaving the comforts of the sanctuary. It is ritual for him to eviscerate the one that is deemed the rodent. He will track down who wrote the letter first, then clean house of all that is deemed depravity. Finally, he will assist in the coming insurgency. He has already departed and will be here in a few days."

Althalos' eyes widened as he contemplated coming into contact with The Dark Horse. *I have heard stories, none of them good. I wonder if Lief will keep his mouth shut...* A loud scream cleaved the air, drawing the attention of both Althalos and Brom. The large cleric was clutching his burning face while the female cleric leaned back on the arena walls. Within moments, Brom jumped down from the ledge with the two buckets in hand. Landing gracefully, and without spilling a drop, he waddled towards the panicked cleric.

Althalos sighed. *I suppose I might as well meet this humpty dump of a cleric.* Approaching the young cleric, he felt sharp tingles around his body.

She smirked while doing the customary cleric salute. "I apologize sir, but the enchantment of my crossbow places a mark on any new male that enters my range of attack." She did an awkward bow.

Althalos folded his arms. "Make it stop this instance."

She scowled at his gruff tone before shrugging; she was about to respond when Brom came in between them. "He suffered some serious burns... but he will be fine once he makes it to the healing quarters. Why didn't you use your crossbow? You should be mastering your skills with it for the dirty vampires."

With her chest puffed out and arms folded she gave both the commanders a look that could kill. "I'm the best shot in this entire facility by far. I have no need to practice. I'm gonna make use of my time here and wield my daggers. Stop badgering me; you're beginning to sound like my father."

Althalos rolled his eyes. *Another female with father woes. Why is it that the male scrubs have limp pecker syndrome, while the females have father compliance issues? This facility is state of the art, yet we have the bottom of the barrel for recruits.*

The young cleric placed one hand on her dagger. "Who are you rolling your eyes at, old man?"

Althalos looked to his left, then looked to his right. He tilted his head back. "You must be addressing Commander Brom. I certainly know you aren't speaking to me in such a manner, scrub."

She strengthened her stance, "The name is Catherine, and I don't have time for this. Are you going to relocate me to your division or not?"

— 14 —

AN ENGAGEMENT
WITH DESTINY

The warm breeze of sundown caressed Zurie's pale skin. Her hands shuffled about while she gazed at the horizon. The city was eerily quiet. Their group of revolutionaries gathered atop the school roof adjacent to the facility. Turning to Oakes with her pistol in her hand, Zurie asked the question on everyone's mind. "Where are the others?"

He muttered a curse underneath his breath. "Some of the groups backed out. Of the thirty-two blood knight leaders and their dens, we now have about fifteen. Half are with us and the other half are with Ragna. The remaining fifteen blood knights have stayed their hand due to Lord Salem's urgings. He pulls more weight than I thought."

A wave of nerves overtook her as she dropped her pistol, which tumbled down off the roof, clinking on impact. Her den looked at her with drooping eyes. *This waiting is killing me. If I'm going to meet the second death, then I rather get it over with. Still, it's odd that there are no night guards around the facility. If I were expecting a battle, I'd quintuple the guard—but to remove them completely?* One of her guild members jumped down to get her pistol, landing with a light thud. He put the weapon in his pocket and ran towards the boardwalk. With her jaw agape, Zurie watched the deserter ran off with her glorious weapon.

She felt frozen. *Did that really just happen? Am I really about to storm the Cleric's Order? What has my life become?*

Oakes nudged her forward, snapping her back to attention, "It's time. We storm through the stables, enter the facility, and spread out into a double wing formation. There is no time to falter and slime your way out of this. We shall have freedom." He turned to what remained of their group. "The clerics look down upon us. They feed us ill-tasting rations that keep us near-famished, and they treat us worse than they treat their cattle. We will be animals no more. Humans and vampires have been at war from the beginning of time. We are bound to take our place atop the throne of supremacy."

The group cheered, raising their hands in the air, but Zurie could taste just as much doubt and fear in their hearts that she did in her own. With one wave of Oakes' hand, the large group of revolutionists were off to face their hated oppressors.

Zurie swooped through the empty courtyard, her eyes zoomed in to take in the elegance of the facility. *Even the grass looks healthier here. But where are the horses? Where are the people?* With her blunderbuss drawn, she and the group creeped into the facility.

They were met with a horrifying sight. An assortment of clerics and mini clerics, all equipped with enchanted bows and arrows, faced their group of vampires. The large mahogany doors shut behind them, and Zurie jumped.

Inside the facility was even more glorious than the outside. The room was decorated in stained glass windows, while the floors were blue and green marble. A Commander-level cleric stepped forward with a jug of triple-X ale in his hand. The fat fellow downed the bottle in seconds, then broke the jug across his forehead. "You lot think you can come into our facility and take us down? You think you can stop Brom?" Brom stomped his feet and the marble tiles beneath rumbled. Zurie withdrew her silver dagger awaiting Oakes's orders.

She looked at the large cleric then turned to Oakes with furrowed brows. Oakes pointed, "You and I will take the big oaf the rest of the group can handle the others." He dropped to one knee, raising his fist in the air, and the air around their feet became lighter. He dashed towards the commander, ferociously fast. Zurie was close behind him, blunderbuss in one hand and knife in the other.

Arriving within range of her weapon, she fired a massive blast of toxic energy.

The blast connected, dealing minimal damage. *A direct hit and that's all it did?* Zurie was too busy in her thoughts to notice a massive fist careened towards her. Oakes blocked the attack with his arms crossed, pushing him back several meters. "Wake up or we're both dead," he said.

Brom beat his own jiggling chest. Grinning, he pulled a pair of golden gloves onto his hands and clapped them together. A massive shockwave forced both vampires to drop to the floor to dodge. A massive hole emerged from the wall behind them. Brom jumped into the air and clapped twice more, causing two more shockwaves to catapult towards the vampires.

Zurie ducked to the left while Oakes rolled to the right just in time. With his eyes burning green, he dashed towards Brom, who had been gearing up for another round of applause. Dodging the fist that came his way, Oakes managed to claw Brom's eyes out before Brom gripped Oakes' hand and slammed him into the ground.

Zurie sent a massive cloud of toxic gas towards Brom's mouth while launching herself towards his groin area. Her dagger pierced into his testicles, and he bellowed. Brom dropped to his knees. Zurie smoothly came up from behind the commander and slit his throat. The ruby liquid spilled in every direction. Resisting the urge to drink, she approached Oakes' body. His arm was bent backwards, his leg broken in three pieces, and he was bleeding from the head. But he would live.

The screams of the clerics and mini clerics echoed throughout the room as the blood knight group sunk their teeth into the necks of their prey, glowing with vitality.

Zurie took a deep breath then called for Dr. Asher to apply one of his magnificent healing ointments. Dr. Asher glanced at the wounds, then at Brom's gloves, and finally shook his head, "My ointments won't speed up the healing of these injuries. Something about those gloves makes their damage immune to outside healing. Our only hope is that he will be able to regenerate naturally through feasting." Dr. Asher examined the gloves closely then pocketed them. "I'll be sure to make good use of these."

Zurie glanced down at the lukewarm blood on the marble floor with disgust. *It's no fun if it isn't fresh from the body, I want my first time to be special. What do I do about Oakes? Do I leave him here? Do I stay and wait for him to regenerate?*

Oakes gripped her ankle for her attention. "Push on, I'll be fine here alone." She nodded and moved forward with what remained of their army. Oakes' summoned crew were silent, in sharp contrast to the heavy footsteps of the rest of the vampires. They traversed a dimly lit hallway with portraits of high-ranking officials of the Cleric's Order both past and present.

Zurie heard a joyful giggle as a silver bolt careened past her eye, lodging itself into one of her fellow blood knights forehead. She watched with jaw agape, while his head combusted into a swarm of flames. The blood knight withered into flakes of light immediately after being impaled. Shivers ran down Zurie's spine, and her hand twitched violently.

She heard a feminine voice out in the distance. "I'm warning you, disgusting creatures of the night. You've overstayed your welcome and overstepped your bounds. You should have just been happy suckling from our generous tits. Now charge at me blindly like the fools that you are so I can pick you off, one by one. You blood knights should be hiding behind a rock right about now. Perhaps if you had your Vamp Lord, you'd stand a chance."

Zurie clenched her hands into two balls of poisonous fury. Purple energy surrounded her as she stormed forward, fangs protruding. *I'm going to suck her carcass dry of every ounce of blood. I will entertain no insults from a human, nor will I allow anyone to speak ill of the Vamp Lord in my presence.* Jumping, ducking, and twirling, she dodged another three bolts of fire. Each bolt that she dodged impaled another blood knight. *It's as if the bolts have minds of their own.*

By the time she was within vision range of her opponent it dawned on her that out of all the blood knights that entered from the courtyard, Zurie was the first one to make it this far. Many had fallen before her and some were too scared to press onward. *I will not let their sacrifice end in vain. This Cleric's Order will feel the divine weight of my wrath.* With brows furrowed, she leapt in front of the female human, who seemed to be amused by her presence. She giggled once again. "Maybe I do need to work on my aim; you should have been a pile of dust five times over. Oh well..."

Zurie in a blazing glory of serpents launched forth with a combination of slashes, swipes, bites, and shots from her blunderbuss. The woman dodged every single attack with ease, only to find herself tripping on Oakes' iron claw.

The temperature in the surrounding area dropped. Snowflakes fell onto Zurie and her companions from the ceiling.

Zurie clutched her body, shivering. *No, he can't be alive. I was sure he would be dead by now; humans aren't supposed to be this sturdy..."*

ICY TEARS

Althalos stormed the halls, taking down every threat that came in his way. His heart kept racing faster as he searched for Catherine. The scum from the main gate were mainly ranged threats, and the two sides were at a stalemate. The Clerics didn't have enough range power to defeat them, nor could they move in to eliminate the threat. However, the blood knights couldn't move in any closer for risk of being withered. It was imperative that a sharpshooter like Catherine be at the main gate, not off galivanting on a solitary mission.

His mind galloped between cursing her out and feeling rare relief. *If she is alive, she will certainly be punished after this, maybe I'll turn her into an ice cube for an hour or two.* He gleamed as he thought of all the punishments that could befall his latest and most unruly captain of the guard. *At least their numbers are much less than expected. With the right range personnel this should be over with minor casualties. I know Brom has held his gate since I have not encountered any threats here, but I wonder if he needs some assistance.* He smirked considering fighting alongside Brom once again. *I am grateful that I have kept up with my training. I give thanks to the light... I can really feel the blood pumping this time.*

Sprinting down the hallway he had a sudden urge to pull out his weapon. And as he did, he turned the corner to see Catherine battling the last thing he ever wanted to see.

Catching his breath, he looked again, straining his eyes. *This wretched, putrid vampire scum Zurie still draws breath in my city. I was too soft to finish her off back when she was first turned. I can only imagine the damage she has caused up to this point. Would that I had listened to Brom all those years ago. Now my heart is as frigid as the winter snowfall. She will perish beneath my boots, former betrothed or not. All creatures of the night will feel my wrath.*

Snow descended on his opponents, who all stopped moving. He could see a group of threats, but none caught his eye save for Zurie. With his hand clasping his mace, Althalos charged forward in a blinding storm of snow and ice.

Zurie aimed her blunderbuss and spoke words that stopped Althalos dead in his tracks. "My beloved... I know all those years ago when I was turned, you spared me out of love. It is my turn to spare you out of love. Please, you are severely outnumbered and outgunned. Step aside and I promise you won't be hurt. Just let us pass." The vampires that surrounded his betrothed held their weapons in the air.

His heartbeat calmed as his energy flowed through him. Glancing down at Catherine, their exhausted prisoner, he took a few steps closer.

Zurie raised the weapon higher, this time pointing it towards the commander's head, "Don't... don't take another step. Don't make me do this..."

Althalos balled his free hand into a fist. "We ceased our engagement the day you turned into one of them. I have two regrets in life and you're one of them. Would that I had died before bearing witness to this monstrosity that stands before me." Tears streamed down the face of the icy commander. His hand twitching, he charged forward once again, this time on a sheet of ice. At blinding speeds he launched his mace into the chest of the vampire scum and heard a loud crunch as Zurie's chest cavity caved in.

Althalos raised several ice pillars from the ground to impale the stomachs of her vampire companions. A short furry creature threw a ball at the commander, who froze it upon impact. With a twirl of his mace he swept up the furry creature in a snowstorm.

Zurie stepped forward, purple light emitting from her every step. Her fangs glistening underneath the light. Althalos stepped forward. *What a disgusting creature she has become. She will never know the pain I feel, for there are many emotions that I cannot show.* Zurie pushed within range of her blunderbuss, letting off two shots within succession. Each missed their mark. Dagger in hand, surrounded by a blaze of striking serpents, the monstrosity dashed forward. A beam of toxic liquid from her hand struck Althalos's shoulder, and he staggered to the floor.

He snarled, teeth clenched, and pushed himself back to his feet. Zurie was upon him, dagger in hand and mouth dripping with saliva. Dropping his mace upon impact, Althalos gasped for air. The dagger inched closer to his chest as the pure strength of a vampire outmatched his human body. At the last second, he managed to divert it to his shoulder.

Blood spewed out. He bellowed in pain from the venom surging through his body. *The facility cannot fall. Everything I have worked so hard for cannot be undone by her.*

He catapulted his fist into Zurie's nose. She shook her head. He reached for his mace with his free hand, only to find the furry creature had kicked it away. Finally, he reached for his pendant, almost touching it before his hand was broken by a sansabonsam. The vampire turned to Zurie and asked a question that sent shivers down Althalos' spine.

"Do you want to feed or should I? An aged specimen such as this should be indulged in solitary. By right..."

A loud screeching noise caused the three scum to drop Althalos. In a crumpled heap, he turned to see The High Cleric, giant axe in hand, charging towards the scum like a mad man. He stepped over Althalos with ease, quipping, "Taking a break?"

Althalos climbed to his feet sluggishly to see Catherine in a bloody pile. He limped to her side, checking for any bite wounds. Upon finding battle wounds but no feed markings he sighed, releasing what fear he had left.

The untouched High Cleric withstood a meager assault from the depleted Zurie, the sansabonsam, and furry vampire. With one sweeping motion of his battle-axe, he caught the sansabonsam off-guard, decapitating the Blood Knight. His body collapsed to the floor, blood pouring out. The furry vamp launched a smoke bomb, effectively blinding The High Cleric, and granting them enough time to retreat. The High Cleric blindly threw his battle-axe in the direction of his fleeing foes. In the distance came a high pitch shriek as metal met bone.

The High Cleric picked up Oakes' head and tossed it in the air. Drenched in blood, he cackled menacingly, letting the head fall. He kicked it around lightly. "Hahaha, looks like Oakes is off the volute board!" He kicked the head as hard as he could, sending it towards the open doors leading to the main hall. "Victory," he bellowed as the head landed against the wall.

Althalos curled his lip but saved his comments for himself.

The damage to the facility was minimal, though the losses were great among the scrubs. Their inexperience showed, as many of them got within biting range of the threats. It was a complete blood bath where the vamp threat was concerned. Nearly all of them were wiped out. The stalemate ended when the High Cleric handed every single cleric an ankh. The simultaneous incantation created a protective shield around the group, allowing them to close the gap with success. A melee battle ensued where the clerics dominated.

Althalos held Catherine's hand. Her grip tightened around his as she awoke for the second time. "What happened? How many did we lose?"

He lowered his head and took a deep breath. "We lost every single trainee that we had. All those fresh-faced scrubs died at the hands of the vamp threat. The clerics suffered marginal losses, but we lost the other two commanders. That..." he took another deep breath, "That drunken oaf Brom went and got himself killed, while that fornicator found himself distracted in the final moments and met the same fate. But enough about them, what is your condition?"

She turned to her side. "I won't be at the practice range anytime soon, but I'm sure I'll be up to premium level in no time. The healer says I was lucky they didn't feed on me. Tell me something I don't know." She rolled her eyes.

Althalos gazed into her eyes, holding her hands. "What is your condition?" he asked again.

She looked up at him, mouth quivering. Removing her hands from his she covered her face and burst into tears. "I thought I was done for. I thought I was going to die... or even worse, turn into one of them. I had never been so scared in my life. My father always said a battle with a vampire would be the death of me, but I showed him. I'm here, and I will live to fight another day."

He sighed and pulled away from her sobbing face. "You can't go around playing savior like that. Being a cleric is about using our group acumen to defeat a foe who is naturally stronger and faster than us. In truth, the fact that they have gained powerful enchantments through black market means disturbs my spirit. We were fortunate that they didn't seem to know how to make bonds with their enchantments. What you did was foolish and not something I would expect from a member of my elite guard. You left your unit to go off galivanting for what? To prove something to your father?"

She sighed. "My father has nothing to do with it. I felt called to take action. I had to trust my gut; it's the only thing that has seen me this far and I have come a long way to be here."

With his arms crossed, he winced as he spoke. "Sounds like something I used to tell the Bishop." *Why am I being so kind? I'm the one they call stern finger. She should be removed from the elite guard and... there are no other commanders to send her to. The hierarchy is all mucked up and that blasted Dark Horse has yet to reveal himself. What a mess my facility has become.*

She tapped him on his arm. "I haven't spoken of my father to anyone save you and Brom... but I feel the need to unburden my soul. Please would you mind lending a comforting ear?"

Althalos raised an eyebrow. "We have the confession priest for that."

She giggled. "Everyone knows the confession priest is the biggest gossip in the facility."

He sighed, shrugging. "I suppose, if I must."

Biting her lip, she shuffled around in her bed. "My father is a notable High Council member who rules his household with an iron fist. My elder brother died at childbirth, and he looks at me as his precious jewel. He always kept me under tight watch as if I was this delicate flower waiting to be blown away at the slightest breeze. One day, after two decades of being spied upon by his people, we got into our final argument where I just lost it. In the night, I packed my things and traveled north as far as I could to this facility. My only wish is to stay here and help protect this facility that has become my true home." She closed her eyes as tears spilled down her face, causing Althalos to grip her hand once again.

A smooth voice called out to him, "Commander Althalos, join me in the Bishop's quarters. We have much to discuss."

— 16 —

A DISH BEST SERVED COLD

Her lungs burned with every step that she took back to the boardwalk. Zurie's legs buckled underneath the weight of Dr. Asher's body. She dropped to the floor, taking the furry vamp with her. Blood stained her top and bottom, pooling around her. Her fangs protruded sharp as blades, thirsty for a feast. She hadn't feasted since her transformation where they indulged in live deer; blood rations would not serve her wounds well. *I wouldn't dare dream of feasting on a member of my den. What kind of blood knight would I be? Besides it doesn't smell that appetizing... something about human blood tantalizes the senses and beckons the being. My first meal from a human will be special.* Zurie struggled to her feet, leaking blood from her jaw. She had a massive gash where the High Cleric had struck her and a shattered rib cage from her former betrothed, but she fared far better than her companions.

She could still hear the taunting words of the High Cleric as she dashed out the stable doors with Dr. Asher in hand. The image of Oakes falling still weighed on her mind. *His head made a low thumping sound when it landed on the ground. Then he kicked it... I can't believe he kicked it. That sadistic fanger. I will get my revenge.* Upon thinking those words, her heart darkened immensely. The boardwalk had no guards at the entrance. Zurie rushed towards the ship. *A blood knight without den mates? Some revolutionist I turned out to be. I will have my revenge.* Her heart was skipping. She truly was becoming one of the undead. When she arrived at the ship her hands trembled, but she carried the body of her last den mate firmly.

Several vamps crowded around the ship, but made no move to disrupt what business she had on it. *They must be making all kinds of presumptions about how it went. If word hasn't already made it back here. I wonder who else survived. Does it even matter? Oakes didn't. Blood will beget blood.* Zurie searched for any emotion save anger, but found none. No disappointment, no sadness, just anger. She ascended to the ship in swift fashion only to see it had been ransacked. Barrels were thrown and broken, while what little blood rations they had was gone. The mast was cut down, and their flag was torn into pieces. The distinct smell of vamp grass—a poisonous substance to vamps and humans alike—lingered in the air. *They must have raided Dr. Asher's stash. Curses, we need his special ointment, or he needs to feed from a living creature.* Jumping into the ship turned her stomach.

Purple energy poured out around her, causing the boat to rock. "I will sever the heads of every culprit and bathe in their blood. I will watch as the Cleric's Order burns down before my very eyes and every single human in this city is flayed till they defecate themselves."

Zurie's voice thundered, and a massive beam of purple light struck the ship tearing a hole from the top down through the belly of the ship. Feeling energy surge through her, she searched in vain for the treatment that her friend so desperately needed. Finally, she checked the pulse of the furry vamp again. He had met the second death. She rocked back and forth with the body in her arms, waiting for the withering process to complete.

For three nights, she had mourned the deaths of the only comrades she knew. The only ones who ever showed her any kindness, any compassion, any support. But the time for mourning was now over. After hearing of the disastrous results, many of the remaining blood knights took sail and left the mainland. Zurie stormed the boardwalk in her bloodstained armor. With her hand on the hilt of her blunderbuss, she pushed by the questioning eyes of the cowardly vampires. Finally, she arrived at the swamp entrance.

Taking a deep breath she catapulted herself towards the underwater cave. Upon arriving, she was met with a sight that could only be described as gruesome. The remaining blood knights were in a circle, watching a clearly one-sided duel. Lord Salem was prodding Ragna's paralyzed torso, mouth, and ears with his rapier. Each touch of the rapier cause sparks to fly out. Serpents left his body and made their way towards Zurie. Lord Salem let out a childish giggle. The other knights in the area simply watched with their mouths covered.

No wonder they show him so much respect. His mode of attack is brutal, and his power levels far surpass anything I've ever seen. In the corner of her eye she saw several coins fall from Ragna's hand. Immediately several fiends jumped forth to grab them, but Zurie was too fast. She charged forward. Upon catching the coins, she heard the childish voice speak.

"What do you think you're doing, last one standing?"

Last one standing? She looked around. Of the entire revolution group she truly was the last one standing. The remaining knights were those that abstained. Her heartbeat increased as the circle closed in around her. She had to think of something fast. *Do I fight, flight, or flirt? He's the reason why they didn't show up. He is the reason why we lost. He is the reason why Oakes and Dr. Asher are gone.* Zurie took several steps towards the illustrious Lord Salem. With a smile on her face, she raised her hands in the air and did a deep bow.

His fangs protruded, saliva dripping down them. "Well... then... it's about time we have a stupid toxin vamp that finally places the necessary respect on my name. I mean..."

With both hands on her blunderbuss, Zurie sent a silver ball of energy into Lord Salem's forehead. The projectiles catapulted him into the cavern wall, followed by a barrage of snakes spewing out from Zurie's person. Blood leaked down his chest as several knights rushed to him. From the corner of her eye she could see lightning rapidly regenerating the large hole in his head at a rapid pace. *I have at best a few minutes. Time to make use of my merchant skills.* She turned to the bloodlust-filled knights with an innocent smile on her face.

"I'm not going to bring up the fact that the lot of you stayed back while your comrades fought for a just cause, because we all know that there is no comradery between rival dens. There is only your den and my den. But there is something that you lot are missing... and that's artifacts. I look at your rag-tag group and I think, why is it that all the broken or weak knights stayed back? Kind of sad, don't you think? Could it be that you were jealous of the other more prominent blood knight leaders? But fear not. I won't berate you for that. I must admit we were outmatched, and the plan had many holes. I'm here to make a proposition to any blood knight leader willing to throw down his meaningless leadership and follow me to the seas, where we will pillage the trade ships of the Cleric's Order. Not just of Titania, but of the entire continent of Europia. I promise you power beyond belief, artifacts of blinding light, and above all... a feast upon humans that has never been seen before."

One of the knights, wearing a ripped shirt and raggedy breeches, said, "You're right... not all of us were sponsored by a more prominent knight, like yourself."

Zurie placed her hand on the head of one of her serpents, which hissed. "Make your point and make it swiftly," Zurie said.

The knight continued. "But why should we follow you into the sea on some fool's errand when we can continue to live a peaceful life as we have here?"

Zurie clutched her stomach in a fit of laughter. "You must really be a fool to think that The Cleric's Order will not retaliate soon. The battle has been lost but the war is far from over. Any creature of the night still in this city by tomorrow's nightfall will feel the wrath of the Cleric's Order ten times over. You don't have to take my word for it. Feel what your senses tell you. Another bloodbath is coming, and this time, it's coming for you cowards."

There was a long silence and then a slew of muttering among the knights. Finally, Lord Salem interrupted the convention with a slow clap. "Very, very good. Quite the appealing speech. I do require more artifacts for my endeavors. I will forgo my den rights to follow you to the depths and back. Just make sure you can deliver... otherwise... I'll have to give you a thorough examination." He let out another childish giggle. *I don't like the idea of him creeping up behind me, but having a powerful lead hand will be necessary if we are to take these ships. I suppose I will just have to sleep with one eye open.* She looked every knight in the eye. Some showed the fear that she knew so well, some showed hatred, and some confusion.

Eventually a cloaked figure stepped forward. "It seems it's just you two. Now leave before we take what we really want... which is that blunderbuss, those coins, and that rapier that Lord Salem holds so dearly. This city is my home, and this boardwalk is our haven."

Maintaining her confident posture, Zurie marched through the crowd towards the exit. She met everyone's gaze one more time. *Is this what I have spent all these decades striving to become? Cowards, the lot of them. My day will come when I will radiate my power.*

— 17 —

INTRODUCTORY LESSON

The scent of lavender permeated from his body and every step he took oozed excellence. With one hand wrapped around his red, gold, green, and black staff and another cupping a golden apple, he led the way to the Bishop's quarters.

Althalos followed in sluggish fashion. The Dark Horse was relatively young, yet exuded experienced wisdom—something Althalos was not used to since the Great War, when scrubs became men within days. While gauging the man's age he unconsciously kept his hand on the hilt of his mace. *I don't like him already. Who does he think he is, waltzing around like that? Smelling of such a sweet scent. It's no scent for a commander. What business do we have in the Bishop's quarters anyways?* He took several deep breaths. *Could I finally be getting the recognition that I deserve?*

His eyes widened as he walked into the room, which he had never seen before. The Bishop's aura lingered as if he were still alive and thriving. Raising his white hood, The Dark Horse turned to Althalos, revealing his dark skin with white markings upon his face. *An Africanus Cleric from the High Council? Quite the rarity indeed. I can only imagine the deeds he must have carried out to have been given his position. It matters not. He will be a useful commander under my leadership.*

The Dark Horse sat behind the Bishop's desk, forcing Althalos to sit in a smaller yet still luxurious seat. "My name is Oko-Iku. I am an associate of the High Council. Do you know why you're here?" He then leaned back and revealed his pearly white teeth with a smile. Oko-Iku was dressed all in white. His sandals were open-toed, revealing feet that looked as if they had walked to their destination on water. *How can he travel such a distance without wear and tear on his clothing or sandals? It matters not. We need to get on with this coronation so I can make the necessary changes.*

Althalos leaned back and nodded. "I have some thoughts on the matter."

Oko-Iku clapped his hands and smiled again. "Excellent, then this won't be awkward. I was hoping it wouldn't be awkward. The ancestors know I'm not a fan of awkward situations. But for some reason they tend to put me in them very often. Perhaps it's an ill joke upon me? What do you think?"

There was a long string of silence as Althalos sat there with his eyebrows furrowed.

Oko-Iku rubbed the side of his ear. "I digress. I tend to do that—you'll have to excuse my quirks. I mean... not like you have much of a choice, as I am your new Bishop." He chuckled and placed a hand on his commander's shoulder, "Together we're going to make this facility the greatest on the entire continent. It obviously won't compare to the centers we have in Africanus, but it will come close. I'm glad I have you as my commander and will rely on you to help choose two more, considering your colleagues chewed the willow tree. I was thinking of simply promoting two members from your elite guard unit. How does Lief and Catherine sound? I'm told they performed well during the little tussle you had with the..." he cleared his throat, "inhabitants."

Althalos shuffled around in his seat. The hand he had on his mace tightened. He clenched his jaw before speaking. "I see. Th... that will be acceptable." Resisting the urge to strike, he thought about the options available. *This man won't last; his demeanor is of a weak nature, and there is no way he will be able to handle the variant personalities that dwell in this facility. A commander position will keep Lief quiet, and Catherine could use some responsibility. But what about me? Is there really a place for me here? I could never have thought of following another Bishop. Perhaps I won't have to...* He took a deep breath.

Oko-Iku placed his staff on his new bed, holding the apple at eye level. He furrowed his brow. "Hmm... it says here you're not satisfied. Why aren't you satisfied? I'd hate for us to have a bad start. Please help me to understand how I can assist."

Taken aback, Althalos released his weapon and ran his hand through his remaining hair. *What manner a person is this? He cannot be serious.*

He replied gruffly, "This is about as good as we're going to get."

The Bishop took the golden apple and gazed into it again. "Ahh... ohhhh... I see. That's a shame. It says here that you're upset that you failed to receive the Bishop position or the High Cleric position. I can see how one would be upset, but with your record, you couldn't have seriously thought you would move past your current station. Did you?"

Althalos leaned forward, glaring icily. He gave the best response he could muster: "What the wandought do you mean by that?"

There was another long silence, and then Oko-Iku's clothing turned pitch black. His staff became a purple bladed scythe. A purple aura surrounded the weapon in the form of six skulls, each calling out a different curse word. His eyes turned from soft gold to dark purple. To make matters more perplexing, his hands enlarged into what could only be described as demonic claws. The monstrosity that sat before him gave a menacing grin. In a deep echoing voice, it spoke, "So you think me weak and impotent? Do you know why they call me the Dark Horse?"

Althalos blinked, startled out of the daze of death that he found himself in, "No... no sir."

The Dark Horse winked. "Because I'm as evil as the things you hunt at night, and I am essentially a work horse for your Cleric's Order. Keep in mind, I am not from the order, though I sit on the High Council. You would be wise to remember the fact that I do not always abide by your rules. I follow the rules laid down by those you might call the unseen. The ones who truly control Africanus. Unlike here, we have a proven structure, which I am here to assist you in creating. But know this, Althalos, none to his name. A curse word brings about a curse in the form of negative energy to both the sender and receiver. This energy is something that I collect... only to send it back ten times over." He leaned in close, emitting the scent of death mixed with decay and chaos something akin to rotting flesh and dirty socks. "You will be wise to remember who you are talking to next time you aim to throw a fit."

Althalos' jaw kept shaking, and his hand quivered, frozen above the hilt of his weapon. Swallowing, he mustered the words he needed. "Pl... please... may I be excused, Oko-Iku sir."

Oko-Iku responded with another wink. "When in this form, the name is Iku-Oko. But yes... I suppose we will have to convene another time. It seems you have soiled yourself."

— 18 —
CAPTAIN IN CONTROL

With one hand on the table in front of her, she glared at her motley crew. With Lord Salem financing the majority of the expedition they managed to acquire eleven vampires, all of whom were poor and rundown. The good news was that they were more docile than the last batch, so she didn't anticipate any sudden mutinies. The bad news was that they were more docile, so she didn't anticipate much from battle. Additionally, there was no alchemist or doctor onboard—positions treasured on any ship. Although the creatures of the night could regenerate minor to medium wounds, the major ones often required assistance. Eyebrows furrowed, she continued to assess the crew they had assembled. *Maybe this is a suicide run, as that bartender called it. But I'd rather die out there fighting for a cause than being butchered like alley rats. Lucky for me, the Merchant's Corner has had a few dealings with those on these trade routes. Got to love a crooked cleric.*

Lord Salem approached abruptly, causing one of Zurie's serpents to coil back. His eyes were half open and he held a beaded bracelet. He smiled, showing his razor-sharp fangs. A disrespectful gesture if she had ever seen one. Zurie grumbled, "You mind putting those away?"

He placed his hand over his mouth, "Oh my, these things seem to have a mind of their own." He clapped his boots together and saluted, "Aye, aye, captain." He giggled. Zurie lowered her brow and clenched her jaw. *He's testing me, for he clearly takes me for a joke. Do I fight, flight, or flirt?* She looked at him, stood up, and moved to walk away without a word.

He sidled up beside her and clutched her hand, nearly breaking her bones in the process. In a childish voice, he said, "I'm saw-ry captain. It's just that I'm so bored."

Zurie shook off his hand with a scowl. "Well, go be bored somewhere else. I have battle plans to go over."

He placed both his hands behind his back. "You're mean. In any case, taking a trade ship is a lot easier than taking a facility. It will be simple: We just need to get within boarding range, and the rest is history. How heavily guarded could it be?"

Taking a few moments to think, she looked up at the night sky. *The sky looks so beautiful out here. It makes me feel as if I have no care in the world, no worries, no pain, just... peace. If only Oakes and Dr. Asher were here to share it with me... to really appreciate it. They say we are immortal beings, but what does that really mean? If we risk our existence for what we believe is right, then the chances of us coming out that door breathing are slim. But isn't the second death a better option than living an existence as a coward? Look at me... the way I am thinking... such dangerous thinking.*

She felt tapping on her greaves. "Are you listening to me? What are you thinking?" The voice of her lead hand tunneled into her skull like a nail.

She sighed heavily. "I was contemplating what the second death would be like and the inner workings of what it means to be immortal."

He widened his eyes, causing electricity to spark all across his body. "Well then, you should have just asked, silly. I can help you with that. I'm widely considered to be the most ancient vamp on the continent. I have contemplated my second death many times over, in fact..." He raised up on his tiptoes. "Some would say I look forward to it."

Zurie looked at this ancient vamp in the body of a twelve-year-old boy. *I know he is ancient... but could he really be the most ancient on the continent? He must have witnessed great catastrophes as well as great deeds—perhaps even caused many of them himself. He will be a challenge to eliminate. My power will have to increase tenfold. But I should learn from him as well. There is so much for me to learn... yet I feel as if my time could come at any moment. One thing I do know... is my heart has gone cold like the dead of night. Lord Salem, The Terror, the entire Cleric's Order... even my betrothed won't be spared. They will all feel the wrath of Zurie Valentine.* She raised her arms in silence with her fists clenched.

Lord Salem raised an eyebrow. "What in the unholy world are you doing?"

Lord Salem's ship was a well-equipped vessel with more than ten cannons. It could house a hundred pirates but currently housed a fraction of that number. With two masts, it was built for speed and evasive maneuvers. A large blue dolphin on both sides indicated the name of the ship. Caressing her favorite constrictor, Zurie gazed out into the distance to what would be their first prey. The trade ship had no cannons and was sailing at average speed. The plan was simple. The Blue Dolphin would approach from the stern and attack from port side, giving them maximum invisibility in the dead of night. She clasped the hilt of her blunderbuss. The smooth handle soothed her mind, but the weight of it brought fury upon her heart.

Tonight, we will strike back a blow towards the Cleric's Order. They will soon fear to sail these seas. May the lord of the night bless me and my den. As they approached the ship, the thirteen members of the Blue Dolphin bared their fangs while the blood in their veins flowed at an increased pace. Zurie was the first to begin the climb aboard the ship. With her superior strength she ruptured the wooden structure with ease.

Landing on the deck of the ship, she smelled the sweet scent of laboring humans. She licked her lips as she roamed the deck for the night's watch. She looked up to see an old man gazing out into the stars from the crow's nest. With her free hand, she waved for her den mate to eliminate the old man. *He will not be my first. I want someone young, fresh, and virile. I want the luscious fluids to flow upon my tongue like a river.* The helmsman was about to signal the alarm when Lord Salem called forth a lightning bolt. The bolt sent shocks throughout his body, effectively silencing him. Zurie followed her senses towards the captain's quarters where she got a whiff of the captain's nature. Her senses wild, she prowled towards her first real feast, a glorious human. Finally, she arrived at the captain's quarters. She nudged the door to find it locked. Blood rushing through her veins, she aimed her blunderbuss at the lock. With a flick of her finger the lock was no more.

She rushed into the room to see the captain was half-naked with a cutlass in his hands. The weapon shook back and forth while beads of sweat dripped down the captain's face. Zurie beamed, revealing her sharp fangs. She swiftly jumped on the desk that separated them. With little effort she pounced on the captain, who managed to slash at the air. Her teeth sank into his throbbing neck. Blood oozed in between her lips. The hot red liquid eased all her qualms and left her with no cares in the world. Her eyes rolled to the back of her head as she embraced her increase in power, stamina, and awareness.

When the body was sucked dry, she dropped it on the floor causing an oddly hollow sound. Kicking the body aside, she stepped on the spot where it once laid. *Once again, it's making that odd sound. It must be hollow.* Jamming her fist into the wooden panel, she managed to open the hidden slot. Her eyes were met with the most tantalizing sight: a chest full of pinyooks, enough to subsidize their voyage for another month or so. In addition to the currency, there was a dark purple enchanted cape. She picked up the cape and draped it over her shoulders, to find that it latched comfortably over her.

Beneath the cape was a large spotted egg. *I wonder what purpose the egg serves. Do I eat it? Or do I hatch it?* She picked up the egg and cupped it under her arm. Next she analyzed the captain's cutlass. "Hmm, it's well made... but not suitable for an enchantment. What a shame; I do need a more viable melee weapon." A slew of footsteps approached from below the deck, causing her to take her spoils and enter the main area. Zurie was greeted with the sight of all her crewmates drenched in the blood of their fallen prey.

Lord Salem had managed to seize a large sack of what appeared to be artifacts, while the rest of the crew each held smaller products for trade. With the chest that rested upon Zurie's shoulder, the expedition was a grand success. *More... I need more...*

— 19 —
TRANSFORMATION

The former Bishop's suit of armor came tumbling down with a loud crash. Oko-Iku was the first to rush out, followed by Althalos and then the High Cleric. The three of them stood there watching the fresh commander Lief fumbling to put the armor back in place. Finally, he glanced at each of the high-ranking members of the Cleric's Order and pulled forth a deep bow. *What a bumbling fool*, thought Althalos. *To think I once thought of him as a son. Now, I only see him as a mere pawn to be maneuvered.*

Oko-Iku was the first to break the awkward silence, "Everything is in order, my child, for this is only a symbol of the Bishop. The essence lives within all of us. As for you coming up here to take your room, there is no need to be nervous. This will feel like home soon enough." Lief nodded fervently as he finished putting the armor back together. Hands clasped in front of his stomach, he beamed towards his superiors. When his eyes fell upon Commander Althalos, he winced.

Their eyes locked for several moments until Lief broke away and lowered his eyes. *Good, he better know his place. Impudent little commander that he is. Brom was twice the man.* The fresh-faced commander approached Althalos, his hands filled with his things from the lower quarters, "Sir... I know you're still mad at me for my indiscretions, but I do want us to work well together as we always have."

Althalos nearly relieved himself hearing such putrid words. He clasped his mouth while gagging, "What has transpired can never be changed. Some may call me set in my ways, but once my trust has been broken it cannot be repaired. The best you can do is stay out of my way and follow my instructions on the rare occasion that they come."

Lief looked up at his senior commander with tear filled eyes. "You're like a father to me... is there no way we can repair this shattered bond?"

Althalos snarled, "I have no need for children..." He thought of Zurie. *I have enough problems to scuff out..* "What I need are comrades in arms capable of neutralizing this vampire threat. Something is coming, and we are far from prepared. I allowed you to become commander for your excellence in shield combat. But make no mistake: Should you fail to uphold your duties as I see fit, I will cleave you down myself."

Commander Lief saluted and marched to his new room. *Why did I give him hope? None should be found when it comes to matters of my heart.* He took a deep breath as he descended the stairs to the food hall. *Perhaps I have really gotten soft since seeing that vampire scum. Next time she won't be so fortunate as to be saved by her comrades. The High Cleric saw to that. I may have my qualms about this High Cleric, but he is an efficient vampire killer. In some ways, the attack was good for us. The clerics are training harder than I have ever seen, and we will have a new batch of scrubs soon. Scrubs from all over the continent are swarming to train under the famed Dark Horse. There was once upon a time when my name had such pull.* The food hall was empty save for Catherine, who had been recovering. The bandages around her body still showed drops of blood; her wounds were more severe than anyone had thought.

Althalos took the seat across from her and gazed at her exotic features and scarlet hair silently as she ate her porridge. *She must drive the other clerics crazy. I'm glad she is focused enough to not let them distract her. She will make a strong commander.* "Why are you in such a sour mood? Something wrong with your healing?"

She huffed, "How would you know? You only came to visit me once. Is this how you treat your elite guard?"

His eyes twitched but he refrained from doing what his mind told him to do. "You're a commander now. I was unaware that you needed to be waited upon hand and foot. The doctor said your healing was on track and that you would soon be doing back flips with your crossbow in quick fashion. Save me the attitude, and let us have a real conversation." *A real conversation? I haven't had one of those in a long time. Why do I crave one now?*

She blushed then revealed her gleaming smile. Tying her scarlet hair back into a ponytail, she said, "Well, what do you want to talk about?"

Althalos donned a rare smile only to cut it off. "I can think of many things, but let's start with how we can improve the facility. It's our duty as commanders to make sure the facility is operating at the highest level it can."

She rolled her eyes and put her hand on his, "I knew you'd say something like that. Why don't you tell me what you do for fun?"

He shuffled around in his armor a bit. "Fun... I'm not sure what you mean by that? Being a commander is fun."

She giggled, squeezing his hand firmly. "I mean, what is it that occupies your mind when it isn't focused on vampires, clerics, promotions, and scrubs?" He bit his lip as his mind struggled to answer suitably.

Eventually he blurted out, "I have a horse."

She stood and pulled him towards the stable entrance. "Now we're engaged in a real conversation. Tell me more about your horse. I want to know everything."

— 20 —
A GOLD PINYOOK
FOR ALL

Their ship rocked back and forth as it absorbed the full power of the demi-culverin cannons' eight-pound ball. Zurie glanced forward as the multi-decked cargo carrier fired upon their ship. This time the cannon ball missed, attesting to their helmsman's skills.

Lord Salem rushed up to the helmsman and yelled in his ears, "Get us out of here now. We can't let my poor baby take any further damage."

The helmsman nodded.

Zurie approached the helmsman and used her boa to grip him by his collar. "I don't recall giving you any orders to flee."

The lowly vamp widened his eyes as he gazed back and forth between Zurie and Lord Salem. A vampire ship could be ruled in many ways. On rare occasions they were led by comradery and friendship. This often occurred when the ship comprised of a single lineage of vamp or a close-knit den. Sometimes, as with the blood knights, they were ruled by voting and democracy. This often occurred when the difference in power level was negligible. However, the majority of the time a vampire ship was ruled with a hand around the throat of every vamp on board.

There were few things that creatures of the night feared, but one universal among them all: meeting the second death by sunlight. Zurie had made it clear that any who opposed her would meet such a fate. The helmsman, finally making his decision, inquired about his captain's orders.

Zurie pointed towards the jagged rocks north of them. "We will hide there. Then take our row boats and row directly at the enemy. With such small targets, they won't be able to strike us down… at least not all of us. Then… we take the ship. I've been thinking… this ship isn't going to do for a knight such as myself."

Lord Salem was about to speak when the master gunner spoke over him, "You're nothing but a crazy toxin vampire out to prove herself. I'm not rushing headfirst into a barrage of cannons. You might as well have me eat a blast of that blunderbuss that everyone is so scared of." Zurie's stomach twisted and turned into a raging storm as she gripped the hilt of her weapon. But this time she paused. *Fight, flight, or flirt? If I kill him… I will lose the rest of the crew for good. There is a time and place for brute force and the time is not now.*

Zurie paced around the master gunner, eyeing the small group that had formed. "We're safe for now, as the ship is under the cover of those rocks. But if that galleon pursues, we will be nothing but boat scraps in due time. Did I mention the fact that we have taken too much damage to repair?" *Good thing the master carpenter is too busy repairing the damage to counter me.* "As it stands, this is our only option. When we succeed, we will be granted a new Cleric's Order galleon ship with plunder beyond our belief. This is our big opportunity to achieve all our goals."

The group became bigger as the master carpenter and a few others joined the discussion. "The damage to the hull has been fixed. We were fortunate that it was above the waterline."

Zurie winced, tapping the top of her armor, "We… well, it's not like we can outrun a galleon of that size."

One of the vamps shouted out, "Throw her off." Another vamp joined in: "Throw her off." Before Zurie could come up with a plan, several vamps had their hands on her to throw her off the ship.

She raced backwards and climbed atop the captain's quarters with her weapon drawn. "If you don't want me as your captain, fine. I will take the galleon myself. I'm not a coward like you lot. I know that to move forward means death, and to move backwards means death. I shall move forward and die with dignity and glory." The vamps watched as Zurie prepared a rowboat for its last voyage.

As she descended into the rowboat, Lord Salem peered down to her, "There has to be at least forty trained clerics on that ship."

She smirked, "It's a cargo ship… they won't all be battle tested. Besides… there is nothing left for me here on this ship. I'm tired of staying in places where I'm not wanted."

He stared at her before jumping down, causing the rowboat to rock, "I'm coming too. Sounds like it will be fun." He raised his rapier and tapped the hilt against his crown, taking one last look at his beloved ship.

The galleon launched several cannon balls at their little boat, each missing by several meters. Lord Salem watched as she rowed in a straight line amid certain annihilation. Every row took them closer to their destiny. Another ball twirled in their direction, this time landing near them. The boat rocked, threatening to capsize. Yet still they pushed forward. With the anticipation of her next feast sustaining her, Zurie rowed with all her might. She looked up at the large ship with the markings of the Cleric's Order. She winced as about twenty gunners pulled out long range rifles and aimed them directly at the two blood knights. She looked to the now-rising sun and turned to Lord Salem with a heavy heart, "They won't be able to track us underwater. I'll attack from the bow while you attack from the stern." A volley came hurling towards them just as they dived underwater. Arms swaying back and forth, she catapulted herself towards the bow of the ship. She poked her head up to confirm that it was clear. As she climbed the bow of the ship, she fought to stay positive.

Victory will come as victory is needed; victory will come, for victory cannot be defeated. Am I simply rushing to my demise? Could it be that I am just some crazy toxin vampire? Shaking her head, she slammed her fist onto the wood, causing it to rupture.

Finally, she reached the deck, where she was met with the faces of over thirty clerics, the oncoming sunrise, and no sign of Lord Salem. She looked up at the sky and inhaled the salty air. *Fight, flight, flirt... or fear?*

Holding her arms before her, she took a power stance. "I want you all to look at me. I am the greatest blood knight to ever exist. Vampires quiver and run at the sound of my name. I instill dread in little human babies before I eat them..." She walked towards the clerics, who all had their weapons aimed at her, "Some of you may be thinking... who the fang is she? Well, pathetic humans, I am the great Serpent Knight Zurie Valentine, and I won't think twice about peeling the skin off every single one of your bones."

A large man wearing the Cleric's Order's traditional blue-and-white coat approached with Lord Salem wrapped in a silver net. He wore a golden gauntlet on his right hand and a left peg leg. "Ho, ho, ho. Some fearsome blood knight you must be. Launching a two-vampire invasion? I'm rather disappointed. Him I know... this is the legendary Kid Salem. A vampire known for his massive appetite for artifacts and paralyzing electric shocks. I had been saving this net just for him. It seems today was my lucky day. But you... I don't know. Never heard of no Serpent Knight, nor do I have any interest in hearing about one. Men... remove her from existence. We have a deadline to meet."

A volley of silver projectiles hurled towards Zurie, who instinctively crouched into a ball. The purple cape wrapped around her front, glowing with bright purple rays of light. The projectiles all hit the cloak with a soft thud and landed on the deck harmlessly.

Zurie slowly raised her head from under the cape, peeking out to see the contorted faces of her opponents. *I'm still breathing. This cape...is magnificent.* She glanced down to see the plethora of silver sitting before her. The serpents whispered to her words that sparked hope. *If you think me powerful enough to complete the ritual.* She responded. Zurie closed her eyes and concentrated on the great waves that crashed against the ship, "I humbly request that the sea god look up from the abyss and grant me a reprieve. May I enter a pact with the great sea serpent Omi." She placed two of her fingers against her temples, and the massive ship rocked.

A giant blue scaled serpent slithered aboard. With its armored scaling and three tails, it was an imposing force. With a snap of her fingers, the serpent blazed forth towards the crew, turning them into specks of blood and flesh. Zurie dropped to one knee in an attempt to catch her breath.

Once Zurie managed to recover, she was upon the captain with her blunderbuss aimed at his head; he held Lord Salem in front of him as a defense. The Cleric's Order Captain shook violently as he mustered the strength to speak, "Hear what words I have yet to speak with open ears. I have precious cargo in the depths of this ship that I know you'd be interested in. If you just let me go, I will take you to it, and we can both be on our merry little way. I wouldn't even need the ship. You could keep it as a gift."

Zurie Valentine gazed at the human, begging for his life, with cold dead eyes. *It seems I truly have gone stone hearted. I used to pity humans due to their fragile nature. Now all I crave is death. I will pull this trigger knowing full well the sparks may engage with that net and send Lord Salem to his second death. Yet I have no qualms; my lust will be abated.*

Just when she was about to launch forth the projectiles, the captain dashed forward and gripped Zurie by the neck, turning it into weighted gold. Her heart throbbed as she fired the blunderbuss into the captain's chest, forcing him back several meters.

The captain chuckled, revealing that beneath his top was solid gold. She dashed forth once again; this time Zurie managed to dodge his attack, only to be weighed down by her gold neck—stumbling just enough for the captain to reach out and grab her greaves and boot.

Zurie limped; her greaves and boot were now solid gold. Eyes wide, she struggled to create more distance. Her back was against the figurehead of the ship as she reached for her dagger with her free hand. *If I fall over, I'll drown... but I wonder if it will be the same for him or perhaps...* The captain rushed forward with a gold aura surrounding his fist.

Zurie ducked his attack and shot him in the stomach with her blunderbuss at close range. The shot catapulted the captain into the air, and Zurie used a python to launch upwards after him, grabbing him in the air and squeezing. Using the momentum of the snake, she swung the captain into the floor of the ship. Upon landing she sent forth a barrage of serpents, each dripping with venom, upon her foe.

With his last breath, he removed his gauntlet and threw it into the sea. *What a scoundrel. Will my pinyook troubles ever end?*

After using her cape to remove the net from Lord Salem's body, she sat there with him for a few moments while they both regenerated, both gazing at the carnage Zurie had created. He smiled and gave her a hug. "I didn't think you could pull it off, but you managed to do something of note while conscious. Quite the impressive feat."

Zurie smirked. "I may not be the oldest or the most powerful vampire, but I am getting better at using my wits. The serpents speak to me as I grow." He nodded. Crossing her arms, Zurie said, "How did you get apprehended with such ease?"

He lowered his head and nudged a human arm. "Let's just say I got distracted by the golden gauntlet. It's a shame that it's at the bottom of the sea now. To make matters worse, my clothes are all ruined." He pouted with his hands at his hips.

She motioned for them to walk, as the sunrise was nearly upon them, "You regenerate at an alarming rate, even while under the effects of silver. Any other vampire would have been dust."

He shrugged. "That's my little secret." While descending the steps towards the hold, she sensed someone calling out to her. It was a weak vibration, but it felt similar to when Ragna infiltrated her mind. Pulling Lord Salem along by his wrist, Zurie made her way lower and lower until they reached a cell.

Inside was a slender masked figure chained in silver cuffs. He had silver chains wrapped around his body and knee-high boots. He leaned against the corner of the cell, a sad face on the mask. "What might we have here? Could this be a pair of salty sea sailors come to season my spice?"

Zurie raised an eyebrow. "What? What do you mean by that? Who are you?"

The captive tilted his head to the side. "It's 'pardon me,' not 'what.' Just because we're vampires does not mean we should lose our manners."

Lord Salem used his rapier upon the lock in an attempt to free him.

Arms crossed, Zurie raised an eyebrow, "He hasn't answered our questions. Why are you trying to free him?"

He scoffed and lowered his voice. "You really don't recognize a legend when you see one? This is the legendary Durriken, of the melodic knighthood. Look at the way he is dressed. Knee high boots, fluffy shoulder pads, tight coat top with a flower at the waist. He even has the violinist's traditional tailcoat." He charged the rapier with electricity to try the lock again, to no avail.

Zurie raised an eyebrow. "The legendary Durriken, my apologies. I thought you had met the second death already. Last I heard you were missing."

The slender figure contorted his body oddly. "Missing is quite different from dead, isn't it, my silver-tongued serpentine of a friend?"

She aimed her blunderbuss at the lock and pulled the trigger, only to have the acid dissipate as the silver projectiles cracked and fall to the ground. Durriken inched his body closer to the lock. "Hmmm... perchance if you went and acquired my violin. One can find it in the crew's quarters. 'Tis quite the alarming accident that I would be absent from my regular duties."

Zurie ran her hand through her curly hair. "Why does he talk like that?"

Salem smiled before responding "I think it's rather fun the way he speaks. Quite eloquent. Unlike the way you speak. He has a certain flare. I'll go look for the violin further down in the crew's quarters—daylight is upon us."

The two remaining vampires stood there staring at each other for several long moments as Zurie tried to figure out what to make of the legendary Durriken. *He isn't much to look at in the flesh. Could this really be the vampire who feasted on a thousand clerics in one night. How dangerous could he possibly be with mannerisms such as this? Even his mask looks foolish in person. The paintings certainly brought out his best side. I'm not impressed.*

She paced back and forth as she continued to size up the legendary creature of the night, "Is it true that you slew a thousand clerics in one night? That most clerics were afraid to leave their houses while you preyed upon their city?"

The voice behind the mask lifted into a higher pitch. "In these lands, one does not become fancy without some fact to said fiction."

Zurie continued to pace, stopping only to ask another question, "How were you captured?"

Durriken's mask tilted forward into the light, revealing a large crack, "Was a sad day indeed... dost thou have time to hear the tale of ten times over?" Zurie nodded with fervor.

THE ENEMY YOU DON'T KNOW

He swung his mace at her head, nearly connecting with dreadful impact. Catherine did several back flips, pulling her daggers from their holsters. With a flick of her wrists, they ignited. causing flames to spew out. With several twists and twirls she launched forth a massive wave of fire at his torso. Althalos stomped his feet causing a giant ice barrier to push towards her, effectively extinguishing the fire. She dashed forward, daggers aimed for his thigh only to have him dodge with ease. "Fighting up close with melee is different than hiding in the shadows with a crossbow. You project where you're going to attack."

With a series of punches, kicks, and elbows, she attempted to land a blow on the veteran commander. He smirked, dodging as the heat from the flames warmed his skin. "You get frustrated easily, that makes you privy to making mistakes." She twirled, launching her elbow towards his jaw only to stop short and sweep her leg across the floor. Just when she was about to connect, he jumped, using his mace as leverage. Her leg hit the weapon, causing damage to her foot.

In seconds she was standing in position with her daggers ready for battle. "Quiet old man, I know what I'm doing."

He snarled, "Old man? I'm still young enough to wipe the floor with you and anyone else in this facility."

The High Cleric started a round of applause, "Is that so? Well, perhaps we should test that theory out. As I recall, it was I who saved you two love birds."

Commander Althalos' face turned red. He tightened his grip around the hilt of his mace, waving Catherine out of the dueling arena. She nodded and took to the viewers corner. Hearing the previous commotion, several other clerics came in to watch the duel, including

Oko-Iku. *I've been waiting for this moment for a while now. Despite my advanced age, I am not useless. I will prove it to all on this day.*

The High Cleric withdrew his massive battle axe and slammed it against the wooden guard surrounding the arena. With both his hands wrapped around the destructive weapon, he smirked. A teal aura poured out of his weapon. The aura oozed towards his body, connecting to his helmet and right arm. He swung his weapon again, this time reaching twice the length of the battle axe via the auric connection.

The overwhelming pressure of the High Cleric caused Althalos to wipe his brow. *I can sense his killer intent; this will not be just a regular sparring match.* With the time he had left, he glanced down at the necklace the former Bishop gave him. The item that he saved for situations such as this. He removed the necklace from his person and wrapped it around his right hand. With his mace in his left he tapped the two together, causing ice armor to form around his legs, waist, torso, arms, and head. The crowd clapped to see the legendary commander in his mythical-level armor. Very few beings, vampire or human, could transcend their bond with their item to reach mythical level.

The High Cleric spat on the floor, snorting, "You'll most likely die from your injuries." he whispered. The dueling bell rang.

Althalos was the first to make his move. He launched forward, mace aimed backwards ready to strike. He launched a swift blow towards the High Cleric's chest. He stumbled and dropped to one knee before swinging his battle axe at the commander. The battle axe connected, shattering the left shoulder of the ice armor, but leaving Althalos relatively unharmed. The High Cleric followed his attack by slamming his fist into the commander's chest.

Pushed back, Althalos repositioned himself, now stretching his right arm as he let loose a rare smile. *I must thank you old friend, for everything you have done for me. Even in death you keep me alive.* From his right hand appeared an ice cleric shield with a cross in the middle and six fleur-de-lis around the edge. He charged forward with his shield held high ready for the incoming blow.

With both hands wrapped around his battle axe, the High Cleric catapulted the weapon onto the shield, making a loud clashing sound. With a flurry of blows, the High Cleric launched his weapon again and again towards Althalos, only to be met with the impervious ice shield bouncing the attack away with ease. Finally, he dropped to one knee exhausted. Althalos approached the High Cleric to deal a decisive blow, only to have sand thrown in his eyes. While Althalos was rubbing the sand out of his eyes, the massive fist of the High Cleric connected with his head, with a ringing sound, effectively breaking the ice helmet.

Althalos staggered back in a daze. While squinting he could see his opponent gearing up for a deadly attack. The aura within the High Clerics body traveled towards the battle axe, giving it a teal glow. The attack came swinging down upon Althalos. With nimble feet and eyes burning, he parried the attack with his shield, following up with his mace greeting the face of his superior. Several bones in the High Cleric's nose broke with a crunch upon impact. His nose oozed blue liquid.

The second and final duelist bell rang, indicating the match over. The High Cleric immediately wiped his nose and made his exit.

As was typical for a public duel, the highest commanding officer would decide who won. Oko-Iku approached the blood-soaked sands of the duelist arena. With his staff in hand, he climbed in the arena, "My heavens, was that exhilarating. I must say I am so pleased to have such elite members of the Cleric's Order under one roof. It makes what I'm about to say much easier. I'll be sending our High Cleric and the three commanders out into the field with a select group of clerics to issue out retribution towards the vampire threat. For too long, people of this city have been sleeping with insecurities. Each and every creature of the night, or whatever they wish to call themselves, will be tied in silver chains. Their trade will cease. Their blood rations will be reduced, and they will be terminated. But above all they will know who truly runs this city. Congratulations to Commander Althalos on winning the duel."

Althalos' eyes still burned from the sand, but his mind ached at what he saw. *Was his blood truly blue? The lighting was dim, making it hard to see but I must trust my eyes and no longer doubt myself. Could he really be a vampire that can day walk?* His body shook violently. *To think there could be vampires roaming around under the protection of the sun. Mingling with us as if they were one of us, eating with us... breathing the same air. Those scum. Who do I tell? Who can I trust? Anyone could be in league with him. What does he want? What am I saying... if there is one there must be many.* Ignoring the outstretched hands of the clerics, he went straight to his room to contemplate the ramifications of this information.

Althalos' eyes darted back and forth, waiting to see if anyone had followed the two commanders he had summoned to the stables. His horse Swan was uneasy on this eve, perhaps feeding off her master. Catherine was the first to break the silence. "I hope you don't have some weird fantasy about us; that would be ill-purposed in many ways."

Althalos winced. "I'm not going to dignify that with a response."

Lief bit his lips. "Ma... may I know why we are hiding in the stables? It smells."

"You'll stand in manure until weeks end if I deem it necessary." To conspire against the High Cleric was punishable by flogging until defecation, followed by having the wounds salted. This process would continue for months until all conspirators were named and dead. *What I'm about to do goes against everything I believe in. Could I really be willing to betray the position of High Cleric? The position that I cherished and sought after my entire life? But things are different from how I wished them to be. So much so different that I can't even recognize my reality.* Taking a deep breath, he started the best way he knew how, "Did you see what I saw during the duel?"

The three looked at each other for several moments. Lief managed to form his face into a pseudo-scowl, "You already made me write and send that letter. What shenanigans do you want to get me into now? I am already losing sleep. Look at me—I think I have grey hairs coming. I'm not used to being a nervous wreck, but every time Oko-Iku sir says greetings, I feel it is as though he knows it was me."

Catherine pulled Leif in by the collar, her eyes fuming, "Did you see the blue blood?"

Althalos let out a deep breath as he exhaled all his tension at once. *I wasn't just seeing things. This is not good... we're set to go out on a mission soon, among his kind of people... perhaps that is when he will turn on us.*

Lief slapped her hand away, "I'm not going to let some woman scrutinize me now or ever. If anything, I should be doing the scrutinizing; I have seniority. How do I know you aren't one of them?"

Catherine was about to speak when Althalos beat her to it, "I have seen plenty of her blood, during and after the invasion. As for you, I have known you since you were a fresh-faced scrub at the age of twelve. If you were one of them, I would have figured that out by now. You two are here because for lack of a better word... you're the only ones I can trust."

Droplets of sweat ran down Lief's forehead. "I wish there was more of us but you're right... I don't even know if we can trust Oko-Iku; he brings about bad visions. What do you propose?"

Althalos lowered his head momentarily.

— 22 —

FLEECED WITH
A SMILE

The night following her return to the boardwalk, Zurie had eliminated all but one of her former den mates. To make examples of them, she left their bodies hanging atop the rafters of the various establishments in twisted heaps of corrosion. The boardwalk was adrift with the rumors of her ruthlessness and awe of how quickly she had dispatched of the vamps who abandoned her out at sea. Vamps would run as she prowled through the boardwalk alone, daring anyone to try her hand. The blunderbuss she held at her waist served her well, time and time again, along with the serpent summons that she had learned to wield with great efficiency. She had become a force to be reckoned with among the blood knights. With a mug of human blood pressed to her lips, she scowled. "One more on my list. Have you come to stop me?"

Lord Salem giggled as he took the seat beside her, "Your serpentine senses have gotten quite sharp. I can usually sidle my way into the path of anyone that catches my eye. No, I wouldn't say that, perchance. Just a word of warning. That pistol of yours is in the hands of a great big meanie—another newcomer such as yourself. It would seem he was the one who convinced that vamp to betray you on the fateful day of revolution. Why don't you forget about the pistol and the stray vamp? You've already made a name for yourself."

Zurie crushed the mug with her bare hand. "You don't understand. It's a matter of principle. For two lifetimes, I have been pushed around and taken advantage of, like the simpleton that I was. I will no longer allow that to be the case. I will take back my power, dignity, and honor; piece by piece. I have a list to fulfill and I will take care of anyone who gets in my way. Their bodies will hang from the rafters just like the others: him and his entire den, if need be. Besides... I feel my power growing as each body drops to the floor. The serpents... they have so much to teach me and I am their willing student. I won't stop now... I can't."

Lord Salem smiled the most mischievous of smiles. "You suffer from a bipolar disorder. I can tell by looking in your eyes."

She raised an eyebrow. "What's this bipolar you speak of? I have been keeping up with my blood feasts."

Lord Salem giggled once again. "It has nothing to do with feedings, silly. Didn't your sire teach you anything?"

She lowered her head before slamming her fist against the table, "My sire abandoned me after turning me. Leaving me to the mercy of my betrothed, who is in the Cleric's Order. I barely know what my sire looks like; it all happened so fast. But I will never forget the sound..."

He furrowed his brows as he reached in and gave her a hug. "It is truly a shame. I have heard stories such as yours in recent years. Vamps aren't following the code like they should. No wonder our people have been reduced to a pale version of our former glory. Did you know that at one point the blood knights were equal in power to the Cleric's Order?"

She shook her head. "How can that be? What kind of force would cause that?"

He pointed to the moon. "I know it is hard to believe, but they are of us, but not like us. We had the support of these beings, but they were as fickle as a leaf in the wind. That is all that I will speak on such matters. Even I am held to tongue on such things. Back to your bipolar. They say toxin vamps suffer from it more than the average vamp; I suspect that has something to do with the toxic energy in your body mixing with the toxins in the air. These energies cause said vampire to be vibrant and aggressive at times, while timid and soft at others. This leads to a decrease in decision making capabilities. When faced with several options, the vampire often freezes and acts irrationally or out of character. Essentially, it is an imbalance of one's own energy mind, body, and soul."

Zurie placed both her hands on her head. "It seems my life continues to be complicated just by my existing."

"I do have a solution. We do an energy exchange... through a mating ritual. You're not at the level of my usual mate but you can still tickle my fancy."

Zurie crossed her arms and furrowed her brow, "I've had no desire to mate with any vamp that I have come across. Oakes was more like an older brother than a potential mate, Dr. Asher was my first real friend, and you... you repulse me."

He clasped her hand gently. "Yes, that's the thing. It's in the air. They spew toxins in the air that even you are not immune to. They reduce the desire for the female and male vamp population to mate, thus causing more in fighting, not to mention the poor excuse for blood. You see, there was a culling where they killed off the vast majority of female vamps. Rumor has it that some of the humans actually ate them. You know how these humans can be perverse with their liberties."

She ran her hand through her hair, only to find her restlessness intensified, "What are you not telling me?"

He clutched her hand firmly this time. "I'd be willing to satisfy your needs... for that blunderbuss."

Zurie nearly struck him with her free hand as she curled away. Lord Salem let loose a maniacal cackle as his irises intensified into a light blue. Zurie's jaw dropped as Lord Salem grew into a beautiful mid-twenty-year-old with long silver hair. His features were exotic, with a light skin complexion. He donned the type of face that could make dreams come true, and his puffy clothing became sparkling light armor. He stretched awkwardly, causing sparks to shoot out. "I haven't been in this form in over two hundred years. But that blunderbuss is calling me. I figure we could make a trade instead of me just taking it."

Zurie clenched her jaw as beads of sweat dripped down her forehead. *I knew I'd have to face him eventually, but not so soon. His power level isn't like anything that I have ever seen. It rivals even the Terror's. There will be a day where I will bathe in his blood, but today is not that day.* With clenched teeth, she withdrew her blunderbuss, gave it a kiss on the hilt, and handed it to him.

He smirked. "Good. I'm taking the cargo ship and all the artifacts onboard as well."

She winced. "You didn't even do anything to acquire those artifacts."

He laughed, "Does it look like I care? Mine... mine... all mine. Now go and find your little pistol, or die in the process. I couldn't care less. I'm done with you, and I no longer wish to look at your face."

Zurie backed away without turning her back on the turncoat. Finally, she made it to a place she felt safe. Her old den in the abandoned cathedral. Zurie sat atop the ledge of the second floor gazing off into space. *Poverty has struck me again: without a pinyook to my name or cargo to sell. I was taken advantage of once again, and I will probably meet the second death against those vamps that have my pistol. What kind of cruel joke is this? I thought I was making progress. Could I truly have risen only to fall on my face?* She looked at the spot where The Terror had let loose his saliva. Clenching her teeth, she thought about all that has transpired since then. Who she had become, and what she had accomplished since then. Standing up, she dusted herself off and dropped down to enter the den that she once called home, "I will devise a scheme worthy of legendary stature. There is no stopping Zurie Valentine, Blood Knight."

— 23 —
WITHOUT HOPE

Catherine glared at the High Cleric. He smirked as their group of high-ranking officials marched in the streets. The Titania Cleric's Order was in full force with the High Cleric, Althalos, Catherine, and Lief leading the charge. Backed by a hundred of the most formidable clerics, the large-scale force was on a mission to fully subjugate the remaining vamps in the city. As they marched in a wave formation by block, they captured the weakened vamps, starved from weeks of drinking diluted blood rations.

The High Cleric grinned, "Remind me to commend Oko-Iku on his tactics. Diluting their blood rations even more was genius. It's like stabbing rabbits in a cage." There was a loud scream from one of the alleyways, and the group rushed towards the noise.

They were met with a cleric who had both his arms severed, blood gushed onto the ground. The High Cleric widened his eyes as he came face to face with a hideous looking vampire. Curling his lip into a grotesque smile, he turned to Althalos, Catherine, and Lief. "I think it's time we see what these new commanders of ours can do. Catherine, Lief remove this abomination from my sight." Althalos was about to protest when The High Cleric shouted over him, "That's an order."

From the corner of her eye, Catherine could see Althalos giving the remaining clerics instructions to make their way to the boardwalk in a spike formation. She could feel the High Cleric's gaze on her body. *Such a deviant. I can feel his eyes disrupting my soul. I will dispatch this creature quickly, then complete my true mission.*

Before them stood a tall, pale ghoulish creature. It opened its jaw, revealing teeth on all four sides of its mouth. The vampire's head was larger than average, letting off the stench of decay. He held a white-and-gold pistol in one hand, and his other arm was deformed into the shape of a claw with a third arm sticking out.

Lief turned to Catherine, who also was covering her mouth from the foul stench. She indicated for him to go first. He stood in front of Catherine and dropped to one knee. With his hand in his satchel he pulled out a single orange leaf. Placing the leaf between his lips, he blew, and it became large enough to cover his body. With his shield in hand, he nodded to Catherine, who aimed at the creature with her crossbow. She fired several bolts, each hitting their mark. The bolts erupted into flames, only to shatter against the vampire's skin a few moments later. The High Cleric screamed disparaging words from behind them. The vampire creature just stood there smiling as he absorbed the energy, growing bigger.

Catherine placed a larger bolt in her weapon and this time aimed for the stomach area. With a pull of the trigger, she launched a bolt that turned into a silver net. The creature dodged the net. Everyone's jaw fell open.

"I missed from this range? How is that possible?" she screeched.

Lief placed a hand on her shoulder. "Hold it together. We have to take this thing down." She nodded. The putrid vampire climbed the walls of the adjacent building, spewing sticky liquid upon the two young commanders. Lief managed to absorb the damage with his shield.

Eventually the vampire tumbled down upon Lief, its heavy weight on him knocking him unconscious. Its fangs inched closer to Lief as the creature struck the shield away. Catherine rushed in with her daggers drawn. She slashed at the eye of the creature, only to have it absorb the damage. The vampire grabbed her by the wrist and held her in the air, its arm stretched as high as the building's roof. *So, it has come to this. Father will know where I am, but of choices I have none.* Her wrist burned just as she kissed the sapphire ring on her free hand. Her body erupted into a fury of blue flames shooting down the arm of the vampire, causing it to let her go. She twisted in the air, managing to gain traction against the wall as she kicked and flipped down between the two buildings. The vampiric creature withered into a tiny sticky puddle before their eyes, leaving behind the pistol and a horrendous stench.

Lief regained consciousness just as she landed atop his shield without a sound. The two turned to their senior officers to see a giant purple bat with teal blades beneath its claws. Althalos' body was on the ground leaking blood, and his head was in the claw of the bat.

At the sight of the monstrosity, Lief and Catherine stood there with their mouths open. The bat creature cackled a blood-curdling laugh, "I've been looking forward to this feast ever since I laid eyes on you two. The bat creature lifted Althalos' head into the air and opened his mouth, smiling as the blood drizzled into his orifice. Tears flowed down Lief's face, while a fury of blue fire circled around Catherine, yet neither made a move to avenge their senior commander.

The bat creature tossed Althalos' head to the side and approached the two rookie commanders. It gripped both of them by their collars and licked Catherine's face, Lief's, "Hmm, which do I want first... something spicy or something salty?" It opened its jaw, oozing corrosive liquid onto Catherine's armor, deteriorating her armor in the process. Just when it was about to sink its teeth into her neck, the creature staggered backwards, dropping Catherine but managing to hold onto Lief. Three constrictors in a triangular formation surrounded the creature's neck, causing it to shake its head in a daze.

— 24 —
IN DUE TIME

urie blazed past the two humans, only to reach her sticky pistol. Checking herself for ammunition, she loaded the weapon. With her pistol aimed at the stomach of The Terror, she fired. A large blast of energy flew out, striking her adversary in the torso. Her adversary staggered backwards once again, this time chuckling to himself. Zurie sneered. "What's so funny? Cracking under the pressure of finally meeting your match?"

The Terror's eyes widened, then returned to normal. "You don't really believe that, do you?" It dashed the still struggling Lief against the wall as it approached. Zurie lifted her chin and bared her fangs. The Terror chuckled once again. "I just find it funny that you came back to me seeking for me to finish what I started. I only spared you out of respect for your sire, but it seems I will have to formulate an apology."

Zurie's face tensed. "What do you know of my sire?"

The Terror widened its eyes. "Ahh, I see… so the rumors are true. She had seeded random humans without teaching them the old way. How does it feel to have an absentee mother and a dead fiancée?" it said, pointing over at the carcass of Althalos.

Zurie holstered her pistol and withdrew her dagger. A massive surge of toxic energy erupted from her body, sending forth a blinding flash of purple light in all directions. Dashing forward with her dagger held high, Zurie was met with air where The Terror once was. "Your sire's blood runs warm through you, and one day you may pose a worthy opponent. I shall savor every ounce of your being. Until next time."

The Terror flapped its wings, making the air around them swirl alarmingly. Zurie's eyes filled with toxic energy as she turned to look at the crumpled mess that was the two cleric commanders. Every step she took produced several snakes. Her rage was uncontrollable as she zeroed in on the humans who failed to keep her betrothed safe. With her fangs primed for a feast, she blocked a volley of silver projectiles with her cape.

Forty clerics, bloody and damaged, prepped for another volley just when Zurie made her retreat. She climbed the walls of the alleyway and disappeared under the guise of night.

With nowhere to go once again, she returned to her former den. The den reeked of vamp blood, another reminder of her failures. As she paced, toxin built up, causing her to shudder. *Is this what it has come to, I fail again to achieve my goal to have it spit back in my face? In place of pain and anguish lie anger and fury. This accursed sire will be another name for my list. Would be that I had never been turned into a vamp to begin with. What would my life be like? I failed the Cleric's Order exam eight years in a row. Would we have ventured off into the sunset? A poor excuse for a human became a poor excuse for a vamp. Fleeced, beaten, and abandoned.*

She pulled out the pistol that she had fought so hard to track down, "What a cruel day fate has played upon my soul. Am I even worth my weight in pinyooks? My dagger still does little in the way of damage; my blunderbuss is in the hands of a child vampire." She caressed one of her many serpents, tugged on her cape, and stomped her boots. "At least I have these."

Taking a deep breath, she thought about her options. *I need to make a trade for something more powerful. Something with which I can eliminate my opponent swiftly. I must risk a chance encounter with Lord Salem and head back to the boardwalk. Then I must get out of the city. I came back due to unfinished business... where would I go now? This place is all that I know. I'm so confused.*

She hopped from rooftop to rooftop, avoiding detection from the clerics that swarmed the streets. While on her travels, she bumped into several vamps fleeing the boardwalk. None could give her any answers for her many questions. Upon arriving at the boardwalk, she was greeted by a swarm of vamp bodies. Pushing forward, she could see in the distance flashes of golden light meeting light blue. Hiding behind one of the few remaining stalls, she gazed at Lord Salem in battle with the Bishop. The two clashed back and forth as clerics watched on one side, vamps on the other. This duel was more than a duel between a Blood Knight and a Bishop: It was a battle for the very existence of the boardwalk, a staple of freedom and rebellion for creatures of the night all over the continent. Shortly after Zurie's arrival, the duel was over, and Lord Salem was apprehended in silver chains. The rest of the vamps watching dropped their weapons and allowed themselves to be chained like the animals they were perceived to be.

The group of vamps that were watching from behind the stall with her started whispering amongst themselves. One of them turned to Zurie with his hands in the prayer stance, "You... you're a Blood Knight, aren't you? The toxic one, Zurie Valentine. I can tell by your cloak."

One thing she had learned about creatures of the night is that they never did the prayer stance to another vampire unless they were about to ask for something ridiculous. As the group of vamps bowed, she snarled, "What of it?"

The leader spoke once again, "Please... do something. If we lose Lord Salem, we will lose everything. He is the symbol of the boardwalk, the epitome of what it means to be free."

Zurie spat on the floor. "Even if I could do something, I wouldn't. The confines of the Cleric's Order suit him fine for his transgressions against my person." The group of vamps snarled and gasped but made no move to engage the feared Blood Knight. The group scattered into the swamp while she continued to watch the night's events.

One by one the vamps were led to the exit of the boardwalk, where they would most likely be made an example of. Her feet ached as she stood there watching the despondent faces of her fellow creatures of the night. Lord Salem looked worse for wear in his usual childlike form. *What do I do? I didn't come here for this... if I let them take Lord Salem, the revolution is all but over. If I engage and try to free him, I will most likely meet the second death for my efforts. That Bishop is not someone I wish to fight face to face.* Her mind danced between options as her body seemed to move on its own.

She charged forward, striking with one of her faster serpents. Before the cleric guarding Lord Salem could respond, she already had her fangs in his neck. While she feasted on the first cleric, her venomous serpent struck the neck of the second.

The alarm went off, and another group of clerics came running towards them. In a frantic mess, she searched the body of the guard for the key, only to see it had fallen out of his pocket and was sinking into the swamp. Diving her hand into the swamp, she grabbed the key and was about to free Lord Salem—only to meet face to face with the imposing figure of the Bishop.

The golden aura swarmed Zurie, freezing her in place. From behind the Bishop she heard a childish voice speak, "Some heroine you turned out to be."

There was a rumbling in her stomach. It had been over two weeks since she feasted on human blood. The extra diluted rations they served only made her sick. She laid crumpled in the corner beside one rather talkative vamp and the nearly withered corpse of another. *My journey will not end here. A captive on a cleric's ship in the middle of nowhere. No, I will not stand for this. There must be a way out.*

Once they lock you up, they never let you out.

The ship's hold was large but not large enough to contain the cargo it carried. Inside the hold laid three creatures of the night per cell. The small cells reeked of blood, guts, and puke from their previous residents. With her hands chained, she gazed at the cell across from her to see Lord Salem had killed his two vamp mates for some reason. She had heard the rumblings but managed to sleep through their screams—not that she cared whether they were in one piece or not. The withered vamp in her cell was different. Zurie hadn't liked the way he was mocking her blood knight status, so she ripped through his jugular with her fangs. She wasn't sure if she should be proud of that. Zurie wasn't sure of much these nights.

There was a creaking sound as the door to the hold opened. The subtle tapping of a cane echoed throughout the area, causing the hundred or so vamps to stir. The vamps covered their ears as the cane came closer. By the time the cane wielder was in viewpoint, Zurie's eardrums had ruptured. Blood leaked out onto her earlobes. Unable to stem the bleeding, she hissed at the cane wielder, who was followed by the Bishop, who had a massive smile on his face. The new man was dressed in a fashion that Zurie had never seen in the city that was her home. He wore a long light grey cloak, with ample arm room, and a cape. The inner collar of the cloak was trimmed with gold, the outer collar of the cape with black fur. The fur cape was connected by a short gold chain. In his hand was a grey-and-black cane capped by a wolf's head.

The cane was a legendary artifact as it gave off unusual energetic patterns. Without thinking, Zurie spoke to who she now deemed was a fabled aristocrat. "What do you plan on doing with us?"

The aristocrat widened his eyes before spitting on Zurie's bare feet. His accuracy with his phlegm reminded Zurie of The Terror.

She tried a different question. "What are you scheming, human scum?"

First the face of the aristocrat spelled fury, then it turned into amusement. "Interesting... an uppity vampire in my presence? I shall rather enjoy beating it into submission." Zurie looked around to see that most of the other vamps were banging their heads against the wall or scratching their ears out. Lord Salem was sitting in the middle of his cell with his eyes closed and legs crossed. It seemed he was trying to cast away the vibration.

It's fortunate for me that I'm in tune with the serpents; certain painful vibrations have reduced effectiveness. I'll be sure to use that to my advantage against his cane. Would that I could get ahold of that tool. I could trade it for something of equal or greater value. The aristocrat gently knocked the cane against Zurie's cell, causing her to fly backwards into the silver bars, creating a massive dent. Her head throbbed as blood streamed down the back of her neck.

The aristocrat spoke once again, this time in a low guttural tone. "You think because of your breed of vampire that it will serve you well. It just means I will be paying extra attention to you. You're nothing but a mutt that will only speak when spoken to." He turned to the Bishop with a gentle expression. "I'll take this one as well as the kid. Perhaps they will learn valuable lessons before I throw them into the pits. You've done well, Oko-Iku, old friend. What will happen to the rest of this vile stock?"

Oko-Iku shrugged as he said, "In manners of utmost secrecy, the Cleric's Order has made it clear that the experiment of that small city failed miserably. We gave the threats a little bit of freedom, and they had the audacity to demand more. Thus, every single vamp from that wretched city is being thrown into the incinerator. We have gathered all of their artifacts, and they will be up for sale at the annual auction."

The aristocrat nodded before placing a single diamond coin in Oko-Iku's hand. "Ugh, my skin crawls at the thought of wearing something a mutt wore. But my mind wavers at the thought of what kind of artifacts these creatures have developed or found. To think they contained the necessary aura levels and intelligence to do such a thing! I'm mildly impressed that their pea brains could manage such a feat."

Oko-Iku chuckled, "You'd be surprised as to what they have come up with in their pea brains. But I ask that you limit your fancy to five or so items. I had my fresh-faced commanders take stock, and they aren't ready to be brought into the other side of doing business in Europia." As their voices drifted away and the door closed behind them, Zurie managed to move once again.

She dropped to the floor with a thud and crawled her way to the edge of her cell. "Lord Salem… are you there? Hello?"

He opened his eyes. "What do you want, failure?"

She closed her eyes, took a deep breath, and sighed, "Never mind."

A BARGAIN DEAL

ief rushed over to Catherine with two large goblets in his hand. With a massive smile, he handed one to her. "We did it! We subdued the vamp threat and are on our way to further growth and prosperity. Yip, yip!"

Throwing the contents of the cup overboard, she furrowed her brows, "Were you not at the ceremony for Commander Althalos? We lost our commander and the monstrosity got away."

He took a sip of the contents while smacking his lips, "I knew Commander Althalos longer than most, and he was a great man, a legendary one even. But I mean... I hate to say it, but he was one cold..."

She slapped him across his face, causing his cheek to turn rosy. He curled his hand into a fist only to release it a few moments later.

With her lips pursed, she pointed in the direction of the other members selected to ferry the captives. "Join them before you say something that will get your tongue burned off."

He rubbed his jaw. "Just because you wanted to fornicate with him and missed out doesn't mean you should take it out on me. You lustful wench." She stood up from her perch and met his gaze with a fist to the face, making him stagger back.

Lief covered his nose as it leaked. "You'll regret that."

She smiled the most innocent of smiles. "The only thing I regret is being stuck on a ship with your daft self for so long. You play this sweet innocent boy, but deep down you're rotten when you don't get what you want. I know your type all too well. Go on and find someone else to listen to your vile words."

He sneered and nodded his head slowly as the wheel of ill thoughts turned.

A few moments later Oko-Iku came above deck with Janpier. His greased black hair and slick demeanor always gave her chills. The two approached her in deep conversation. Janpier did a bow, forcing Catherine to take the Cleric's knee. She dropped to one knee with her head bowed low and one arm across her chest. He raised an eyebrow.

"When your Bishop told me that you were here under his charge, I had to see so for myself. Your father has been worried sick, sending scouts all over the continent for any knowledge of your whereabouts. To think that you had joined the Titania Cleric's Order of all places. I was just telling my good friend here that such a place is hardly for people of your caliber. The capital city is much better suited for talented ones of your ilk. May I know why you ran away from home?"

She squirmed in her armor as she rose to her feet. *A curse on this aristocrat and his questions. Every time we have encountered each other he would give me these lecherous looks, only this time it is a look of pity—as if I have gone daft myself. It's the capital city and the high-born people that are the problem, not me. But I would be a fool to give words to my thoughts, especially to this aristocrat. The one with the wolf cane.* For the first time in Catherine's life, she had to use something that her teachers often preached: tact. She mustered her brightest smile as she looked Janpier dead in the eyes momentarily before lowering them, "I'm ashamed to speak in front of such nobility. I have not seen you since I was a child. Some might say I am still as such."

He chuckled and placed a hand on her shoulder. "I will not judge you; please explain." It sent further chills down her spine. *Damn, if I fear his judgement. The only things that scare me are my father and his plans for me. But how can I tell him that?* She held firm to her convictions and resisted the urge to explode in a mad rage.

With her hands in front of her, one hand atop the other, she spoke again. "I ran because I wanted to experience what it was to be a member of the Cleric's Order: the organization that has kept nobles like yourself from destitution and obscurity for quite some time."

He chuckled. "Yes, your tongue is as sharp as ever. I have always enjoyed such pleasantries. I am quite the noble am I not? Though I have yet to rise to the High Council, things are looking to be favorable this year. But I shall not bore you with politics, as I'm sure you'll hear plenty of them when you arrive in the capital. I have been debating on whether or not to send word to your father."

A sense of dread filled her as she stood there, barely listening to the words coming out of his mouth. *I knew this moment would come, but what will be worse? The fear of the outcome or the outcome itself? Anxiety is truly a silent killer.* Janpier finally removed his hand from her shoulder and turned to Oko-Iku. "Perhaps I could ask for another favor of my good friend."

Oko Iku raised an eyebrow, "Depends on what that favor might be. Like I said, there are some things that I cannot procure without a flurry of questions."

Janpier waved the Bishop off. "No, nothing like that. I ask that you free up Miss Catherine and yourself for dinner tonight in my quarters. I'll have my slave whip up something absolutely fantastic for us."

Oko-Iku nodded his head. "I suppose that can be arranged." Janpier clapped both his hands then tapped his cane on the floor slightly.

She could hear the faint screams of the vamps stored below deck. While tapping his cane rhythmically, he said, "I know how you high ranking officials like to dress, in dreary armor and such. I'd appreciate it if you raised the hammer, so to speak, and came dressed in attire you would wear for a splendid peruse in the city." He chuckled to himself, "Well not a night from your city. Pretend we're in the capital. Perhaps now that the vamp infestation has been taken care of, your city can be turned into something worthwhile."

Oko-Iku folded his arms together, "Have you been doubting my abilities? This wouldn't be the first time I have turned a cesspool into a vibrant functioning city."

With his hand in the air and a gleam in his eye, Janpier responded hastily, "I wouldn't dream of doubting your abilities. If not for your skin color and where you come from, you would be the most influential member of the High Council, and not their work horse. Just know there are things that have transpired which require me to ask certain things of you... but I'll save the rest for dinner."

The cabin was small but functional. It had a small lavatory and a medium-sized bed. The room was decorated in the traditional Cleric's Order fashion: lavish under normal circumstances while remaining efficient and effective. Catherine placed her dagger in the bucket heating the water, then removed her armor and washed her body by dipping the rag in the boiling hot water. As the scolding rag caressed her skin, she thought about a time when she truly was happy. *I have never been happy. What is happiness? How does one find such a thing? The closest thing was the brief moments I spent with Commander Althalos. Perhaps the thrill of battle—that was something that brought extra beats to my heart. My father would have collapsed to see me in battle against a vampire, much less a whole horde of them. But those*

moments were fleeting, something akin to a flutter in time sent forth by the light to keep me going. I know not what will fill this emptiness in my heart, but I do know that I just want to be happy. Can Catherine Goldcrest of the Goldcrest family truly achieve such a thing? Or was it only Catherine that had a chance at such bliss? One thing I do know: Life is too short to live it under the thumb of someone else's expectations. She dried herself off and sprayed what was left of her most alluring perfume, a parting gift from the capital of everyone's beloved continent. Hands resting on the wall, she took several deep breaths as the world around her spun. "Not again." Her heart rate increased while her breaths became short. As she staggered to the bed, her mind spun around in a daze. Finally, after several long moments, her symptoms subsided, and she managed to stand.

She put on her favorite dress, one of the many that her father had bought her. As she dressed, she realized she had lost some weight, while her arms had become more powerful. With a sigh, she finished dressing just in time for dinner. On her way to Janpier's cabin, she was approached by several of her comrades, "Look at miss Goldcrest; didn't know ya cleaned up so nice. Care to come by the common area when you're done? We got something for what ails ya." *I wish I had my crossbow on me. Every day I spend on this ship is a reminder of how men can be just as bad as the vampires. Good thing I brought a dagger with me. If one of these poor excuses for a cleric even touches me, I'll jam it in their eye.* She walked by another group of clerics, and this time none murmured a word: As if they had never seen a woman before.

Eventually Lief came running towards her with a white shield. "Mind if I escort you the rest of the way?"

Catherine stopped and raised an eyebrow, "Of course I mind... you probably think I'm about to get fondled or something of that ilk. I have no interest in you or any other man on this ship. I don't date clerics. You're all too...unrefined around a true lady."

Lief shook his head. "No, I know it's some kind of special dinner. Oko-Iku was seen wearing something unusual as well. I just wanted to apologize and show my appreciation for what you did for me. You saved my life back there and I know it hurts that we lost track of the High Cleric. But I promise that when we get back, we will find it and give it the worst death imaginable.

Catherine stood there for a few moments. "Fine you may escort me, but don't touch me." As they walked the group that was staring started to cheer for Lief as if he had won some kind of prize. Ignoring their cheers, the two walked the remaining distance without any incident.

Upon arrival he did an awkward bow. "I will wait out here if you don't mind… to escort you back of course." She nodded and opened the door to the special quarters. It was twice as large as her quarters and much more glamorous than she could have imagined. The walls were made of oak, while the floors shone as if made of ice. *Who knew a cargo ship could contain such glamor?* She did an awkward curtsy as her eyes met with Oko-Iku and Janpier. She sat across from Janpier and he smiled, revealing diamond canines. He snapped his fingers, permitting a hunched figure to enter with a platter of the continent's finest meat. The hunched figure smiled broadly showing its missing fangs. She bowed, nearly touching the floor, then turned around without a word, entering the small confines of the closet behind the bed.

Catherine shuffled around in her chair. "I see you use defanged vamps as servants. I suppose not much has changed in the capital."

Janpier licked his lips. "They are quite cost efficient once you tame them. Only need to feed them blood rations once a week, and they clean silently while you're sleeping. When one wakes up, the whole castle is spotless. I've had this old hag for five years or so without incident. But of course, they must be routinely defanged to ensure they lose their aggression and their bloodlust. Did you know that a large portion of their bloodthirst comes from their fangs, in addition to what they consume? These beasts truly are fascinating creatures." Oko-Iku placed a handful of lamb in his mouth. Catherine did the same. The three sat in silence as they each enjoyed their meal of fresh lamb and bread.

When the meal was finished, Janpier was the first to break the silence, "I hope you have enjoyed my hospitality so far, as the night has just begun." He clapped his hands together. The vamp servant left the closet and went into the kitchen. Upon returning she brought forth a large cheesecake, placing it gently on the table.

The dinner party immediately dived into the rare delicacy, leaving little room for breathing. When it was finished, they all wiped their mouths and spoke the customary words to end a high-class meal, "Valor in all endeavors; peace be onto those that have sacrificed for this meal."

Oko-Iku leaned back and adjusted his pants. "That was absolutely delicious. Your slave can cook."

Janpier smirked. "Yes, this one was an excellent acquirement. I plan on putting those two to good use as well." *What are they talking about? Has he purchased more vamps? I thought these ones were to be sent to the furnace by order of the High Council. To sell them into service of the noble class would be a cruel fate. To defang a vamp is easily the most gruesome of acts one can inflict on their kind, monster or not. Nothing deserves such a fate.*

Oko-Iku shifted the conversation to imminent matters. "Your words haven't fallen on deaf ears. Perhaps now you can tell me what mysterious favor you have to ask of me and one of my commanders."

Also leaning back, Janpier snapped his fingers. The servant emerged with a piece of parchment and placed it in the hand of her master. He took a deep breath and shook his head before placing it in the middle of the table. A red hand was painted in blood on the parchment. Underneath the bloody handprint, it read in cursive, "Janpier Donvalve." Eerie silence swarmed the room, causing Catherine to adjust her dress. *A red hand on parchment. It doesn't take a genius to understand that this is some kind of threat. But why is he so scared? What does this have to do with Oko-Iku and I? This silence is starting to become a nuisance, perhaps I should say something.* She leaned forward to get a closer look at the parchment. "May I know what this means?"

Oko-Iku placed his clenched fists on the table. "Here I was hoping this would be a smooth journey. As always, the High Council and the aristocrats have their secrets that they must keep from me."

Janpier shook his head, "The High Council doesn't know. I can't afford for them to know about this. Not everyone in the council is a friend of mine. They would use this threat as a reason to deny me from my deserved position."

Catherine picked up the parchment and studied it. The blood was clearly human, but it had an odd scent, as if layered with something sweet. *Perhaps a female sent this. Could all this be over a mistress of some kind? I know how these aristocrats are nothing more than walking peckers.* Janpier lowered his head, tears flowing down his face, "This red hand means I have been targeted by the one and only vampire organization recognized by the High Council. There are common blood knights, and then there are these five, who make the rest seem like the play of a child. The High Council has yet to identify what even one of these elite blood knights look like."

Catherine widened her eyes as the air around them seemed to leave the room. Struggling to speak, she managed to muster a few words. "What will you have us do?"

It was as if a massive weight had been removed from Janpier's shoulders. He released a breath before speaking. "I would like you two to commission yourselves to be my personal guardians."

Oko-Iku glared at Janpier for a few moments. "You ask when the deed is already done. Otherwise you'd be sweating up a mighty storm right about now. I know you all too well. What did you do? Speak truthfully or our dealings will be null."

Lowering his head, the once-proud aristocrat was forced to plead his case. "You caught me grey pawed. In manners such as this it does serve one to come with the dice well loaded. I admit I have already spoken to Catherine's father under the guise of hiring her to take care of my stable of vamps. While you Oko-Iku... I contacted your patron in the High Council..."

The eyes of Oko-Iku turned as black as his clothes, and a dark aura surrounded his body. The creature before her thundered, "You go over my head another time, and your head will be under mine in a sack. Additionally, the price for those two vampires has tripled." The aura seeped into her body, freezing her where she sat. Urine leaked down her thigh, dripping onto the chair.

Janpier nodded fervently. "I would apologize, but we both know an apology means nothing. I did what I did because I felt it was necessary to acquire your skills."

Her legs shaking, Catherine managed to stand up, "May I be excused? It is rather late, and it seems our business is over."

Janpier grinned slyly. "Not a problem, my dear lady. I look forward to having you on board as my guardian."

She curtsied awkwardly and stumbled out the door as quickly as she could. *What did I just agree to? But I had to get out of there. Such suffocating energy.* Her chest heaved up and down as she attempted to gather her bearings.

Lief popped out of the night with a smile on his face, "See, I waited. I couldn't abandon you on such a night. Some of the boys are still on deck gambling and whatnot. Aren't you glad I waited?"

In her hurry to brush off conversation, she muttered, "Sure." She walked in silence as Lief was rambling on about how his shield maneuvers had improved and he looked forward to future battles with her. Amid the conversation, he mentioned how beautiful she was three times.

When they arrived at her quarters, she opened the door to enter. "Thank you for walking me to my quarters. I do appreciate it."

An odd expression crept across his face. "You're not gonna invite me in?"

Catherine managed to hold her laughter in. "Invite you in? Why would I do such a thing? I wouldn't want you getting the wrong idea..."

Lief stomped his foot and scowled. "You wore that tight dress to show off your body, and you're not going to give me what I deserve? I waited four hours while you flirted and ate your way to a cushy guardian position. Yeah, I was spying, so what?"

She tried to close the door when Lief pushed himself in. He grabbed her by the arm and tossed her on the bed. With his body atop her, he reached for his belt buckle. "I bet you aren't even wearing anything under your dress, nasty bar wench."

Managing to free one hand, she punched him on his jaw, making him pause for a moment. She wound up for another strike, which he blocked. He landed a punch to her nose. Involuntary tears leaked from her eyes, causing her to squint. He took his hand and pushed it up her thighs. "See you're already wet for me." She scowled, raising her knee into his groin. He staggered back. Just as she removed the dagger from underneath her dress, he jumped atop her with lustful eyes. The dagger pierced his chest. As the life faded from his eyes, he mustered one word. "Why?"

— 26 —

THREATS A PLENTY

The prisoners were pulled up from the base of the ship into the evening light. Each was chained to the one in front. Upon seeing their destination, Zurie was in awe at the odd shapes and sizes of the buildings. Their structures defied logic. Varying in size from large to massive, they were all made of some sparkling material that blinded Zurie the longer she gazed at it. The aristocrat approached her with a key in his hand. While handing it to a hunchbacked vamp, he smirked. "Poor thing, you're going to be in a lot of pain in the next coming weeks. But I must prepare you for the arena. You understand, don't you? Stupid thing, do you understand me?"

Zurie sneered, "I understand you clearly. Why should I fight for you?"

The aristocrat chuckled, "The name is Janpier Donvalve of the Donvalve family. First lesson, when you speak to me you will speak with the utmost respect or else…" He tapped his cane on the deck of the ship causing all the creatures of the night to shuffle around uncomfortably. He then leaned in closer, his piercing grey eyes reminded Zurie of her betrothed. Janpier poked Zurie in the left eye, then gazed at her tongue. He turned to his vamp slave, "We will need to add something to her tongue, something a bit more appropriate. See what you can find in the market."

The slave nodded, then hobbled off to her duties. Zurie furrowed her brows. "What?" Janpier gripped her tongue and twisted it swiftly. Just when she was about to bite her new master's hand, he let go, causing her to bite her own tongue.

"That old hunchback once had a tongue… every month religiously she cuts it out herself. Perhaps you would like to join her? It's not "what," it's "pardon me." It will take you some time to adjust, but adjust you will."

Janpier removed a light grey handkerchief from his pocket and wiped his hand. He approached Kid Salem and caressed his fair skin. Kid Salem stood still with his hands behind his back and a slight smile. Janpier smiled. "Now he is a good little boy, how are you feeling?"

He did a half bow in the chains. "I am feeling confident that I can be of service to you my lord. I won't cause any trouble."

Janpier patted him on the head, "Ah, what a wonderful pick. You will make for an excellent servant. That hunchback will be cooking for more people and thus won't have as much time to clean." Kid Salem beamed.

Oko-Iku sidled up beside Kid Salem with a firm hand on his shoulder. He said gruffly, "I told him you were one of the most powerful vampires I had ever encountered, but he took it for a joke. I will be watching you. One step out of line and it will be your head."

Kid Salem did another half bow. "No trouble from me sir. None."

The new arena knight and servant walked with their patron deep into the city until they arrived at a large grey castle with a wolf sigil above the gate. The castle glistened like the other buildings. As Zurie walked through the gates, she dropped to the floor in agonizing pain. The same thing occurred to Kid Salem.

Janpier laughed violently. "Ah yes. Every building in the capital is warded for creature-of-the night-threats. Causes crippling pain unless the head of the household turns it off. Let us continue." He clapped his hands causing the glittering and the pain to stop. They entered the building to see an extravagant castle with art decorating the ceiling and the floor. Most of the images were depictions of Janpier conquering vamps and odd creatures. He had sculptures of himself in glass cases with artifacts in silver cages. Some were rare; some were legendary. Ultimately, they were better than anything Zurie had ever laid her hands on, save for that odd cape.

Janpier lead them upstairs to a room with a reinforced lock. He opened the door, revealing a feather bed with silk sheets, silk curtains, and marble tiles. The large room smelled of vanilla. He spread both his arms in the air, donning a smile. "I trust you are pleased, Kid Salem. This will be where you sleep when you are not working. Or, if you prefer, I can procure a pink box for you, as I know you vamps like to sleep in those boxes of yours."

Catherine spoke for the first time since arriving in the capital. "They like to sleep in coffins, sir. Similar to how our dead are often placed in them."

Janpier shuddered. "How gruesome. But yes, we can order one of those coffin things for you. As you will learn I am quite the generous master. Most masters treat their slaves worse than mold. All I ask is obedience and loyalty." Those words sounded odd coming out of his mouth.

Zurie's thoughts ran rampant. *At least I will find myself sleeping in a soft bed. Better than the floor of a ship or a straw bed. Though nothing has yet to come close to a well-made coffin. Perhaps I'll request a purple coffin. That's the least he can do with all this wealth of his. I'll have to figure out a way to get my hands on some of those artifacts before I make my escape.* She glanced at Kid Salem, who seemed to be in the most pleasant of dazes, as if the cane vibrations popped his brain. *Never mind him. I'll leave him to his fate. I have my own skin to think of, and getting out of here won't be easy. That female commander is no slouch, plus they have their Bishop who subdued Kid Salem. Fighting my way out of here won't be ideal. I'll have to use my illustrious sneaky tactics.*

Kid Salem smiled innocently. "The bed will be fine, thank you milord."

They made their way back downstairs and outside at the back of the castle.

Zurie next found herself outside in a large field of poppies. The cold breeze of the capital struck her like a dagger. Gazing at the colorful flowers, she winced; their scent caused her nose to ruffle. Janpier led the group to a small cabin connected to the castle. Upon opening the door, her senses were overwhelmed with the stench of feces and some unknown substance.

Janpier smirked. "This is where you will sleep when you're not training for the arena. There is much work to be done—and don't expect to be sleeping much either. During the evening you will train with Catherine, and during the night you will train with Oko-Iku." *I know how to fight; I don't need their training. But I do know I'm not a match for this Oko-Iku. Maybe if I can critically wound him in battle, I can find a spot for my release. This training may be useful... learning the official tactics of the Cleric's Order could serve me well in the future. I will bide my time and play the fool to catch the wise.*

Catherine tapped her on the shoulder. "I know what you're planning, vampire scum. If you think I'll let you harm my patron or make an escape then you are surely mistaken." Zurie rolled her eyes and turned back, only to receive a hard slap at the back of her head. *Just for that they are all on my list. Kid Salem, The Terror, Janpier, Oko-Iku, and Catherine. They will all feel the wrath of Zurie Valentine. I will never forget the humiliation of being captured and forced into servitude by humans. I'm sure Oakes, Dr. Asher, my betrothed, and my old denmates would be having a fit if they were around for this. But I will have the last laugh.*

She raised her chains in the air, "May I know more about this arena sir?"

Clapping his hands, their master did a little jig, "The arena is a grand event. Every Saturday the aristocrats, the High Council and some wealthier common folk attend the event. We put up our creatures of the night in death matches against one another. You win three matches, and you're done for the week. You lose and well... I think you can guess how that would go. My last three vampires failed miserably against my..." He clenched both his fists. "... nemesis. Someone with strong ties to the High Council. The worst loss imaginable. Thus, I procured you, Zurie Valentine. I had my cook investigate your battle history and it seems you're quite handy with toxins and corrosive-based weapons, particularly ranged ones. However, you have a notable failure against a more well-armored opponent. The Terror, I believe, was his blood knight name.

"I have an artifact that I think will suit both our needs. You take down this enemy of mine, and I will reward you greatly. Every victory will make you a superstar in the eyes of myself and the crowd. There is much glory and joy to be found in the arena, and it is up to you to take it. Lose and you're nothing, a nobody. Just another vampire that met her second death. I also notice you have the blood knight marking on your shoulder. That is good. We will be able to procure for you an excellent suit of armor. I admit it baffles me to this day, but your kind has managed to enchant certain armor for only blood knights. Quite the feat." He chuckled to no one in particular.

Zurie clenched her teeth. Shaking, she managed to contain the bulk of her ire. *There is no way that I'm going to be working for this human as a slave knight. I will be a grand blood knight, and it won't be in some putrid arena for sport. May the great Vamp Lord see fit to shine down upon luck and prosperity as I cleave my way piece by piece to this aristocrat's heart.*

— 27 —
ARCH NEMESIS

She woke up in the middle of the night drenched in sweat. She tugged on her loose-fitting undergarment. *Another night terror. Ever since the gruesome death of Althalos I have seen specters grasping at my chest as if they want to take me to the abyss that follows the wicked. Then with the murder of Lief.* Her thought process trailed for a few moments. *Do I tell the Bishop about my transgression? To murder a fellow commander and dump his body in the sea is a crime above all others in the Cleric's Order. I was defending my maidenhood as I should. But who would see it the way I see it? Men are not like women. We hold different things in high regard. No, I rather think not. I will not reveal my hand. I am in a good position here. I can be of great service to a reputable person in the community while staying out of my father's demanding clutches. But am I so fortunate as to walk away from this crime left unpunished? Perhaps these specters are of the mindset to do what the human hand cannot?*

Catherine's restless night continued as she rolled back and forth. Her legs felt heavy, while the rest of her body felt light. Using her arms for leverage, she rose from the king-sized bed. She gazed out the window to see Zurie training with the Bishop. The two were engaged in a brutal clash, but it was obvious to any keen observer that Zurie was outmatched. She was using a clunky cursed halberd that Janpier had been saving for a more suitable vampire. The legendary weapon was powerful indeed, but extremely heavy and not suited for a vampire of Zurie's build. *She will never succeed in the arena with that weapon. The one thing she had going for her was her speed, and that's all but nullified with that heavy weapon.* Something in her made her desire a closer look at the battle.

As she reached for the door handle, she heard Janpier's cane tapping about. She opened the door and greeted him. "Milord Janpier, I wish you had summoned me to escort you to wherever it is you're going."

He smiled, "Not to worry, my fearless guardian. There will be no head hunting on this night. I could never dream of being attacked at my beloved castle. It is an impenetrable fortress. My only fear is for when I am out and about on the streets. In any case, I heard the first day of training going on outside, and I had to watch. A more intriguing conversation is: Why are you up? You've always been a deep sleeper from when you were wee high." He pointed low to the ground.

She laughed. "I haven't been wee high in quite some time. I do remember you used to always give me those sweets with the wolf heads."

His piercing grey eyes seemed to look far into the past of distant failures. "Yes... that was when my brother was of this world. It would have been quite the canary if you had met him. Sadly, I am now the last of my blood."

"You mean to tell me you have no family left?"

"Not that I know of. My brother is gone, my sister is missing and so are all my cousins. I've searched for those of similar ilk, but those endeavors have born no fruit. If you were one of us, I could sweep you under my wing and teach you all I know." Catherine raised another eyebrow. *What does he mean? Does he mean an aristocrat? I mean, as far as I know, being a High Council bloodline is revered just as much if not more than an aristocrat.*

Shrugging his intentions off, she continued. "I do have some things I wish to know, but there is so much that my father doesn't want me to understand. I love him, I dearly do. But he casts such a shadow over all that he gazes at."

He paused for a moment. "Your father is the greatest member of the High Council by far, so I can see how his demeanor might overtake anything that you wish to do."

She shook her head. "It's more than that. When I wanted to learn about the art of battle and follow in his footsteps, he forbade any teacher in the capital to show me. He sees me as this delicate flower that must be protected or else trampled by the world of men. But you, you see what I'm capable of. I appreciate you granting me a guardian position."

"Well, keep in mind your father believes you are here under false pretenses. He is hoping that I will change your mind from the path that you are on. Though I can tell that is a war long lost. Come, let me show you the armory, the training sessions aren't going anywhere." They took a left turn into the grand hall of the armory, where Zurie had retrieved her cursed halberd. It was filled with weapons and armor, enough to meet the needs of about three hundred able-bodied warriors. She dropped her jaw at the array of legendary artifacts on the back table. Legendary artifacts were so rare that the entire Cleric's Order was said to only have about a hundred in total. But here Janpier was with twenty to his name, including the cursed halberd. He beckoned her over to the glass table where he pulled out two round golden crossbows. The legendary weapon wasn't enchanted, and it would be an easy switch to imbue it with a fire stone. *I can feel the power of this weapon; no blood knight would ever get away from my sights again.*

She beamed at him. "Is this for me?"

He nodded, pointing at a pair of boots with a firestone imbued in them. "Now, these aren't as fast as wind boots, or as easy to maneuver in as lightning boots, but these lava boots will allow you to stick to walls. You can pull off some incredible angles with these while keeping yourself safe from harm."

Placing the golden crossbow on her back in a holster she wrapped the belt of bolts around her waist. *I'll have to count them later, but it seems like about four hundred bolts here. They're so light, it almost feels as if I'm faster with them around my waist.* Janpier clapped his hands before rushing over to a jewelry case. "Now, the crossbow and the boots are because you are my guardian, and I have to make sure my investment is equipped with the best possible weapons, but this is something that I'm giving you because our families have been friends for so long."

He picked up a ruby bracelet and put it in her hand, "This bracelet is something that was popular when my people were flourishing. When your life is in critical condition, you can pull and break the bracelet, and you will return to a preset location. As you can imagine, there aren't many of these left, laying about." He showed her his wrist, which held five of them. He took his cane up and walked towards the door. "It sounds like they are finished with their training. You should get some rest before breakfast; we have a long day ahead of us."

How did he hear them? I couldn't hear a peep out of them the entire time we were in there. Perhaps I was too focused on my new equipment. She smiled and nodded.

The smell of breakfast wafted into Catherine's room. She hadn't got much sleep since returning to bed—this time out of excitement, rather than the fear that had kept her awake only a few hours prior. She rose, placing her armor on piece by piece as she sang. Her lovely voice filled the room as an angel's song would. As she progressed down the hall with her new boots, bracelet, and crossbow she glanced at the decorated wall. The walls were filled with portraits of the Donvalve family. *How can such a large family be all but wiped out? Could there have been some kind of epidemic? A family feud perhaps? I don't think I should ask; it seems to be a sore place in his heart. Let the past remain where it rests, just like with mine.*

Just when she was about to sit down, Kid Salem rushed forward and dusted the chair. "That was the last spot for me to clean milady. All done." He gave her an awkward bow followed by a bright smile. *I know that collar on his neck limits his powers to the bare minimum, but I don't trust this brat. He nearly wounded the great Bishop. I'll have to keep a close eye on him—no way a blood knight that powerful would accept servitude. I know I wouldn't if I was one.* She looked at the glorious meal spread before her. *Bacon, eggs, poultry, beans, cabbage, cheese, and wine. Everything one could want to start the day. I almost forgot what it was like to have a bevy of options for breakfast.* She turned to Oko-Iku, who was devouring his poultry and cabbage. "Better than what we get served in the Order don't you think?"

He turned to her with heavy eyes, "Our chefs do the best that they can with the sanctioned ingredients. This is only temporary. You'll be back to eating unseasoned mutton in no time." He rustled around in his cloak. "Speaking of Cleric's Order business, why didn't Lief see us off? You think it has something to do with him not being the acting High Cleric while the High Council finishes its investigation?"

Catherine wiped her brow. "Could be, I wouldn't know. He and I didn't talk much."

Oko-Iku raised an eyebrow. "Really? He said you two were practically joined at the hip. Arse and bench, as they call it where I come from."

Catherine shuffled in her seat. "He had a schoolboy's crush on me. When I turned him down, he stopped speaking to me. Apart from that, it was a professional relationship, as I keep all of my relationships within the Order."

Oko-Iku nodded, "Yes that does explain it, I suppose. In any case when I get back, I'll have to teach him a bit about upholding the Order's divine law and how to keep it in one's pants. I remember when I first arrived here from Africanus, me-oh-my, did many a maiden fly the roost. But the Cleric's Order is quite the peculiar organization when it comes to one's sexual urges."

Catherine's cheeks turned a rosy red. "I do have urges sometimes, but I am saving myself for someone who can truly light a fire in my soul."

Oko-Iku widened his eyes and pulled out his golden apple. He glanced at it for a moment but then placed it down. "Ahh, I am about to forget my position. There are some topics that need not be invaded. I shall have to take your word for it. Now on to bigger and better things. Janpier, what grand mission do we have for us today? I am well energized after the training session." Janpier clapped his hands together causing Kid Salem and the hunchback to clear the table.

With one hand tapping the table, he said, "How can you forget? Today is the day of the auction. I do have to thank you once again for a sneak peek at what the Cleric's Order will be contributing, but I have also received word of a few other items that I need to procure if we are to be successful in the arena. How comes along our little blood knight?"

Oko-Iku cleared his throat and leaned forward, "Yes, well. I've been meaning to broach the subject. She is having issues maneuvering with that cursed halberd. It's a wonderful legendary piece but it's bulky and weighty. She is a vampire so she is able to carry it, but without real sustenance she can't manage. Perhaps an axe or mace if damage is what you're going for, but a halberd that is cursed may not be the best way. Especially when you factor in blood knight armor which is typically heavier than the average, we're not looking in good shape for the arena."

Janpier slammed both his fists upon the table. His eyes fumed grey smoke. "No, that will not do. It must be that halberd. I have studied all the artifacts that I have obtained and that is the only one that can defeat that... I can't even say the words. Just know that you have three weeks to prepare our Blood Knight for the arena. I will not be embarrassed again by that scoundrel." He growled low as his eyes darted back and forth from Oko-Iku to Catherine.

Catherine, Janpier, and Oko-Iku walked through the bazaar towards the auction house. *How can we protect him from anything like this? We're shoulder to shoulder with any that would be threat.* The bazaar was filled with rare delicacies from all over Europia. Food from Africanus was rare, as it was thought to be unclean. The inhabitants of the capital often stared at Oko-Iku and would sometimes throw insults his way due to his origins. But none dared to press the matter any further, for his face was well known and his power well respected. Catherine had her hand on the lever of her golden crossbow as she perused the area for any Red Hand threats. *How would I even know what one looked like? I suppose they'd be*

a vampire wearing red... if they wish to cause us convenience. When they arrived at the auction, she dropped her guard slightly. There were two behemoth clerics standing at the gate, each holding a tall halberd. Upon seeing Janpier, they both took the knee. The golden doors to the auction house opened. Just when Catherine and Oko-Iku were about to enter the guards stopped them, "No weapons allowed. Auction policy."

Catherine clutched her weapon. "Not letting this out of my sight. I only just got it."

Janpier stomped his foot. "What's taking so long? We have items to procure."

She sighed and pointed at the larger of the two guards. "If this goes missing, I'll have my boot up your arse and my finger in your eye." She couldn't tell what the guard was thinking as he had a helmet on, but she took the silence to mean he got her point.

After Catherine handed in her crossbow and daggers, the group finally entered the auction house. It was true to its grand stature. There were artifacts from all over the continent and some from farther. The legendary ones were few and far between but reminded Catherine of her precious crossbow. They sat in the front row where a blue velvet barricade blocked them off from the common folk, as Janpier had put it. *In all my time living in this capital I have never experienced such extravagance and luster. Father truly has kept me from living a thrill-filled lifestyle.* As the cushioned seats filled up with the common folk, Catherine noticed two spots still available in their VIP section. She leaned towards Janpier beside her. "Are we expecting more?"

Janpier looked to his far right. "I hope not. The only other aristocrat that would be caught dead at these proceedings would be my arch nemesis. Everyone else sends a slave vamp. Oh, how I loathe him from the bottom of my soul and the heart of my mother."

Catherine turned around to see many vamps with collars of various colors around their necks. Each with missing fangs. "I suppose you will defang Kid Salem soon enough."

"Yes, of course. Thank you for reminding me. It is the law after all—though a sweetheart such as he could never betray my trust. Nor do I think he is foolish enough to invoke my wrath. We will have to defang him soon. Now quiet. The festivities are about to commence."

The announcer, a slender man with a tall top hat, came on stage. He waved at the crowd, who merely grumbled in return. Finally, he acknowledged Janpier and his escort.

As he shuffled a few pieces of paper, his eyes diverted to the door. "Welcome, welcome. Please come in. I'd like to welcome Alistair Crumble of the Crumble family." A few of the vamp slaves started to whisper amongst themselves; some were clearly distraught.

She looked at her patron with heavy eyes. "What's wrong? Why is everyone so skittish?"

He sighed and leaned back in his chair. Beneath his breath he murmured, "The Crumble family is now the wealthiest family of all the aristocrats. They have two members on the High Council, and Alistair Crumble, the eldest brother, is known for simply outbidding everyone on all the items then selling most of them at marked up prices to Africanus warlords. Then he buys their raw materials at dirt cheap prices, only to have them made into artifacts which are once again sold at a marked up price. It's the shadiest of all commerce and should be illegal. But the royal families turn a blind eye to it for reasons not known to me." Catherine could see Oko-Iku struggling to maintain his Oko form.

The short man approached Janpier with a massive grin on his face. He wore a ring on each finger and a silk shirt with silk pants. His face was unusually disfigured. It was an odd face. It wasn't ugly but it wasn't attractive either. At best, one could describe it as unusual. On his arm was a tall blonde woman wearing the most extravagant of dresses. She additionally had a belt containing enchantment stones of every type, from wind all the way to critical death.

Alistair inspected every member of Janpier's party then scoffed, "The young Goldcrest girl and an Africanus workhorse as your escorts... how perverse." He turned to Oko-Iku then nudged him with his tiny body, "Move over, workhorse. I want a close view of my good friend's tears as I take all his favorite little trinkets." Oko-Iku winced but vacated his seat.

All eyes were directed up front for the beginning of the auction. First was a purple cloak that would defend the user whenever they were about to receive critical level damage. First bid went to a bubbly vamp slave in the back, second went to Janpier, and then the final went to Alistair.

This process continued for the entirety of the auction, until they reached blood knight armor that could only be used by a toxin vampire, the rarest and weakest of all the vamp classes. The enchantment on it was a paralysis technique considered one of the most difficult enchantments to master. Alistair grumbled, "What dingbat would put such specific enchantments on such a beautiful piece of armor? It's almost a work of art. It's too specific for someone to wear and too beautiful to melt down for raw material. Blah, my head hurts. I don't know..."

A thought dropped in Catherine's mind. *If I remember correctly that Zurie used toxin in the alley way. Yes, she is a toxin vampire, perhaps this is the armor that we need.* She tugged on Janpier's coat sleeve and whispered in his ear, "Zurie is proficient in toxins and corrosives, perhaps paralysis will be useful."

He raised an eyebrow, "Are you sure paralysis is a good fit? I'd hate to be stuck with another piece of artwork, I have so many as it is. Ever since the Crumbles amassed such a fortune that's all I've been able to procure." She nodded with fervor. A vamp wearing a red collar placed a bid on it. Just when he was about to win, Janpier placed his own bid.

Alistair shot their party of three a dirty look, "What do you plan on doing with it? Placing it in your viewing lounge?"

Catherine shot him a dirty look in return. "That's none of your concern, you don't even want it."

He stomped his feet repeatedly against the floor, "Anything I want is mine. Even the things I don't. I bid forty noble coins."

Janpier raised both his hands in the air, "How does he still have forty left? All I have is thirty-eight in total. He outbid us again."

Oko-Iku reached somewhere in his cloak to pull out three noble coins, "Take it and win the armor. I hate that little shite as well."

Janpier placed the bid of forty-one noble coins on the armor.

His arch nemesis' eyes widened as he searched his pockets for more noble coins. "Do you... do you take pinyooks? I still have pinyooks."

The announcer shook his head, "No sir, you know we exclusively take the premium and only tangible form of currency which are noble coins. We don't take that fiat money backed by nothing."

Alistair's teeth were grinding as he caressed the belt of his female companion, "You'll regret this Janpier. This isn't over; I will have the last laugh. Just watch."

Janpier raised his hands, "I don't know what you're talking about. Don't be a sour puss, we all have our off days. I mean, ninety-nine percent of the artifacts at the auction is so unlike you—but sometimes one finds themselves faltering." He shot him an obscene gesture as the three directed the auction carriers as to where to bring their item.

— 28 —
WHAT'S MINE IS MINE

She still hadn't gotten used to the stench of the cabin where she was held. As she tossed and turned, she devised a strategy that would grant her victory in the arena and against the members on her list. *Every night that I face this Oko-Iku, I realize how far outmatched I am against the members of my list. I need to get more powerful. This cursed halberd is a great addition to my arsenal. Would that it weren't so heavy, or should I say, that I weren't so weak in carrying it. Perhaps Oko-Iku is right. Although it repulses me to no end, I must work out. A vampire working out. That is unheard of.*

She dropped to the feces stained floor and did two hundred pushups. One for every blow she would deal to her enemies. Sensing a group approaching, she got dressed in the rags that she was forced to wear while a slave. Sitting there she took a beetle from the bed and placed it on the windowsill. *Would that I was a beetle and could fly away, watch in awe as all my problems die away.* She gazed outside the window, feet dancing as she anticipated her release.

At the lock release, she pulled open the door—only to be slapped across the chin with Janpier's wolf cane. "Where are your manners? You're no longer a wild beast crawling about in the slums. When someone opens this door, you sit on the bed patiently. Or have you forgotten day one training already?"

Zurie winced, curling her hands into balls. "No master, I was just... excited to sense you." As soon as the words left her mouth, she had to stifle all the bile in her stomach from erupting volcanically.

Janpier beamed. "Excellent, my little pup is learning. Come out; we have a special surprise for you."

She emerged from the confines of the cabin into the evening sky. *Though I may have less than before, I still count my blessings knowing I'm not in the furnace.* As she thought the words that had kept her going since her captivity, she saw Catherine and Oko-Iku standing next to enchanted blood knight armor.

Janpier caressed the exquisite piece of armor with a mischievous grin. "I'm told this armor would suit you well. A paralysis enchantment would suit you, no?"

Zurie nodded.

Her master clapped his hands together, "Good. As for how you're going to wield this armor and halberd effectively that is up to you and Oko-Iku. Know that if you fail this training regime…" He raised his cane and unscrewed the wolf figure, revealing the sharp blade of a fencing sabre. "Well, my little pup, you're not as stupid as you look. You already know what will happen should you fail me."

Shedding what little pride Zurie had left, she knelt to her master with the wolf cane. After several long moments of holding the position she raised to her feet. Her master smirked, turning to Oko-Iku with a grin on his face, "I told you. All creatures of the night submit before my wolf cane." He looked down to the floor briefly, "It's a family heirloom… or I suppose the correct term is, it was. I have no one to pass it down to."

Oko-Iku placed a hand on his patron's shoulder. "You're still young. You can still seed an heir." Janpier's face turned pale, as if he swallowed a mug of blood rations. He shook his head and left without saying another word. Oko-Iku met Catherine with his face contorted.

She simply shrugged. "Perhaps he can't have children?" Oko-Iku shrugged too before assuming his battle stance.

Zurie had gotten used to the Bishop's odd weaponry. The sun apple was a psychic device of some sort where, given enough time to communicate to it, he could predict her next five moves—even if she hadn't thought of them yet. What made matters worse was that the apple could launch forth a beam of pure sunlight that, were it to touch her person, it would disintegrate that part of her body instantly. There was no quicker path to a second death she had ever seen. The sun apple could also heal Oko-Iku from severe wounds. The staff was another troublesome piece of weaponry. If she entered the radius while it was active, she would be hit with a sudden wave of drowsiness, essentially putting her to sleep. *I must avoid the sun beam while preventing him from communicating to the apple. But staying in his range too long would be treacherous, less I be placed under a sudden slumber. Up to this point I have only been able to deal minor cuts and bruises. Perhaps I should make use of my sea serpent. No, I shall save that as my trump card.*

Catherine yelled out, "Cripple the vampire already, it's getting late." Oko-Iku crossed his arms as his apple balanced atop the staff.

Studying Catherine, Zurie murmured, "She'd make a better vampire; one day I'll turn her." Assuming her battle stance with her cursed halberd in position she launched forward at a steady pace. Feeling the weight of the halberd slowing her down, she used her momentum to attack. Oko-Iku easily sidestepped. Zurie followed up by kicking her leg out, nearly landing a blow. After dodging another attack, Oko-Iku's staff emitted a sweet scent of lavender, forcing Zurie to back off.

She circled her opponent several times, as she would in a blood knight duel. *His speed is greater than any other blood knight I've ever encountered so I only have one shot at this.* With all her might she charged forward, the halberd gleaming under the moonlight. Every step she took dug into the soft soil of the land. When she arrived within striking distance of her opponent, she focused her energy on a snake double. *Which will he choose to strike? If he makes the wrong decision, I have him.* Beads of sweat dripped down Oko-Iku's face as he catapulted his staff into the head of the snake double, causing it to explode in a flurry of acid.

With her halberd jammed into Oko-Iku's ribcage, Zurie smirked. *Maybe I'm not so unworthy after all.* Blood oozed out of the wound as Oko-Iku's eyes widened.

"Perchance was that a snake double?"

Zurie strengthened her stance, "The battlefield is no place for conversation."

Oko-Iku patted Zurie on the head. "Good, you remember lesson number two. We will reconvene in two weeks. The day before the arena. Until then all you must do is workout wearing these." He pulled off his cloak to reveal black bandages all over his arms, chest, torso, and legs. As he unraveled the bandages, Zurie could feel an immense amount of cursed energy ooze from his body. Each part of his body he unraveled depicted a foreign tattoo. As the cursed energy swarmed around his body, Zurie took several steps back. Oko-Iku dropped the bandages on the ground, causing the earth to shake.

She cupped her jaw before speaking. "How... how heavy are those?"

Oko-Iku shrugged. "They will always weigh twice your body weight. Perfect for training, especially for a vampire. You will gain strength at a quicker rate because of what you are, while at the same time it won't disrupt your figure. This is your chance to find meaning in your life. I suggest you train hard."

Zurie squinted, "What do you mean by that?" Her posture softened as she got used to the pervasive aura of the dark energy.

With his arms folded he leaned in closer. "I don't need my apple to read you like the open tome that you are. You have feelings of inadequacy; you're not accepted by vampires, nor are you accepted by humans. You're a misfit not unlike myself. This life that Janpier has proposed to you may not be what you expected when you were first turned, but know that it is the best thing on the table."

Zurie nodded and dragged the bandages to her cabin. *I will never submit to a life of servitude. I don't see how good it could possibly become.*

With her back erect and legs firmly on the ground, she smirked within her armor. The once intimidating art was now hers to maneuver at her will. Zurie walked up to Kid Salem with her hand caressing the waist of her armor. Kid Salem gazed at the work of art. "I like... I really like. Though it doesn't seem as sturdy as the armor made for men. You will be of use to us."

She waved the child off. "Yes, I have noticed that all the armor for female blood knight's seem to be rather... eye catching. It's almost as if whoever is enchanting these suits of armor don't want female blood knights."

He giggled. "It's best not to think about such things. It will only hurt your brain. In any case you must win many battles for us, for your priority is to serve our master. I hope you have not forgotten how good a team we make."

"No, I have not forgotten. I have not forgotten how foolish trying to save you was, as it got me caught up in this mess. I have not forgotten how you have spurned me for conversation every chance you get. So, I ask you, when did you become an you and I?"

He did a twirl in his puffy servant's suit. "Ever since you gained some power, armor, and a cursed weapon. You somehow seem more... respectable. Join forces with me, and we can complete my mission in bloody fashion. I have somehow underestimated our opponents' power levels. The Red Hand commands your fidelity."

She took several steps back, "You speak of the illusive and illustrious Red Hand as if you are familiar. What do you know of the Red Hand?"

He raised his tongue to reveal a red hand tattoo on its underside. "I know that I am one with their order, and their order is one with me. I suppose I should formally introduce myself. I am Lord Salem Swiftbolt of the Swiftbolt clan. Middle finger to the Red Hand and for all intents and purposes, your only way out of this predicament."

She tightened her grip on her cursed halberd. "They say all creatures of the night are bound by the allegiance to the Red Hand. Even more so a blood knight. But after meeting you, I'd rather take my chances alone. I know what I'm doing." She turned her back upon the lightning child and made her way to the dining area, where she was served undiluted goat blood.

Janpier walked in with his cane tapping lightly. "Kid Salem seems to have polished you nicely. I'm glad. You look worthy of the arena champion title. I know the cabin is a hell hole, but it was necessary for your training that you wallow in such conditions. You win the three matches today, and you will be relocated to a castle room. How does that sound, little pup?"

Resisting the urge to verbally assault her master, she bit her tongue. "I feel ever so grateful for the opportunity to make the Donvalve name proud, milord. The arena soil will run blue with the blood of my opponents."

Janpier clapped his hands with glee. "Excellent, just as I would expect from an arena victor. Now remember today is just the preliminary rounds. But you will be facing one of the scoundrels' vampire in the third battle, should you make it there."

She drowned in her goat blood. "I shall make it."

The arena was soiled with the blood and guts of her vampire brethren. Taking a deep breath she gently clasped the collar around her neck. *If I'm to free myself, this might be the best place. There are few guards here, their collar is subpar, and I can hide within the large crowd of people.* From the corner of her eye she saw a section for the aristocrats where Janpier was sitting with Catherine and Oko-Iku. On the opposite side of the arena was what she presumed to be the High Council, each dressed in white cloth with a cross and sun marked upon their clothing. Each member of the High Council was veiled, with a marking to indicate identity. The announcer stepped to the middle of the arena with the referee at his side.

"The rules are simple. When the bell rings, the two of you will enter the middle of the arena, where you will fight to the death. If a member of the crowd so much as gets a scratch from an attack of yours, our sun beam will inflict a pain that is beyond comparison." Both vampires looked up at the massive long-range rifle. There were two people operating it, one to navigate the angle and one to pull the trigger. The announcer's voice boomed throughout the arena. "In the white armor, wielding the cursed halberd of dismay, we have Zurie Valentine fighting for house Donvalve. She is a vicious and demented Blood Knight who hangs the bodies of her enemies for sport."

It wasn't for sport; it was to prove a point. Their research could use some work.

The announcer pointed at a behemoth of a vampire almost twice the size of The Terror. "In the orange armor, we have Tiny Tim. He is a recently turned vampire under the patronage of the High Council." Tiny Tim wore the armor of a barbarian with skulls all over. It was clear that he had recently feasted on human blood, as his bloodlust was at an all-time high. *He will have the added benefits of increased speed, strength, and endurance.*

Zurie looked at him mildly. She lowered her head and assumed her battle stance. With her massive halberd resting against the sand of the arena behind her back, she took several breaths. Two venomous serpents appeared, wrapping themselves around the weapon. The behemoth came charging towards her, the ground thundering beneath every footstep. He launched one massive fist where Zurie was standing.

Zurie quickly cleaved the inner thigh of her foe before walking away. A massive cloud rained acid on the behemoth, melting his body to the horrible tune of his cries. He quivered and rocked as his body dropped to the floor. His soul left his body; his eyes rolled to the back of his head. An orange essence left his body and flew into the Halberd's eye. *I see, so that's what that eye was for. Perhaps that's why they call them cursed weapons. They consume the souls of fallen foes while draining energy of the wielder at an alarming rate. But for what purpose does it serve? In any case, I'll have to improve my stamina if I'm to survive longer battles.*

As she analyzed the inner workings of her weapon she felt an odd tingling sensation, followed by chills down her spine. Her body tensed as her strength, speed, and awareness increased significantly. *It feels as if I had just feasted on a human. Quite the interesting weapon. I shall make good use of it.* She glanced at Janpier, then Oko-Iku, and Catherine, who could be seen clapping rapidly.

As Zurie stood waiting for the next opponent to be brought in, the cheers of the crowd rained down upon her like a thundering storm. "Valentine! Valentine!"

She raised her weapon in the air. *Is this what it feels like to be loved? It feels so...good.*

Her celebration was cut short when a hooded vampire emerged from the shadows of the arena gates. The announcer called out the name Sir Visor the Shadow Weaver and blared his horn.

Sir Visor approached Zurie with a ball of shadow yarn in his hands. "I see you are a fellow blood knight. May this battle be honorable and respectable." Zurie tried to nod but was unable to move. Her eyes darted below her where she saw shadow strings attached to her legs, torso, and neck. Within seconds, she was tangled in the energy draining strings. Sir Visor lifted his hood to reveal two rows of rotten teeth. He sucked in the shadow strings, bringing Zurie closer to him.

Could this be how I meet my demise? Eaten by a rotten-mouthed vampire. No, I can't let that occur. Especially not after experiencing the warmth of the crowd. I crave to electrify them once again. This armor is enchanted with a paralysis stone, perhaps... if I focus. She closed her eyes and focused her mind on sending paralysis through the strings. A spark lit, turning into a wave of energy hurling towards her opponent. Upon seeing the attack, her opponent released the strings connected to his mouth.

Focus, I cannot meet the second death here, not now when I have felt something to make me feel alive. Zurie channeled her energy to access the fields around her body. As she drew in her energy field the shadow strings dissolved, freeing her of her temporary captivity. After breaking free of the confines, she assumed her battle stance. She launched herself towards her opponent. Sir Visor was quick, but Zurie was quicker. After dodging her first blow by the skin of his teeth, the second struck him in the stomach. Blue blood leaked out onto the ground as Sir Visor jumped back creating space between them. "Darkness falls!" echoed throughout the arena.

Zurie's vision became pitch black. *What's going on?* A low cackle erupted from an unknown place, "Those who rely on their base senses always fall prey to my tactics. I'm glad I was matched up with a lowly toxin vampire. This battle will be over quicker than I thought." Zurie clenched her hands around her mighty cursed weapon. Feeling the weapon feeding off her rage she charged the most destructive attack she had made to date. *He's right. I am a toxin vampire. I don't need my vision to sense him. I can use my serpentine senses.* She focused her energy on the arena, breathing in sequence with the energy of her halberd. Sensing, touching, embracing its life source, she twirled around the weapon and launched a massive surge of energy in the form of a snake towards the running Sir Visor. The attack traveled across the ground, unearthing the sands beneath it until it reached its destination. The surge connected with its target and exploded his body in every direction. A black essence traveled from what was left of his heart towards the halberd, where the eye opened and consumed it.

She shuddered; a surge of vitality caused her to roll her eyes in ecstasy. The trance lasted several minutes. *I see, so different souls give me different effects, but one thing is sure. The more I kill the stronger I get. One can truly get used to this.* The crowd continued to chant her name, causing something in her to stir: something only known to one in the arena.

The announcer clapped in awe. "This Valentine is quickly becoming a fan favorite. However, we do have last week's triple winner who may have something to say about her short career." He handed a lightly armored male the orb of projection.

"I spit on the career of this Zurie. She will fall to me as many have before her."

The crowd cheered for this opponent, causing Zurie to stir. *What... what about me? I thought they loved me.* After witnessing firsthand, the fickle nature of the crowd, she charged her weapon with as much energy as she could muster. She sent a surge of energy towards the stranger. This opponent was much quicker than the last; he jumped to the side with time to spare. He reached within his pockets to pluck out an egg.

She reached out with her free hand. "That's mine. Give it back this instance. It was stolen from me when I was taken captive."

Her opponent returned her demand with an obscene gesture. "I possess it, thus it is mine."

Zurie clasped her hands around her weapon. "Just because you possess a stolen artifact in your hands does not mean it wasn't stolen. Hand it here and your death will be swift." With another obscene gesture, her opponent dropped the egg and kicked it. Glowing bright red, the egg opened from the middle. A six-foot reptilian creature with harness and light armor appeared. At the top of its head and Achilles tendons grew sharp green feathers. It screeched, causing many in the arena to cover their ears. The long-ranged sun rifle immediately turned and aimed at her opponent. He raised his hand to the air as he approached the creature. It snapped at him several times, but he managed to mount it without injury.

Valentine yelled at her opponent, "What for fang's sake is that?"

A spear emerged from his palm. "Don't you pea-brained vampires from that desolate city know anything? This is a raptor. They are native to Africanus and notoriously difficult to train. But once you tame them, they are loyal for life." The raptor reared its head to shake its rider off but only received a strike on the head for its efforts.

Acid rain swirled around Zurie as she stood in the middle of the arena, her energy shooting in every direction. She clenched her fists as she spoke. "Retract your previous statement."

There was a long silence before her opponent pulled out his pecker and urinated on the sand in front of Zurie. "That's what I think of you, pea-brained vampires from that cesspool of a city. All who participated in that hair-brained revolution are nothing but failed blood knights if you ask me."

It's painful enough as it is to think that Oakes and Dr. Asher will be remembered as nothing more than footnotes in the grand scheme of the revolution. Their names will fade away in the sands of time under the names of the fallen. But I will not let their memories be sullied to my face. This, I cannot stand for. Zurie charged forward with her weapon poised to impale her opponent's throat. The man on the raptor dodged the attack easily as the raptor sprinted across the arena, launching six feathers at Zurie. She managed to dodge the first three but was struck in the neck by the second three. She felt blood ooze out, followed by a numbing sensation in her neck and chest area. As she struggled to move forward, her opponent returned from the rear atop his raptor, his spear aimed at Zurie's upper back.

The rider impaled his spear into Zurie's back, piercing through her armor as if through butter. He carried her forward, ramming her into the wall of the arena. A serpent lashed out in defense of its owner but had its head bitten off by the raptor. With a loud thud, Zurie's body dropped to the floor in a crumpled heap. The rider turned around and did another lap around the arena before coming around with a golden spear in his hand.

By this time Zurie had managed to stand.

The rider launched his golden spear towards her left arm, impaling it against the arena walls. Zurie bellowed as the weapon twisted and turned inside her arm causing her to drop her weapon. The rider came around once again with a silver spear. He cackled as he launched it at Zurie's chest. This time she was ready for him. She caught the spear just as it was about to pierce her chest. *I have unfinished business to take care of.*

Her eyes a toxic fury, she pulled herself off the wall and picked her weapon up off the floor, "Is this what the capital has to offer? Is this all you have to show for your superior wealth and servitude?" She clenched her teeth.

The rider spat on the floor, kicking the raptor. The beast charged forward at insane speeds. With another silver spear in his gloved hands, the rider charged, aiming for her throat.

Zurie launched herself more slowly than normal towards the speeding raptor. A constrictor emerged from her weapon, wrapping itself around her opponent's neck. She agilely leaped into the air then cleaved the rider in two, leaving the raptor unharmed.

The crowd erupted into a wild frenzy, giving her a standing ovation. The announcer walked towards Zurie who was breathing heavily. Using her halberd for leverage, she coughed up a glob of blood.

The announcer clasped Zurie's free hand and raised it in the air. "This week's arena victor, Zurie Valentine of the Donvalve house. Prepare yourselves for next week when she will take on another set of three vampires. Should she survive that is." He turned to Zurie with shallow eyes. "As an arena victor you may take one artifact from your fallen prey."

She responded, "That raptor is mine."

— 29 —

BLOOD MOON

There was a long pause as Catherine read the letter that had just arrived for Janpier. It had been six months under the patronage of Janpier, and there had been no attack. The training was going exceptionally well, as the vampire beast had been undefeated in the arena. Each victory was more convincing than the last. The audience had even begun calling her Lady Valentine the Untouchable, a name that concerned Catherine. With her brow furrowed, she read the letter again to make sure everything was correct. She marched down the hall to Janpier's bed chambers.

Kid Salem was outside the door, dusting the handle. Another member of their "family," as Janpier liked to call them, that she had concerns about. The child vampire glanced up at Catherine with that innocent smile he always had on. A sudden rage of fury built up in Catherine's mind. *Oh, how I long to kick his teeth in. Make him swallow those pearly whites. I know he above all is up to something.* She was about to knock on the door when Kid Salem whispered, "Milord is sleeping."

Catherine drily responded, "I didn't ask you."

She knocked heavily on the door. A few minutes later, Janpier opened the door with his hair in a mess. The cane wasn't in his hand as usual, presumably due to how quickly he rushed to the door.

In a hurried voice Kid Salem spoke, "Milord, your room is a catastrophe, allow me to clean it." Without giving Janpier time to respond, he was already picking up the clothes from the floor and folding them.

He chuckled. "That kid certainly takes his job seriously. So does Zurie. She has won me a bucket of noble coins. Are you familiar with how people of the finer tastes operate?"

Catherine shook her head. "No, I am barely familiar with how the Cleric's Order operates. My father shunned me from such things."

"I see. You should see him soon. We have been in this city for too long, and I can't keep giving him excuses."

She nodded. "I didn't know you were under such a burden. I will see him as soon as time permits. Perhaps after the next arena fight."

Janpier chuckled once again. "Hehehe, more noble coins for me to collect."

She handed him the envelope, and he raised an eyebrow, "Oh, an official request to fight in the arena. We haven't had one of those in a while. I'm sure it's another one of those lesser houses of which we are no longer a part."

His hand trembled as he read the letter out loud, "Greetings to my fellow noble house. House of Donvalve, it has been a while since our interaction at the auction house. I have missed you dearly. It pleases me greatly that through your arena victories, your house has risen into the top five noble houses. Such an outstanding feat for one filled with mutts and pups. I hereby challenge you to Avido de Terra for the equivalent in noble coins for your house—if you win, that is. Nothing would please me more to see your house turned into rubble, with the riff raff that reside in it sent to the furnace. If you weren't aware, Avido de Terra is a duo competition between vampires, and as such you will need to find a partner for that unholy serpent-wielding blood knight of yours. Should you accept the challenge, you have three weeks to find and train a partner. We will initiate the Avido de Terra at the Blood Moon festival, when the vampires' powers will be at their peak. It shall make for a wondrous event. Should you fail to accept this challenge, all the aristocrats will know what a bumbling coward you are, which, as you could suspect, is fine by me. Sincerely, your best of friends, Alistair Crumble. Personal statement, your cane is ugly, and it smells like dog urine."

Janpier dropped the piece of parchment upon the floor.

Catherine was about to speak when he excused himself, indicating for Kid Salem to leave the now clean room. He sidled up beside Catherine. "What's wrong with milord? Does he need some tea? I can have the hunchback make him some tea." Catherine glanced at Kid Salem, his bright doe eyes and innocent features. Grinding her teeth before she spoke Catherine asked him a question that had been burning her mind since they first met. "I wasn't there for the battle. But did you really fight toe to toe with Iku-Oko?"

Kid Salem swayed back and forth, "Who, little old me?" Catherine gripped the child by the collar of his servant's suit, causing Kid Salem's eye to change into something unworldly momentarily.

She looked the child in the eyes with nothing but contempt. "You're the reason why I have trouble sleeping. It's my duty to protect milord and your prancing around all innocent disturbs me. Oko-Iku hasn't been the same since he fought you. He's almost melancholic, as if you took the flair out of his wind. Did you really go toe to toe with Iku-Oko, his alternative form?"

Kid Salem smirked. In a more mature voice he said, "I find it rather amusing that I cause you sleep disruption. Perhaps you should strengthen your willpower. Then I wouldn't be on your mind so often. As for the great Dark Horse—yes, I did stand toe to toe with him for a few moments. However, as you see my best was not enough. I'm here, and now so are you. What happens next only the fates can decide. Just know that there will be blood...and a lot of it."

Catherine clenched her fists, "You're right about one thing. There will be blood. Perhaps it will be yours. You're going into the arena in three weeks. I hope you like fighting alongside Zurie because if you lose the entire House of Donvalve will be extinguished, and your lot will be sent to the furnace as you so rightly deserve." She smirked. "Perhaps a loss is exactly what is needed. The world would be better off without the likes of you two."

Kid Salem's face returned to innocence. "Whatever did I do to displease you? Could it be because I'm more handsome and younger? They say worry makes a human age a degree or two, what could it be that ails you? Perhaps thoughts of your father, and having to face him after breaking your engagement with a special aristocrat. I heard that marriage would have set your family up for generations to come. Would also have solidified his position on the High Council... did you know that the High Council doesn't like poor degenerate gamblers on the council? I mean..." Catherine raised her hand back and slapped Kid Salem across the face. The noise echoed throughout the hall. Kid Salem tried to unleash his fangs, but they had recently been removed. He made no other move to engage.

Good thing they have those collars on their necks. If they dared to attack a human, it would activate and instantly electrocute their brains. But why did those words make me so angry? How did he know about my engagement, and can our family really be that poor? It seems the things Father fails to tell me are endless.

The arena was brimming for the Blood Moon Event. Unlike the regular arena events, fans could place wagers on the winner of the outcome. Although Zurie had beaten an array of opponents up until now, she and her duo partner were not favored to win. With ten-to-one odds against them, it was heavily believed that the Crumble family would come up victorious. Alistair Crumble approached the group with Durriken the Maestro by his side.

Alistair rubbed his grubby hands together, addressing Janpier. "I'm going to enjoy setting your little house on fire. I'll frolic in the poppy leaves as a maiden blesses my tulip. Then I'm going to watch as all your precious art incinerates, just so I can see the look on your face."

Janpier squirmed in his expensive clothing. "You're a cruel, vile thing. You will go nowhere near my precious artwork!"

While the aristocrats were engaged in heated conversation, Zurie and Kid Salem seemed to be in an amicable one with their opponent. "What happened? We freed you. How can you be the arena champion?"

Durriken lowered his head, "Alas, it is another long story for the strong and the strangled. Would that fate weren't a stringent keeper I could not escape. I'd wish you luck in the arena. But it seems we are destined to intertwine our blades in a rousing battle. I'd ask that you preserve the memory you once had of the legendary Durriken and not this washed up arena fighter."

Zurie raised an eyebrow. "To be an arena fighter is the greatest thing a vampire can aspire to. Look at you, the crowd cuts themselves in your name. I'm a great arena warrior, and I have never felt such love before. I've had humans rush to kiss my bloody boots. Men and women clamor to touch the many serpents of this arena victor. I have never felt such joy." She looked up to the sky, basking in the night's smoldering heat.

Durriken lowered his head as he tapped his fingers against his violin. "It seems your master has gotten to you. Know this. Only an unworthy blood knight would find solace in the confines of a human's whip and mercy. We are blood knights and you are not unworthy, no matter what your situation dictates."

Catherine pushed herself in front of the two. "Enough of that. There will be no talks of rebellion or you'll both meet an early end to the night."

With both conversations ending abruptly, the Crumble party went their way.

From the corner of her eye, Catherine saw her father dressed in his typical white gown with sun in the corner, accompanied by an array of his personal guards. She rushed over to him and embraced him. The old man patted her on the shoulder as he embraced her firmly back. She lowered her head. "Is it true? Are we really poor?"

He leaned in further, bringing his voice to a mere whisper, "It's all taken care of. We will be placing a sizeable wager on the Donvalve family."

She took a step back, "Is that what this all has been about? You two planned this from the beginning. Have the Cleric's Order train your vampire slaves so you can take a bite out of the Crumbles. What better way to have me close by your side then as the guardian of some aristocrat I barely know. Was the Red Hand even real?"

Her father whispered again, "If by real you mean whether we sent it or not, then the answer is yes, it is real. But it is most likely a ploy from the Crumble family. I can't imagine that group of vampires actually giving out warnings before they strike." She looked at the increased number of guards. "Are you in danger as well? Why the increase in guards?"

He patted her on the head. "There are some things a lady does not need to know about. These are High Council matters."

Catherine clenched her fists, tears flowing down her face, "Stop treating me like a child."

He tilted his head back. "We will continue this conversation another time." He was about to leave when an arrow zipped by, nearly connecting with his eye. Another careened in his direction, but Catherine managed to jump in front of it. Protected by her armor, she stood up and surveyed the surroundings as the guards circled around their patron. As if from the shadows, another arrow came flying, striking a guard in the neck. The guard collapsed to the floor as his body shriveled up. The crowded bazaar emptied as the people rushed towards safety. Oko-Iku soon arrived with his staff and apple drawn. He tapped the base of his staff, causing bright light to shine around their group. An orb of protection surrounded them. Moving as one cohesive unit they made their way to the arena entrance. "What about Janpier? Shouldn't you be protecting him?" she asked.

"I did protest, but he said the slaves would be enough should anyone attack him. He puts a lot of trust in the vermin."

She nodded. "I just hope his trust does not end badly... for all of our sakes."

— 30 —
WHAT'S UNDERNEATH?

The arena was reconstructed for the grand event, as the Blood Moon was seen as the sacred day of the vampires. An occurrence once every hundred years, it marked a certain victory for the humans to bask in vampires killing each other on a sacred vampire day. In addition to the symbolic attributes of the Blood Moon, there were practical benefits retrieved from it. The red moon somehow granted creatures of the night additional powers. This being the case, the guard was doubled around the arena, and certain restrictions were put in place.

Zurie caressed the feathers of her glorious mount, "What do you mean, I can't ride her into battle?" Her fangs protruded involuntarily.

The guard crossed his arms. "You heard me, vampire scum. You better win. I put my last pinyook on you and your mystery duo partner."

Zurie furrowed her brow. "When I win, it won't be because of you and your needs, human filth. I'm the greatest blood knight this arena has ever seen." She struck a victorious pose.

A few minutes later Lord Salem sidled up beside her in his full form, wielding a black-and-blue rapier with a lightning bolt sigil to match his forehead sigil, which glowed a bright blue. His eyes were the kind of light blue that could sing a many maiden to sleep. His recently grown fangs shined.

Zurie shivered as she glanced at him. *So much for being the greatest blood knight... based on power levels alone he would still mop the floor with me. Though I do have something going for me that no other vamp has. The serpents' council has granted me an entirely different kind of sight. I have become something more than just a toxin vampire wielding the serpent's power. I am one with them. When the time comes to cross him off my list, I will be ready.*

Lord Salem smirked at Zurie. She tightened her armor. "What's so funny?"

He licked his lips. "I ever tell you how delicious you look in your armor? Good enough to just swallow every drop..."

The arena announcer called forth the two blood knights, "Fighting for house Donvalve we have the crowd favorite and a common face in these parts. Zurie Valentine the Untouchable. Fighting along with her, we have Lord Salem the Lightning Assassin.:

He smirked again. "It's been a long time since I've heard my blood knight name called out loud. Usually it's whispered in secret among the soon-to-be-dead."

She gripped her halberd firmly. "Are you... are you the assassin from the Red Hand? What are you planning? I have no interest in playing a part in your play."

Lord Salem looked grim. "You'll play your role or be devoured like the rest. When it comes to creatures of the night, the Red Hand is your be all and end all." They entered the arena only to be met with a bloody Durriken. As he struggled to reach them, the crowd buzzed. Both Donvalve knights approached slowly, analyzing the body of the legendary vampire. He soon collapsed on the ground in a pool of his own blood.

There was silence as the crowd, Zurie, and Lord Salem stood, puzzled as to who could have fatally wounded Durriken.

The ground rumbled, and both Zurie and Lord Salem to brace themselves. With a great gust of wind entered The Terror in full form. The giant bat-like creature was twice the size from when Zurie last saw it. Its purple fur now had a golden tint while the teal blades had doubled. In the middle of its chest was a glowing red topaz. The aura around its body screamed death, while the expression on its face told many a tale.

Lord Salem stood there, weapon in hand, and applauded. "You did well. You found the Vamp Lord's topaz. The key to bringing him back to us. The Red Hand applauds your efforts. Now hand it over so we can carry out the necessary ritual."

The Terror chuckled. "I never said I was going to revive my sire. I only agreed to retrieve the stone. I rather like being the most powerful vampire walking around. The Vamp Lord would only serve to stifle my brilliance. Besides, his topaz looks better on me, don't you think? I am the new Vamp Lord. I suggest you bow before me."

Zurie's body shuddered under the weight of The Terror's power. Sweat dripped down her forehead as she struggled to make a sound. *Focus. He is just another opponent. Exactly like the rest. You must avenge the fallen.*

She pointed her halberd in The Terror's direction, "Easy for you to say when you're in a collar and chains just like us. You're just another slave to the humans."

The Terror cackled once again. "The only ones who know my human identity are my ally and patron, Alistair, and you two. I live as human by day and hunt as vampire by night. The best of both worlds."

Zurie thought about all that she has lost due to The Terror and its selfish plot. *Betrothed, would that you had lived, we could have come to some kind of understanding. At the very least, you did not deserve to perish at that creatures' hand. It should have been mine. Oakes, would that I weren't a coward and I had stayed and fought. I was not strong enough when we fought The High Cleric. Finally, Dr. Asher, I need your council as I stand here, about to make a decision that will alter the rest of my second life eternally. I have tasted the love of the arena and know what it feels like to be wanted. But this cannot be real love. Real love is not as fickle as a leaf in the wind.*

It was at this point that Lord Salem sheathed his weapon and leaned against the corner of the arena. Zurie looked at him with eyebrows raised. "What is the meaning of this?"

Lord Salem shrugged. "While I will certainly not bow to this treacherous beast, I cannot fight the creature that holds onto the red topaz. He is essentially right; he is our Vamp Lord. But a reprobate such as yourself should have no qualms at breaking vampire protocol. You'll have to fetch it for us."

Zurie withdrew her weapon, "I have my own reasons for pushing forth. When this is all over, we will settle our score."

Assuming her battle stance Zurie rushed forward. Her weapon clashed against the double blades of The Terror while a black mamba lashed out at it. Easily fending off both attacks, The Terror let out a loud screech. The vibration shot out in all directions, giving Zurie pause. The sun rifle aimed directly at The Terror, silencing it. Holding her halberd up, Zurie sent a massive surge of toxic energy at her opponent. It connected, causing minor damage to the golden-furred monstrosity.

Zurie summoned her colossal sea serpent, entwining it with The Terror. She leaped forward and jammed her halberd into the eye of The Terror. While blinded in one eye, The Terror bellowed out as it swiped left then right, connecting with the neck of her sea serpent. The creature disappeared in a puff of blue smoke.

Zurie attempted a retreat, but before she could, she was gripped by the foot. A slash of her stomach nearly killed her instantly.

With what little strength she had left, Zurie jammed her halberd into the groin of The Terror, only to be met with armor. The Terror chuckled as it sent forth a devastating kick, launching Zurie into the wall of the arena. With a loud thud, she crashed into the edge. The Terror stood there dusting off its wounds, which only served to infuriate Zurie further. *Do I ask Lord Salem for help? What can I do... I don't think I can defeat this... monstrosity.*

As she stood there bleeding and drained, she did the one thing that came to mind. She asked the serpents for help. The earth trembled as The Terror approached, but she remained steadfast. A calabar burrowing python appeared. *Perhaps I can be of assistance.* As it coiled around her, she felt the hard scales of the python become her own. Her damaged blood knight armor dropped to the floor; reinforced snake scales took their place.

With purple corrosive liquid spinning around her body the blood knight Zurie approached The Terror with a menacing grin.

The Terror raised an eyebrow. "You smile as you meet your second death?"

Zurie shook her head. "No, I smile as I send you to yours. The fallen will be avenged, and their names forever engraved in my mind." She charged forward, then disappeared in a flash of toxic rain. Using the massive rain showers to cover the entire arena, Zurie made her way towards The Terror, eventually landing several strikes upon its body.

Severe corrosive damage to The Terror's tough skin made it bellow in agony. The Terror staggered but remained on its feet. In an attempt to fly above the acid clouds, The Terror took to the air, only to be shot down by the humans for code violation. Their sun rifle tore a large hole into The Terror. While tumbling to the ground, it managed to find its balance, landing on one foot.

As it stumbled, it charged a vast amount of purple aura. With a quick release it sent forth the aura in every direction, striking Zurie in the chest. With a ferocious growl, it approached Zurie. Saliva dripped down its mouth as blood oozed out of its chest, neck, and stomach. "I can't remember the last time I had this much fun. But it would seem the fun ends here."

Zurie struggled to her feet, using her weapon as leverage. Just when The Terror was in striking distance, she flashed forward, slashing each leg three times, followed by six corrosive beams of light. Zurie supported this attack by wrapping several snakes around her opponent's neck. The snakes pierced their fangs into its neck, causing The Terror to stumble once again. While on her knees, Zurie charged her last remaining energy, focusing it all into the palm of her hands, creating a single ball of concentrated toxic energy the size of her head. With a flick of her fingers, she sent the ball catapulting into the chest of The Terror. The ball expanded rapidly, exploding from within The Terror. Pieces of his body flew in every direction. Drenched in blood, Zurie lay there as giant teal essence floated towards her weapon.

Lord Salem managed a minor smile. "You're not done yet." He took out a golden key and unlocked his collar. The sun rifle immediately aimed at Lord Salem and fired. He dodged the enormous beam only to pick up the red topaz and unlock Zurie's collar. Lord Salem put her over his shoulder and carried her to the exit where the gate was already open. One of the guards nodded as he raised his left hand, revealing a red dot in the middle. As they rushed outside, the guard handed Zurie the reins to her raptor. They were met with a group of vampire slaves, who escorted them to a nearby haven.

The abandoned sewers were a far cry from the castle where they were used to staying. It leaked when it rained, and it sizzled when it didn't. But they stayed there as free vampires. Zurie sat in silence as she feasted on the blood of a human civilian for the first time in a long time. As she sucked the body dry, her eyes rolled to the back of her head. She licked the blood off her chin. A former vampire slave approached the great Zurie Valentine with both arms across her chest and a slight bow: the traditional symbol for submission amongst creatures of the night.

With her eyes now alert, Zurie perused the female vampire. *She isn't a blood knight, hence the fear she holds towards me. What is there to fear but the specters of fear itself? I have conquered my greatest fear, yet I somehow feel hollow... the pendulum of joy ever swaying back and forth.* The female vampire dragged the human carcass away with a forced smile.

Naturally she would fear me. I have killed many a blood knight in my short time as one, with the crowd aroused by every blow struck, their raging screams energizing my every step. Who would have thought that I would gain such joy from the human species? Would that my own kind held me at such a high regard. Now that I have bowed away from the public eye, what is left for me? To wallow in this abandoned sewer. It has been months since I last tasted fresh air. Though I must admit... the restlessness in my heart has nothing to do with my outer condition. This time under such conditions has given me much time to think, a consequence of my heightened tendencies.

What does a vampire do when she does not love herself? Have I ever loved myself... could I even dream of such a thing? What does such a thing mean? Where is the cause that will fill my cup? How does one find a person they can trust? What could possibly satisfy my needs?

Lord Salem's distinct footsteps approached the room where she wallowed in. Rustling in her scaled armor, she gripped the base of her halberd. *Would that now were the time to remove his head from its lofty perch. My very condition stems from his refusal to revolt—only for him now to have started one destined to lose. How can we go against the ruling class of the entire capital city? The High Council, the Cleric's Order, and the Aristocrats are searching for us. We are but a handful of vampires in a city full of adversaries.* Pointing at Lord Salem, who stood in full form, she grumbled, "What do you want with me, foul abductor?"

He raised an eyebrow. "It's time to move. It took some convincing, but you have been selected."

Not moving an inch, she responded, "Selected for what? Free me from your vague sentences with their hidden meanings and ulterior motives."

He huffed, "Must we do this now? Here I thought you understood your position." He leaned in closer as the scent of honey filled her lungs. "You will do what the Red Hand asks of you, even if that is to cut off your own head. We are the true rulers of the creatures of the night, not the prey that is the human species."

With her eyes throbbing she stood up and walked past him, "Could have fooled me." As soon as those words left her mouth, Lord Salem called forth a lightning bolt to strike Zurie down. It was immediately absorbed by a large boa constrictor.

Zurie appeared behind Lord Salem with her halberd resting on his neck, "Would that I could kill you right here and now. But you have me curious as to what the Red Hand has selected me for." He caressed her hand gently, causing Zurie to release him. He led towards a wall marked with a red hand and wings. He placed his hand on it and spoke several incantations, causing the wall to dissipate.

Entering the hidden facility atop her mount, Zurie's jaw dropped immediately. She was met with an entire underground vampire city filled with human blood facilities, blacksmiths, training centres, and even a racecourse for both vampires and mounts. Lord Salem beamed.

"Welcome to Sovereign city. The largest vampire city in the continent, and the city that rivals the capital for dominance."

Zurie dismounted, approaching a blacksmith, "I don't have any pinyooks, but what would it take to get my weapon sharpened and upgraded?"

The blacksmith's laughter could be heard from the other corner. "We don't accept those dirty human coins down here. We work on the barter system. I'll sharpen and upgrade your weapon for an autograph. You're the famed Zurie Valentine, ain't ya? Plus, you're the new pinky finger? It would be my pleasure." Zurie nodded.

Lord Salem sidled up beside him and nodded. "Yes, this is Zurie. However, she isn't officially the pinky finger yet, and it was supposed to be a secret."

The blacksmith chuckled. "Me and my big mouth. If you are chosen, agree to only come to me for all your weapon and armor needs. Leave that glorious cursed weapon here, and I'll have it back to you by the time you come back." Zurie handed him the hefty weapon.

As they progressed through the vampire city, she noticed Lord Salem was eerily quiet. "Why are you so silent?"

He flashed back to reality. "I was just thinking about my sister. She had a temper that could rival a storm, but when calm, she was the sweetest thing. Almost like you."

She shrugged, changing the subject. "I see. So, I am in the running to be the pinky finger of the Red Hand? What meaning should I place on such a thing?" They arrived at a large, glistening red-and-black castle.

Lord Salem clapped his hands several times rhythmically. The glistening toned down, allowing them passage. Within the castle, they were met with the scent of honey and lime. A golden vampire lay down on a large gold sofa facing them. A swarm of honeybees surrounded him.

The vampire drawled, "Hmm... fresh honey on the summers eve. How delightful. Lord Salem... the middle finger of the hand has returned. How frightful. Oh, and he has brought a new plaything. Or perhaps this is the infamous Zurie Valentine?"

Zurie stepped forward. "I am she."

The vampire took a handful of honey from the vase in front of him and slathered it all over his face. "How exhilarating."

Lord Salem rolled his eyes, grabbed Zurie by the hand and pulled her up the floating stairway. Each step seemed to grow larger. Upon arriving to the next floor, she was met with a vision of pink and purple furniture with a myriad of large bouncing balls. He guided her through the bouncing balls, paying them no mind, towards a large white door. He knocked on the white door four times, then opened it to reveal a massive room lined with books. Zurie felt a prick at her lower back.

"Don't move."

Lord Salem stomped his feet. "We don't have time for your jokes; let her pass." The sword removed itself from her lower back, causing Zurie to relax.

A masked figure wearing a white cape and white cloth appeared in front of them, "I was only being facetious. I haven't seen you in such a lovely form in quite the long time. This must be the corrosive one." He patted Zurie on her shoulder, "Nice armor. We shall have to duel sometime." Zurie nodded slowly. *Duel him? Each level I go up, the air becomes heavier. How powerful are these beings?* Lord Salem pushed her forward as they passed shelves after shelves, stopping at a glowing white bookcase. He plucked one spine in the middle and the bookcase vanished. Next they entered a room filled with a cursed aura so dark that her eyes couldn't adjust. She did, however, sense another being in the room.

Lord Salem was the first to break the silence. "Great thumb of the Red Hand. I have brought in front of you the infamous Zurie Valentine. A blood knight who has proven herself by surviving the massacre at the Cleric's Order of Titania and by eliminating powerful vampires in the arena, most noteworthily The Terror. She is a blood knight of a great lineage and would make an excellent pinky finger of the Red Hand."

A raspy laugh echoed throughout the room. "It's not me you have to convince. She barely believes she is worthy. Perhaps she should be devoured right here and now. Save me the trouble of doing it later." Zurie could taste Lord Salem's fear—something he had never exhibited up to this point.

She took a step forward. "It is true that I have doubts within my heart about my personality. But I no longer doubt my abilities, nor what I will accomplish, if given the chance." The voice was silent for a few moments before clearing the darkness to reveal a bright white room and a floating orange ball of essence.

The voice returned. "Take this cursed essence. It is all that's left of the last pinky finger. Should you survive while using it, you will become the pinky finger to the Red Hand. If not... then good riddance to you both."

Lord Salem bowed, leading Zurie to do the same. She grabbed the essence and swallowed it.

Nothing happened. She was about to speak when immense pain shot through her entire body. Her eyes turned orange as the energy surrounded her hands. Her heartbeat increased rapidly.

She could faintly hear Lord Salem's words. "Don't fight the cursed mark, embrace it." Her eyes rolled to the back of her head as she dropped to her knees. Zurie's heart exploded.

CONDITIONS GALORE

atherine held a firm grip on her crossbow. Her body was tense. There had been numerous attacks on several aristocrats since the Blood Moon Festival. It was estimated that half of the slave vampires freed themselves, while another quarter revolted against their masters in violence. *The economy heavily relied on slave labor to take care of the commonplace tasks. Without most of the slave vamps, several industries must have been shut down or severely crippled. I can only imagine what's going to happen next, now that sanitation and food preparation are at a standstill.* As she stood outside the Trading Area Oko-Iku approached her person with his staff and apple in hand. "How are you holding up?"

"A bit tense. All this waiting around in the open has me feeling all manner of ways. It would be nice if they hurried up with their meeting."

Oko-Iku nodded. "I agree, but this is the exact middle ground between their two castles. Neither wanted to give an inch in such a trivial matter."

Catherine sighed. "I wonder what Crumble did to Janpier. He seems so reasonable for most things, yet when it comes to Crumble, it's almost as if he completely loses his mind."

Oko-Iku lowered his voice to but a whisper, "I'm trusting you with this secret, for having knowledge of it may allow you to do your job better."

She nodded. He moved in closer. "There was a point in time where Crumble and Janpier were the best of friends. They did everything together, especially visiting the auction. It was a sight to see, considering the aristocrat houses were traditionally always at ends. None of the houses trusted each other, and each was vying for power and supremacy. But these two young lads transcended that rift. Things turned to the worse when one day Janpier's older sister moved back to the capital. Alistair immediately fell in love and began to seek out her affection in secret.

"At first, she spurned him for, as many a lady, she enjoyed the chase. Eventually it was said she fell for his lavish gifts and promises of superiority. When the two announced their union, Janpier was joyful. That was until his sister left Alistair standing at the alter and she embarked on some far-off journey to some distant land. Alistair was distraught. His family was furious; how could the Crumbles be made a fool of by the lowly Donvalves? So Alistair devised a plan. He used his brother's influence in the High Council to have the Donvalve family dismissed from noble status. The Donvalve family, broken by their fall to normalcy, split up. At the time it was Janpier, his younger brother, and his older sister. The younger brother could not handle life as a normal family and committed suicide. The older sister is somewhere off galivanting and enjoying life. Janpier was left to pick up the pieces. Thus, you have the Janpier and Alistair feud. It was actually your father who reinstated the Donvalve family, putting them in good standing once again."

Catherine placed her hand to her mouth, "Such an evil little man."

Oko-Iku nodded his head. "If you only knew the half of what that man is capable of. He has brought down just as much evil and pain as any vampire I have had the liberty to cleanse." She was about to inquire what he meant by that when the flap to the tent opened. Janpier emerged from the tent first with a pale expression.

He glanced down at the sand beneath their feet, refusing to make eye contact with either of them. In a whisper he said, "Catherine... your father has sent word through Alistair."

She raised an eyebrow. "Why would he send word to me through him?"

Janpier bit his lip before handing her a piece of parchment with her father's seal. She clasped it gently and opened it with trembling hands. While reading it aloud her voice quivered.

"Dearest daughter. It is my hope that you have grown ten-fold during your time with the Cleric's Order. As you know the High Council presides over the Cleric's Order, which serves as the continental military force. As you read this letter, know that it comes with a light hand and a heavy heart. I am sure by now you have heard the rumors. I will confirm one of them. I have lost our immense fortune due to my gambling habits. Because of the circumstances, it is important that you understand the gravity of our situation. Due to the altercation at the arena during the Blood Moon festival, I was unable to place the bet in time. My debts are substantial to the point that I will be removed from the High Council if they are not repaid in a timely fashion. In addition to said removal, I will be banned from the capital: a fate worse than death. The good noble Alistair Crumble has agreed to pay the debt in exchange for your hand in marriage as his second wife. I ask that you consider this agreement as Lord Alistair will take great care of you. Should you not accept, which is your right, I will have to invoke my right to commit suicide, for living such a despondent life would be too much to bear. Signed with duty and affection. Patron of the Goldcrest house."

She read the letter once again to herself. As the words swirled in her brain, heat filled her being. She crumpled the piece of parchment and shouted, "You little shite, get out here. What kind of crackpottery is this? My father is not such a man that would commit suicide over losing his position. Also, how much of a coward is he that he could not tell me this to my face?"

Alistair Crumble emerged from the tent with a smile on his face. "Oh, you're fiery... I like that. But I would never sully my good name by wedding a dame with such foul tactics, such as some people. I merely suggested to your father that I clear his debts. It was he who jumped at the thought of marrying you off to me. But I mean who could blame him, I am quite dashing and daring."

Catherine attempted to raise her crossbow as Oko-Iku gripped her arms stifling her. Finally, she collapsed to the ground, breathing heavily. Her chest ached while the world around her spun in a circle. *This must be an ill joke. How can my father be so reckless?*

She used Oko-Iku as leverage to stand. "Janpier, I hate to ask but can you not take everything that I am to be paid, and use it to clear my father's debts? I will even ask you to loan me money in order to pay his debts."

Janpier lowered his head like a beaten pup. "Would that I could. The debt far exceeds what my house is worth. Even with the proceeds from the arena. Truth be told... out of all the aristocrats there are only a handful that could pay the debt without breaking their bank and Crumble is the only one that is on good terms with your father. I hate to say it, but I don't see any other option. Save for saying no."

Catherine tightened her fist as she sniffed to hold back her tears. Alistair creeped up beside her, caressing the leg of her armor. "Don't worry my love. Alistair Crumble will never fumble the precious jewel that is your heart." He grinned as he twiddled his grubby hands.

Fighting the urge to purge, she swallowed, "I'll do it... but under one condition."

— **32** —

PAST WOUNDS

An insatiable thirst swarmed over her. Struggling to stand up, she settled for speaking, "Blood." she whispered. She waited a few moments before repeating herself this time louder. "Blood please."

From the corner of her eye, she could see light blue boots rustling. As she lay on the floor with her mouth open, drops of human blood oozed down her throat. When her body had regenerated, she sat up in a sluggish manner. She glanced over to see that her savior was Lord Salem.

He inched closer to her, "How do you feel?"

She took a deep breath, "I feel as though I have been struck by my betrothed's mace a thousand times over and beaten into a pile of vampire dust. I feel empty. I feel as though I have been chasing this imaginary thing called fulfillment only to find my pockets are filled with rocks weighing me down."

Lord Salem sighed, "It seems it falls on me to impart some age-old wisdom. In this world there are few who ask to be turned and zero who ask to be born. There are those who wallow in their despair, those make the best of their situation and even those who choose to control their destinies. I have come to learn that for a man, fulfillment derives from pursuing a purpose or passion. For ones of a feminine nature, their happiness comes from finding meaning in devotion to something greater than themselves."

She crossed her arms. "What's the difference?"

He sighed once again. "How troublesome you've become. The difference is that the former is internal, and the latter is external. Of course, this rule only applies to the majority. There are always exceptions."

A pleasant tingling sensation rained upon her body. *What is this sensation? It feels heavenly.* She glanced at Lord Salem, who shared her bewilderment. "It must be your heightened aura. All members of the Red Hand have one." He jumped into the air doing several backflips, "It seems your heightened aura grants speed and acrobatics to you and nearby comrades. You should look at yourself; you'd be surprised as to how your body has changed."

She looked down to see her forearms and hands covered in a light coating of purple and white scales. The rest of her skin was seamless, elegant, even beautiful. Her hands transformed from their usual stubby form to something more delicate. Even her figure was rounder and more robust. She shimmered like the serpent woman that she was. The biggest change was to her vision and other senses. She could feel the vibrations of over a thousand vampires going about their night. She noticed her appetite was atrocious as she craved more blood than ever.

Lord Salem brought her another bowl of the precious elixir. "I'd imagine this serpent form of yours requires a lot of fuel. It is like that with all of our transformations. It will be even more noticeable when you start wielding that cursed weapon of yours."

She nodded as she drank the sacred elixir. "What are those numbers floating around your head?"

He perked up. "Excellent, your second sight has fully activated. As a toxin vampire you can read your opponent's statistics due to your connection with the other plane. The top number is their projected health until their demise, the middle number is their fatigue level until exhaustion, also known as their energy level, while the third number is their power level in comparison to yours. The fourth number Ragnar was trying to figure out before his untimely demise. I only know about these numbers since Ragnar explained them to me. The ability to read statistics is why toxin vampires had gained a reputation for being weak and cowardly..."

She cut him off, "They would run away when they saw the power level was out of their threshold."

He nodded, "Precisely. Not a bad tactic when one wishes to remain immortal. However, there are ways to defeat stronger opponents, as you have demonstrated repeatedly. Every opponent you have faced in battle up to this point was more powerful than you, yet through cunning and strengthening your connection with your serpents, you managed to defeat them. Additionally, it seems your condition comes with certain benefits that you have learned to harness by being in tune with the toxic chemicals in your body. This is what the Red Hand lacks: a certain wild card. We have been lacking your resolve to topple a superior foe and overwhelming numbers."

Zurie raised an eyebrow. "But who can rival the Red Hand in terms of power? I don't need this advanced sight to sense that the Red Hand are more powerful than any human walking around. Especially the index finger and the thumb."

Lord Salem erupted into a fit of laughter.

He clutched his stomach as he continued laughing. After catching his breath, he proceeded with his explanation. "It's not the Cleric's Order that we are wary of, nor is it the High Council that truly holds power on the continent. I mean, yes, the Cleric's Order has some notable humans who give us pause. Oko-Iku is one of them. But it's those... mangy wolf shifters that hold a vice grip on the capital, and as such own the continent. They hide behind their status as aristocrats and manipulate everyone from top down towards their own endeavors."

Zurie raised both her hands in the air. "I'm confused."

He rolled his eyes as he sat down.

Grimacing, he tried to explain once again. "You recall stories of the Great War correct? Where the Vamp Lord perished at the hands of the Bishop at the time. But before he perished, he managed to turn the Bishop, causing his own clerics to turn on him. It dealt a catastrophic blow to their psyche and nearly won the war for us. Do you know how we lost?"

She shook her head. "No, I have been wondering since I first heard the story."

"The Lycanthropes betrayed our cause. They were supposed to attack the clerics from the rear, effectively pulling off a pincer attack, which would win us the war. But when they saw our beloved leader of the night meet his end, they got it in their tiny wolf brains that it would be a better idea to side with the clerics."

Zurie sat there with her jaw agape, "How come I have never heard of these wolf shifters before?"

He gripped her by the shoulders, "There were very few of them to begin with, as it is rare to successfully turn a human into a lycanthrope. After the war they went into hiding, so much so that vamps just assumed they killed each other off. But the Red Hand knows better. They broke up into small packs due to their inability to function as a unit. We've had two objectives since the Great War. Our primary objective is to revive the Vampire Lord in all his splendor. Our second, to eradicate every remaining wolf shifter."

With her hands clasped together, Zurie leaned forward. "This is a lot for the mind to grasp. Especially after my newfound transformation, it's like my mind is in a swirl."

He gripped her by her scaled forearms. "The Yellow Moon is coming up soon. This is a sacred day for these wild brutish creatures. It is rumored that once every decade on this day the leaders of each wolf clan gather together. It's one of the few times they come out of hiding and turn into their true form. We'd be able to catch them off guard."

Her eyes intensified. "I see."

"There is more..."

"I'm sure there is."

"Janpier is one of them." There was a long pause as she digested the information.

"Why is that of import?"

He gripped her firmly from behind, gently caressing her neck with his finger. "Because I know you grew fond of him during our time as his slaves. But it is better to live restless as a free vampire than it is to live comfortably as a slave."

She shrugged him off. "When your sympathy was needed, you were nowhere to be found. Free me of your kind words. When your hand was needed for a revolution, your rapier was nowhere to be found. So, free me of your gentle touch."

Lord Salem took a step back, crossing his arms, "What will you have me do? Shall I pay for the casualties of my mission until I draw my last breath? I thought it was obvious, but I suppose I must put words to it. I could not support an open rebellion while The Terror was in the Cleric's Order searching for the Bishop's pendant. It was imperative that we found that gemstone in order to revive the Vampire Lord. I honestly didn't think it was worth the risk."

She summoned a black mamba to wrap around the back of her neck, ready to strike, "Well, it was. Enough with the history lesson. What do you ask of me now? I know this information comes with an ulterior motive."

He gazed at her for a few moments, "My, how you have grown since when we first met. Would that things were different. It's very simple. We need your readings on their statistics before we engage. We will engage the strongest wolf shifter first, causing disruption amongst their pack."

She nodded, "If Janpier is one of them like you say... I wish to be the one to end his life. I know you think I've grown soft upon his spirit, but the opposite is also true. He is on my list for confining me and lowering me to a mere slave. I will do what I must to remove him from it. Through him I caught a taste of what I'm searching for, but through the Red Hand I have found power and liberty; I will continue down the path of the Red Hand in hopes that it will bear fruit for what I truly desire."

He gazed at her glowing purple eyes. "What might that be, Zurie Valentine?"

She bit her lip before responding, "I will seek out this cause, person, or activity that I can fully devote myself to. My hope is that I recognize it when it is found."

$$— 33 —$$

SLEEPLESS NIGHTS

Another sleepless night washed over her as she stood at the window in the middle of the night. She opened it, allowing the snow to sprinkle upon her body. As she peered over the windowsill, she contemplated the very thing that placed her in this predicament. *To jump would mean I am weak like my father. To receive destiny's heavy hand, only to take an easier route. Besides, who is to say that death is the answer? Perhaps the afterlife would revel at my weakness and pain me ten times over.*

She tugged on her silk night gown. *No, I think not. Giving up is not the answer. I'll figure something out by the hand of my own will. Something that has always served me righteously.* The room was filled with lavish gifts from her husband in pursuit of entering her loins. Steadfast she held him to his word. To wait one year before they consummated their vows.

She sat down and ate the rare chocolate that he had purchased for her. It was shaped like a wolf. *What's with these aristocrats and wolves? Janpier had wolves plastered all over the place.* She thought of Janpier and her guardian position: one that she truly enjoyed, to be of use to the highest degree guarding against a dastardly opponent. Now she was in the confines of a dastardly fellow. One who ruined the economy for the needy, in the name of greed and vanity.

She could hear hard knocking from outside her door. She approached the door, only to grab a dagger and hold it behind her back. As she opened the door, she was met with Alistair's first wife. *She wears that belt twenty-four seven as if to tell me she will always be his number one. Why should I care? I'm only doing this to be of service to my family. If only in this first year I could convince him to seek his perverted pleasure elsewhere. These older men see me as nothing more than a sexual object to gratify their base human pleasures. If only I could find someone who wanted me for me.*

His first wife rolled her eyes as she spoke. "The grand lord Alistair Crumble requests your presence for dinner on this special occasion. Dress with some class."

Catherine winced but nodded. *The way she speaks gives me pause. I want to pull her tongue out with my...* She stopped herself. Taking a deep breath. *If only I could still act on my aggressive tendencies. I should not need to hide an entire side of my being to please a man. Should not one covet their personality in fullness?*

She looked at her armor, which had accumulated a large amount of dust, then a blue dress that he had bought for her the day before. She sighed, "I remember the last time I wore something this tight. It didn't bode well for me nor those in my direct vicinity."

As she descended the stairs to the dining area, all the guests stared with wide eyes. *I didn't expect there to be so many people. Good thing I wore the dress instead of the armor. I would feel completely out of place.* She took the seat to the left of her husband and beside her brother-in-law, whose eyes would not be deterred from her bosom. As she sat, she touched her inner thigh to make sure her weapon was still there.

Alistair Crumble beamed his crooked teeth at her as he held her hand firmly, "Isn't my wife just lovely? She is wearing the brand-new dress I bought her. Notice how it compliments her hair? I have good taste, don't I?" The crowd at the table started to sing his praise.

Alistair begun by introducing everyone that she didn't recognize. First were his two younger brothers and their wives. They had six between the two of them. Then he introduced her to a dashing man with the noble eyes of a wolf. His yellow eyes instantly caught her attention while his polite demeanor kept it. Throughout the dinner the two kept locking eyes while the rest of the group ate and talked. *He is so arousing... to think I'd meet such a man to make me feel so warm inside.* She squirmed within her tight dress attempting to keep her focus.

While taking deep breaths it was Alistair's first wife who was first to take notice. The blonde woman gripped Catherine by the arm and excused them both from the table. As they walked towards the nearest bathroom, she spoke, "Listen here you mugpot. That man you have been ogling all night is the only one who lights a fire between these legs. I will not have you with your younger face and tighter body come mess this up for me. You already have the affection of Bumble the Crumble, quit while you're ahead."

Catherine pushed the woman back. "Unhand me. I have way too many things on my mind to be worrying about you and what my desires may affect. They are my eyes, and they can look where I want them to." The woman released a low guttural growl as she launched her sharp claw-like fingers at Catherine's eyes. Not having time to react, Catherine stood there frozen.

The woman smiled, revealing silver canines. "After tonight you and I will revisit this conversation, when you're better equipped to handle a woman such as myself." The two walked back to the table in silence. Catherine's mind was abuzz, drenching her in a river of fear. She sat with her head held down and continued to eat her soup. Her legs shook and trembled with every heartbeat. *After tonight? What's supposed to happen tonight? What's so special about this Yellow Moon?*

Suddenly everyone at the dinner table had finished their meal. *Why does it feel as if everyone is staring at me?*

She looked up to see all members of the group staring at her with glowing yellow eyes. Their faces were transformed into those of wolves. Simultaneously they all raised their heads into the air and let out a blood curdling howl.

Catherine closed her eyes in a daze.

— 34 —

DAZED AND
CONFUSED

The eerie glare of the yellow moon troubled her deeply. It seemed especially odd under the heavy snowfall. With both eyes forward she continued to trudge through the wilderness. Pushing through bushes, she had a disturbing thought. *This isn't going to go well.* She turned to assess the large group that was with her. Lord Salem and the ring finger were part of her group, while the index and the thumb each led their own. The plan was very simple, but if successful, it would wipe out the lycanthrope threat. They would swarm in on their enemy with a triangular formation and overwhelm them with superior numbers. With a three-to-one advantage, it should be a journey in the meadow.

Her mind wandered from the battle plans to the sight of Catherine being carried like a mere rag doll. *I wonder what those beasts plan on doing with her? Why do I even care? She is just another human who looked down upon me and my kind.* She watched as the group of animals placed her naked body on a large stone tablet. Lord Salem turned to Zurie with furrowed brows, "Do you see their power levels and stats?"

She nodded, "But they all look the same. It's going to be hard to separate them in battle. What if they don't scatter like you suspect?"

He withdrew his rapier, causing sparks to fly out, "These beasts are cowardly. They will run. But if they do not, we will fight and win."

The golden vampire floated between the two of them with his vase of honey in hand. "One would think this might not go as planned. Who would have thought they would have replenished their numbers to so many? How suspenseful." He pointed towards a hill where another pack of lycanthropes joined the one that held Catherine captive. The leader of each pack growled at each other but made no move to attack.

Zurie gazed into the green eyes of the recent additions. "Well there is Janpier donning his house crest around his waist."

Lord Salem shrugged, "What's more interesting is that smaller one, wearing the house Crumble crest. Who would have thought that the entire Crumble family would made of those beasts? I suppose that explains their rivalry. But it matters not. We will eliminate them like the mangy beasts that they are." He turned to the free vampires, "Remember, their bite is toxic to us, resulting in the second death. Additionally, their blood is of a toxic nature as well. It causes severe burning. Finally, do not look them in their eyes."

Zurie shuffled around slightly. "Should I say something? To rally the troops... I feel as though I should rally the troops."

Lord Salem shrugged. "We have trained for this for a long time. These are not the vagabonds from that puny excuse of a city, filled with poor excuses for vamps."

She bit her lips before turning to the group of restless vampires, each brandishing their own special artifact. "I know you've trained for this and I know this may be unorthodox but..."

Lord Salem raised his weapon high in the air. "Charge." Their vampire unit charged forward into the open clearing where the two wolf packs convened.

Lowering her head slightly, Zurie turned to the open clearing and charged forward towards her destiny.

Upon arriving at the clearing, she was met with the distinct scent of lycanthrope. The scent filled her nostrils causing her to gag. While coughing, she was met with one of the large beasts. On closer inspection each beast was akin to The Terror, only possessing less raw power. *What kind of stats are these? Do I fight or flight?* Zurie's heartbeat increased rapidly and her hands froze as she gazed into the eyes of the grey-eyed creature before her.

With one swipe of its claws, she was hurled across the plains into the stone tablet where Catherine laid. Feeling her back crack as she stood up, Zurie shook herself to her senses. The beast was upon her, baring its claws. She blocked the swiping attacks of the beast with her halberd. It let out a high pitch yelp as Zurie shoved her halberd into the exposed underbelly, the beast swiped at her chest in an attempt to pierce her scaled armor. Zurie summoned several clouds of toxic gas to stifle her opponent. The gas had no effect.

Dashing forward again with her halberd held high she heard the vampires' horn for retreat. As she looked around, she saw that their forces had been depleted to half while not one lycanthrope was severely injured. Black smoke shrouded her being, hiding her behind a veil of nothingness. Using her newfound nothingness, she rose towards Catherine. *My only hope is that the veil will shroud us both.* While picking up her body, the black smoke extended causing Catherine to be nothing as well. The lycanthropes had their noses to the ground in vain. While tiptoeing past the creatures she analyzed them closely. *I have seen those artifacts before. This isn't good.*

By the time she arrived, she was met with slumped shoulders and heavy breathing. Lord Salem approached her with his wound still bleeding. "Why'd you bring her?"

She tensed up. "I have my own reasons. It doesn't concern us right now. What concerns us are those pendants that they wear."

The ring finger floated towards the two of them. "Honey, honey, honey. What about them?"

She explained that the gold pendants were ankhs that The Terror had stolen from her den: artifacts from Africanus used against vampires.

Lord Salem jammed his weapon into the snow. "Ankhs... I have heard that word before. They are said to be like the crosses that the clerics use, yet different."

The golden one interjected, "Hmm... now that we are on the topic, some of the more powerful ones wore both an ankh pendant and a cross bracelet. How protective?"

Zurie raised her head. "it's not that they were more powerful... it's that they made us weaker."

With the great losses that they undertook, there was much doubt and fear among the vampires of Sovereign City. Some vampires wanted to leave the continent and make a home for themselves in Africanus, while others wanted to regroup and make another attempt at a revolution. A select group concocted the idea that they should move for peace negotiations with the High Council, and in consequence end their long-lasting animosity towards the lycanthropes as well. It was well-remarked that the humans now placed at least an ounce of respect on the abilities of the vampire population, while the lycanthropes must be feeling confident.

Ultimately, each creature of the night was to make their own decision. However, most awaited the decision of the Red Hand, recognized as the five most influential blood knights on the continent. Zurie sat in the corner as the Red Hand threatened to become a splintered division of fingers. Each member of the Red Hand had a different opinion on how to progress. Most daring of all was Lord Salem, who wanted to strike at the heart of the Lycanthropes and engage Alistair Crumble. "Our strategy was sound, just the execution was poor. Now that we know who some of the lycanthropes are, we can approach them at their homes while they are alone."

The golden ring finger poured honey out of his vase into his mouth. As he gobbled the elixir, he let out a low moaning sound. "Honey, honey, honey. How excellent. What if matters were left up to Zurie? Her cunning must surely surpass all of ours."

Why me? Why'd he have to mention my name? I'm sitting in the corner for a reason. Such a ghoulish creature, this golden glob of honey. Always drinking out of his vase. Such a weakness, to be addicted to blood, severely allergic to the sun, horrendously weakened by silver, and to have to avoid the cross like the plague. Perhaps these wolf shifters have a weakness of their own?

Zurie made her way to the middle of the room where the other four blood knights stood. While pacing, she asked the question that none had the wherewithal to ask. "What are the weaknesses of these wolf shifters? Humans have some weaknesses, as do we. Thus, they must have some as well. Something that we can exploit to our benefit." The rest of the Red Hand grew silent once again.

It was the honey-swarmed ring finger who broke the silence. "Perhaps we should ask the human who so graciously takes up dominion on my floor. Hmm?"

Zurie winced but nodded. "I suppose one of us should retrieve her."

The ring finger dumped another helping of honey into his mouth. "I suppose that one should be me. Since it is my floor. Hmm?" The rest of the group gazed at the odd figure that was the honey-soaked blood knight.

A few moments later he returned with Catherine tied up and drenched in honey. Her voice was crackling like the pit of fire that she was. "Unhand me, you filthy blood suckers. If I had my crossbow, I'd send two right in between your teeth—improve that grin tenfold."

The group of blood knights each licked their lips in sequence save Zurie, who clenched her teeth before speaking. "Why is she slathered in honey? How do you expect us to get information from a captive when we're all thinking about feasting on her?"

The ring finger clapped his hands, "You have quite the lip for a newcomer. Perhaps I should show you a more appropriate place for those lips to flap."

Zurie's eyes glowed bright purple as she gripped her halberd. "Retract those words or I will have to retract your tongue." The snake around her arm hissed. Another coiled itself into a circle in preparation to strike.

The golden ring finger poured the last remaining bit of honey out of his vase then glared at Zurie with piercing eyes, "You dare to challenge me? Hmm? You think you can defeat the great ring finger? Hmm? Lucky for you I'm not in the mood for a fight on this eve. It's time for my honey bath. I retract my statement. Whatever the Red Hand decides is fine with me. I shall retire to my floor, now that the scent of dog is absent. Conversation is done." The ring finger turned and floated away with his shoulders held back. Zurie smirked and sheathed her weapon while stroking her serpents.

With a new set of clothing and a bath, Catherine's demeanor was slightly more pleasant. She ceased the insults and was quietly sizing up the blood knights.

Her eyes darted from the thumb, to the index finger, to Lord Salem, and finally landed on Zurie, "So it was you who saved me. Based on their demeanors, I can tell each one of them would rather see my head on a pike and my body thrown to the wolves. Why am I here and not being ravaged or turned? Perhaps you ought to let me free from these ropes. My arms are aching."

Zurie leaned in close, her fangs protruding, her breath smelling of the sweet venom that coursed through her veins. "It would be a hazardous mistake to take me as an advocate for your cause. It is very simple. I had the sense that you would be useful. So, make yourself useful." *I truly wonder why I took her from that stone tablet. Why the urge to turn her into one of us? It is as though her and I are similar in some regard. Shall I ask permission as the code dictates?*

Lord Salem poked his head in between the two. "What can you tell us of the cross and the ankh artifacts?" With the tip of his sword, he urged Catherine to answer.

She contorted her face in all types of ways. "Why should I help you to dethrone those wolf creatures? As far as I'm concerned, I've been plucked from their grips only to be handed to a beast that is just as vile." Zurie shifted her eyes from the hungry looks of her companions.

Softening her posture, she said, "Think of what they were going to do to you. They were going to turn you into one of them or use you as a sacrifice. Why else would they bring you out into the middle of nowhere and place you onto an altar?"

A coral snake poked its head out of her scales, causing Catherine to stir. "Can... you put those things away?"

Zurie tapped her feet. "Don't you understand your situation? We may be vile creatures of the night, but your entire order is corrupted by these beings. The fact that the ruling class of aristocrats is writhing with them should cause you concern, no? I mean you did take a sacred oath to uphold the purity and values of the Cleric's Order. Yet take a gander at the hypocrisy of it now. You are tasked with controlling and hunting one beast while taking orders from another. The High Council has two Lycanthropes that we know of while the aristocrats feed the pockets of the Cleric's. I know Althalos my love must be turning in his grave."

Catherine clenched her fists. "You will not mention his name again. He was just as sick with you and your existence as he would be with the current state of affairs."

Zurie winced but responded calmly and evenly, "Perhaps... you should be keen in remembering we both failed the night he was murdered. At least I managed to reap the benefits of obtaining revenge. While you, what? What have you done this entire time, but be broken down into a victim, such potential wasted? How strong you must have become to wither under the weight of the Crumbles. Join us in open arms and assist us in exposing the Lycanthropes to the world of humans. These beasts must remove themselves from the shadows and enter the light." With her hands opened wide, Zurie erupted into a rare smile.

Catherine took a few steps forward then spun, kicking Zurie in the face. Zurie's nose bled. Catherine followed this attack with a kick to the stomach, but a boa constrictor emerged to block the attack. Zurie threw herself forward, gripping Catherine's hands as the boa constrictor wrapped itself around her arms, breaking them. Catherine screamed out in agony as her arms snapped in two. She shot Zurie a ferocious look as she knelt on the floor, weakened.

Zurie's eyes were burning a bright purple and her voice echoed of venom. "Tell us the weakness to the ankh and the cross, or I will break every bone in your body one by one."

Through gritted teeth Catherine managed a response. "I don't know much about the ankh. I do know that it has a powerful vampire repellent when activated. It can cause a vampire to run away in a fit of fear, allowing them to be picked off from behind. But above all the ankh is a regeneration artifact that speeds up their healing twice fold, making them near invincible. Or so the fables said. I couldn't imagine for a minute that the lycans truly existed. The cross can either be an offensive weapon or defensive one depending on who wields it." She paused as she glanced at her broken arms, "If I tell you everything I know, what will happen to me?"

Zurie looked to the thumb, who floated towards her.

The ball of smoke looked sad. "You have seen too much. Your options are to become one of us or make your peace with death."

—35—

A FEAST FOR THE BEAST

Janpier winced with every step he took. While descending the stairs, to the dining hall he mumbled underneath his breath. The pain he received while he was in lycan form diverted to his human form, as expected. With his eyes locked upon his conniving sister and her family, he swallowed his saliva. He took his seat at the head of the table; his sister was at the foot.

Why has she returned? A power play perhaps? Could she truly want what I have rebuilt? He leaned forward, steepling his fingers. "What brings you to my humble abode, my good sister? Also, it would seem you brought a whole brigade of what should I call them? F-a-m-i-l-y?"

His sister used the knife and fork to eat her deep-fried vampire leg. He watched as she indulged in the succulent vamp meat as it caressed her tongue. As per usual she was elegant in her silence. The other members of her pack sat there eating their vampire parts. The one he assumed was her mate sat there glaring at him with fury.

The scar-faced being irked Janpier. He sneered, "What are you looking at? Have my glistening facial features caused you to forget your manners?" The scarred being made no movement save to glare.

Florence finished eating and thanked the loyal hunchback vamp. She was elegantly dressed with a ring on each finger and five bracelets on her right wrist. She wore one necklace with an ankh pendant. Her facial features matched her attire in its elegance, but she gave off a certain air of superiority.

With one hand pressed against the fork and another wrapped around her napkin, she smirked, "Oh dearest brother. No need to be ill mannered."

He stood up and flipped his plate, wincing in the process. "Who granted you permission to re-enter the city after abandoning my pack? Who gave you the authority to intervene at my meeting with the Crumble Pack? And who said you could tell my goddamn slave to go through the arduous task of cooking and seasoning the fallen vamps?"

He stood there breathing heavily with his fists clenched, "Finally, who told you to bring a pack of mangy mutts into my territory? Especially your mate! He has been seething to rip into my throat since the Crumble meeting."

Her sharp green eyes glowed, reminding him of his past, when she would rip into his flesh for fun, "I did. I need no other authority than my own." The mutts at the table smirked. Janpier took his cane and spun the head a click to the left.

Florence raised a finger and wagged it in the air, "Silly pup. I wouldn't do that if I were you. If you cause my pack pain, I will be forced to choose between you and them... and it would be ill-gotten to spill the blood of our gracious host. Perhaps you should use your words like papa taught us."

Janpier slammed the head of his cane against the table several times. "I want you all out! Get out of my castle."

Florence stood up and made her way towards her brother. Upon arrival she stood nose to nose with him each scowling, "You would cast out your only sister from the home she was raised in because of what? Sibling rivalry?" She twirled around, raising her hands, "Look at what you have accomplished. The rebuilding of our grand house name. You are recognized as an aristocrat and will soon be on the High Council. After the show of force we demonstrated, the Crumble family will think twice about stepping on our toes. Don't you see? We make a good team."

Janpier strengthened his posture. While taking short sharp breaths he mustered a few words. "Why return now?"

Florence smirked once again. "Now we're getting somewhere. You've decided to ask the important questions."

As he sat back in his jewel-encrusted chair, he sunk his head into his hands, "Have you come to take your place as the head of the household? Like Father always wanted?"

She nodded. "I suppose it is as simple as that. It is time for me to burden myself with the wants and needs of being a noble. I have spent so much time in obscurity that it seems a whole lifetime has passed me by."

Janpier pulled out several strands of his hair. "Is there no reprieve for me?" he said as he looked up at the ceiling. Florence and her pack erupted into laughter.

"What's so funny?"

She rubbed her younger brother's shoulder. "You're just as gullible as ever. I wouldn't be caught dead fraternizing with these so-called elite. They aren't fit to pick up my scat. You'd be the face of the pack during the day, while I, the face of the pack during the night. We're here for one reason and one reason only: unity."

Janpier raised an eyebrow. "Unity? Unity of what?"

Florence leaned forward, a rare smile revealing emerald canines, "Unity of all Lycanthrope kind—and you're going to assist, dearest brother." Mouth agape, he peered into her eyes as if he could see the future unfold.

Instinctively, he took to his knee and lowered his head, "What will you have me do?"

— 36 —
A PIN IN THE BALLOON

Zurie watched in silence as another name was crossed off her list. Catherine had decided that to live out her days as a vampire would be worse than death. While Catherine had pressed her sharp blade against her own throat, she had yelled, "The Cleric's Order will never die. You lot will find your demise in short order." With one last menacing glance at Zurie, she slid the weapon across her throat, spilling blood onto the sewer floor. As her body collapsed into the puddle of water, the iron scent of human blood filled Zurie's nostrils.

Lord Salem was the first to succumb to his thirst. The other members of the Red Hand watched as he feasted upon the body of the young cleric woman.

Zurie leaned back against the sewer walls. "She could have died a more honorable death."

Lord Salem paused momentarily, "She made her choice. What death more fitting for a cleric than amid the piss and shit that her kind has forced us into? You'll be wise to remember who the enemy is. I don't know who I dislike more: the brazen Clerics with their superior artifacts or the uppity lycanthropes posing as aristocrats."

Zurie curled her lips, "Just because you hate all clerics and all wolf shifters doesn't mean we have to stoop to their level. If we're supposed to be the superior race, shouldn't we provide them better deaths than they would give us?"

He crossed both his arms, "Since when did you grow a bleeding heart for our food source? The way you're talking, it's as if you feel bad that she is dead. Perhaps you had other motives for bringing her here." He squinted. "You're a simple-faced one, that you are. I suspect you wanted to turn her."

Zurie clenched her fists, "So what if I wanted to? We need more powerful vampires in our midst. Ones that know how to fight and are knowledgeable of the cleric's ways."

Lord Salem stomped his feet. "Never. No more new vampires will be created while I walk the muck that is this continent."

She clenched her teeth before speaking. "What power do you have to prevent vampires from being created?"

The thumb floated in between them. "As the middle finger of the Red Hand, Lord Salem is charged with damage mitigation. Our top priority is to revive the Vamp Lord. But the legends may very well be correct. We may be extinguishing the entire vampire race by reviving him from the second death. If that is the case, we don't want to add more vampires to the list."

Zurie's jaw dropped. *These weak-willed creatures. Damage mitigation? Yet they hold the keys to our liberation in their hands and they have kept it paused out of fear. How are they no different from me up until now? All this time I held the Red Hand and blood knights in reverence, only to find that they are the ones that are truly unworthy of my praise. I thought I was the one that could not live up to the lofty standards set before me when my own standards are the only ones I must meet. It's no wonder vampires in this continent are slaves and kicked about like playthings. Our leadership is faulty. To possess such power, yet to be kept back by fear. What a waste.*

With her hands balled into fists, she gazed at each member of the illustrious Red Hand. "How does one turn a human, anyways? I mean, as far as I know, my generation of vampire is the latest, and that was forty years ago. One day our bite ceased having such an effect on the humans."

Lord Salem took a step forward. "That is not something that you need to know."

She took a step forward.

As the two locked eyes, the index finger parted them. Brandishing one sword in each hand, he turned to Lord Salem. "Each of us must live by our code, for that is what keeps us from falling into the squalor that we have been thrust into. One thing I will not stand by is secrets amongst us. We are supposed to be the light that shines in the dark for all vampire kind. Had I known this was knowledge that you possessed, I would have inquired ages from whence I came."

Lord Salem's eyes intensified as he pondered his next move. He looked at the thumb, who donned an angry face.

Zurie broke the silence. "What if we only turn the humans who volunteer to become a creature of the night? If I'm not mistaken, there are several hundred humans who have been working with the Red Hand for various reasons. I'd take a guess and say that a large portion would relish at the idea of entering our ranks."

Lord Salem went silent for several moments until he nodded his approval. "I suppose that would be acceptable." He stuck out his tongue and pulled out a small dagger from his bootstrap. With one clean motion he severed the end of his tongue. He handed the slimy organ to Zurie, who curled her lips.

He motioned for her to eat it. She placed the severed tongue atop hers and leaned back. The organ traveled down her throat with ease as she swallowed it whole.

Gagging, she clasped her mouth, "There, I ate it. Now what?" The other three vampires of the Red Hand gazed at her, wide-eyed and mouths open. They erupted into laughter.

Heat formed around her face. She asked the question while already knowing the answer, "What the fang is so funny?"

The index finger removed his mask to reveal a hideous deformation of the mouth. "Can't believe you actually ate that. There is no way to turn a human. That ability dwindled soon after the second death of the Vampire Lord. When we revive him, it will either be the greatest thing to happen to us or the worst. When he first revives, he will be in a weakened state for many moons. It is best that we neutralize this lycanthrope threat first. In all honesty, a good laugh was required. We have been at a loss for ages without a pinky to poke at, since the thumb broke the last one."

So, I'm to be the butt end of their jokes in exchange for what? The privilege of being a Red Hand? I may not have met any blood knights more powerful, but I have met a few that were smarter, wiser, and more capable. This will not do... this will not do at all.

Lord Salem adjusted his helmet. "My plan is very simple. We simultaneously attack the lycanthropes individually during the day. Our day-strong rings will pose useful in this regard. Some will be in public while others will be in the confines of their own home. The transformation takes a lengthy amount of time during the day. That should give us ample time to cut them down where they stand. Some will be hesitant to transform if they are in public, which we will also use to our advantage. There are three major groups. The one's from..." Zurie turned around to see what had caught his attention. A blinding light piercing through the above sewer grating, followed by the removal of the stone manhole. The four members of the Red Hand, under the shroud of nothingness, walked towards the entrance of Sovereign City.

Zurie's quarters remained in the basement of the Red Hand castle. The small cavern leaked water that smelled like raw fish. A scent that would be bearable if not for her heightened senses. She groaned as she rummaged through the former pinky finger's things in search of artifacts. *Becoming a blood knight was supposed to bring me greater prosperity, but it seems the poverty gods favor me. I can barely afford to feed myself, much less my mighty steed.* She took stock of her valuables. The tongue ring that janpier's slave had procured for her made it easier for her to create, manipulate, and be in synch with her serpents, the cursed halberd that had taken many lives to date, and her beloved raptor. But above all, her natural ability to produce toxins, manipulate corrosive liquid, and communicate with serpents. All these had carried her far, farther than anyone could have imagined, but she was still poor. *Perhaps I should be grateful for what I have accomplished. From when I was first turned my sire left me for dead at the hands of my betrothed. Little did she know that I would one day become a member of the Red Hand.* She raised both her hands into the air, "Look at me now my great sire, are you not pleased?"

One day I will be face to face with my sire. I will cleave her down where she stands and strip her of her artifacts. The blur that was my turning experience has granted me clarity, and in that is my growth. I will achieve greater things because of my nature, not in spite of. To be the rarest of all the types of vampires is something I shall wield as a badge of honor. For I now realize the rest of the world does not know how to handle one of my ilk.

A memory dropped into Zurie's mind. *Lord Salem mentioned something about my breed or stock, something of that ilk. He must know something about such matters, but why has he kept quiet about my sire up to this point? My faith in these people dwindles with each passing night.* She placed her halberd on her person and summoned her precious serpents back to their resting places. While ascending the stairs to the ring finger's floor, she took one last look at the place that was given to her as a dwelling. *Perhaps one day this habitat will feel like home.* The next level was oddly vacant. The scent of honey still ran strong as she ventured to the next floor. Lord Salem's floor was also vacant. *Could they be having a meeting without me?* She knocked on the large doors to the index finger's section.

When the doors opened, she was met with the other four members of the Red Hand. Zurie clenched her fists. "Why was I not informed of a meeting?"

Lord Salem raised an eyebrow. "Oh, how odd... I told Honey Dew to inform you. He was supposed to tell you to come up from your... little dungeon there." The Hand members chuckled to themselves.

Honey Dew drank from his vase, "Hmm, was I? Perhaps I was? Well, you're here now." Zurie's eyes shifted into snake slits momentarily. *Death, death, death,* the serpents whispered. The four continued with their conversation.

Lord Salem handed out day-strong rings to each member of the Red Hand, "These rings are necessary for our success. When the time is ripe, we shall strike upon the..." Several of Zurie's snakes emerged from her palms. Lord Salem raised his hands while curling his lips, "Did you really have to do that during my speech? Now I must start over again."

She glanced at the serpents, who were dancing oddly. "Something's wrong. I think we've been infiltrated."

The thumb turned into an angry face. "None could ever bypass my illusion. I knew it was a mistake to let you in. Truth be told we only needed someone with popularity amongst the lesser vampires to improve our good name. It was dwindling after the actions of she who need not be mentioned. The fact that you stand in our presence should be good enough for you. To think you'd need to be included in meetings is laughable. But now you feel you have rights and a say? This I cannot stand for. Now be a good little toxin vampire and keep your toxic mouth shut." Zurie's eyes twitched violently as she assessed her situation. *The shadow vampire is one that is immune to physical attacks, but in return deals low physical damage, relying heavily on nightmare and fear-based attacks. Nothing I possess would harm such a creature. I must retreat... for now.*

With her fists clenched she spoke one last time in front of the Red Hand, "Maybe not today, maybe not tomorrow..."

Lord Salem interrupted her with his sharp tongue. "Would you just shut your mouth? You've embarrassed me enough as it is. Go back to your dungeon and we will call on you when it's time to fight. Know this: the only time a female blood knight is worth her weight is when she is fighting or fanging."

Just like that, the true nature of the Red Hand was revealed.

As she patrolled Sovereign City, her mind pondered many matters. *If we really have been infiltrated it will just be a matter of time before the clerics rush in here full force. Or perhaps the Lycans will do the deed themselves as payback for our failed attack on them. Maybe both. I suppose now would be a good time to breakdown into a heap of despair.*

To join the Red Hand, only to be relegated to a mere vanity prop. I will not live such a life. But what kind of life should I live? All I have ever dreamed and aimed for was to be a blood knight. I achieved that and I am neither satisfied nor happy. Then I entered the arena, where I still felt a void. Followed by the putrid toxicity of the Red Hand, rivaled only by my own venom. Is this truly the life I am destined to live? Am I foolish for even believing that I could find peace in these accolades? What is power without self-love? What is prosperity without family to share it with? What is respect without peace of mind?

These are my misgivings and mistakes. But now I must ask myself, is it too late for a toxin vampire such as myself?

A tapping on her shoulder caused her to turn around with her fangs protruding. A short, stocky human handed her a note from the steed master indicating that she should return to the steed shop immediately. As she rushed towards the steed shop, her stomach twisted. Her breath heaving, and dripping beads of sweat, she arrived.

There she was, her precious raptor, lying on the ground with two eggs by her side. As she clutched the body of her once-mighty steed all she could think of was: *Would that I could cry. The pain I feel, I'll never be able to show.*

The steed master lowered his head, "As you knew she was ill already, I was surprised that you didn't show up to check on her. She was tearing up a mighty storm during your absence."

Zurie raised her head, "What do you mean? This is the first I'm hearing that she was ill."

He raised an eyebrow, "That's odd. I had given several notes to Honey Dew. He said and I quote, "How ill-proposed. I'll see that they are delivered.""

She stood up exuding purple energy. While picking up one of the eggs she turned to the steed master and said, "I trust the other one will suffice as payment?" He nodded fervently. While marching towards the Red Hand castle, her mind swirled, but it was filled with one concept, *Death.* She went over battle scenarios and possibilities.

Not knowing what to expect of Honey Dew's abilities, she did know one thing. His stats said that he was vastly more powerful than she was. But none of that mattered. What mattered was principle. There were few things that Zurie Valentine could stand for in this treacherous world, but principle was one of them. With artifacts prepared and ready, she opened the door to her destiny. "Honey Dew. Where are you? Reveal yourself, you sweet-to-the-nose but foul-to-the-mind poor excuse for a blood knight."

Honey Dew twirled around in his sofa to reveal him licking his honey dipped fingers. "How perverse. Words like that ought to get a little girl killed. But I'm hungry, so I shall let you flap your gums." Zurie stormed towards the bulbous creature. She catapulted her clenched fist into the golden vase that Honey Dew carried wherever he went. The vase split in two, leaking honey all over his body. Eyes blurred a honey yellow, his bare feet touched the floor for the first time since joining the Red Hand.

The other members of the Red Hand emerged from their floors to watch the battle. Honey Dew clapped both his hands together, connecting a glob of honey. Bees emerged from his mouth and belly button. With their sharp stingers pointed towards her, they launched forth a devastating attack. A serpent emerged, absorbing the attack, then disappearing in a puff of purple smoke.

Zurie charged forward with a serpent on each side and her halberd aimed at Honey Dew's massive head. He caught the halberd with his bare hands while being bitten from the left and the right by the venomous serpents. As they poured venom into his body, honey spewed out back into them. The honey hardened, turning them into golden statues. With a twisting of his body, Honey Dew swung Zurie into the air, relieving her of her mighty halberd. Taking the weapon and dashing it to the side, he opened his mouth to release a swarm of wasps. They initiated forward, doing dazzling displays of acrobatics as they dodged the piercing snake attacks that came their way. Zurie inhaled and released a massive puff of toxic gas. The purple gas dropped the wasps, causing Honey Dew to close his eyes in agony.

Upon landing on her feet, she directed a blast of toxic energy at Honey Dew. The attack landed, causing him to kick and squirm in pain. As he dropped to the floor, he turned himself into a ball of honey. While recovering her halberd, she watched as the massive ball of honey glowed bright yellow for a few moments before shattering into several pieces. What emerged was none of human, bee, nor vampire, but something only the most powerful of blood knights ever achieved: an ascended form that embodied what it meant to be a creature of the night.

Its wings were that of a bee, while it had three stingers—all aimed at Zurie. Its stubby arms and legs made it look almost humorous, though this creature far surpassed The Terror. She shuddered as she thought about The Terror and how she had to dig deep within her essence to send it to its second death. *A weakness. It must have a weakness. Bees. Bees have five eyes. Perhaps that means they will be more receptive to vision-based attacks.* With her arms tense she closed her eyes and summoned the longest snake. "King cobra, I ask that you grace me with your presence. I need your assistance."

Her tongue ring glowed bright purple as the summoning took effect. A circle surrounded her while several markings appeared. In a puff of purple smoke, a large purple king cobra wrapped around her, guarding her. Their minds melded.

Three stingers nearly struck the serpent. Zurie twirled in the air, moving as one with the serpent as they attacked in sync. The tail whipped back, careening across the back of the bee monstrosity. While dancing in slow, rhythmic fashion, the eyes of the cobra and Zurie locked with Honey Dew. The three swayed back and forth repeatedly, neither wanting to give up the mental battle. Slowly Zurie's eyes closed. She shook her head to snap into focus. Honey Dew's eyes closed next as the rhythmic humming swayed him to sleep. With his eyes firmly shut, he tumbled towards the floor, creating a large crater upon landing.

Zurie stormed forward with bloodlust in her eyes, ready to strike the final blow upon her adversary. Just when she was about to land the killing blow, she sensed a massive army swarm into the city. She lowered her weapon and took off Honey Dew's day-strong ring. The rest of the Red Hand stood before her as she was about to open the gates to the outside.

Lord Salem was the first to speak. "Where do you run off to? It's best if we stay here and defend the castle."

She curled her lips. "How can your selfish words fall off your lips with such ease? It seems it's truly the policy of the Red Hand to secure their own selves before that of their city. You are no different than the High Council and the people we call our enemies. I have a list to finish, and for now that is good enough for me. Just know that I put a curse on all of you and your destinies."

— 37 —

TACTICS

Although it was nighttime, the bazaar was bustling with activity. The street vendors peddled their exotic fruits from their tents while the clerics instilled order. Janpier could see out into the distance a child plucking a star apple from one of the foreign vendors. He smirked. *There was once upon a time I had to employ such tactics.* Risking the hand penalty, he would appropriate whatever he could get his hands on. For those who have experienced hard times, it is their greatest fear to return to such poverty. At least so it was for Janpier.

He tapped his sister on the shoulder and pointed to Alistair Crumble at a nearby table eating couscous royale: a rare couscous dish served with lamb, chicken and meatballs from Africanus. He was accompanied by his first wife, who often wore his belt of enchantment, one of the most powerful artifacts known to the continent of Europia. Alongside his first wife were his brothers from the high council and his most esteemed guards. As he munched away, his eyes solely focused on his meal, it was clear to Janpier that Alistair had grown soft. The Alistair of old never would have eaten in public, nor would he have left the confines of his grand castle without at least an accompaniment of twenty.

Ultimately, he wouldn't have done it on a predictable day each week.

Florence grimaced, "It truly has been a long time since I have spoken to him in this form. It would seem Father Time has not been his most pleasant supporter." Janpier's body tensed up as Alistair raised from his seat and beelined towards them, causing several bazaar patrons to redirect their path.

Upon his arrival he spat at Florence's feet before redirecting his attention to Janpier, "Does she follow you everywhere you go now? Who knows what depravities have befallen my beloved Catherine? I extended an olive branch to you by inviting you to the transformation ceremony and you repay me by bringing..." He surveyed Florence from top to bottom. "Her."

Janpier took one step towards Alistair with a mild expression. "It's a new dawn, Alistair. Florence has returned, and she brings with her great news from the south. A way to unite all Lycan kind, starting with our three packs."

Both Florence and Alistair laughed.

Alistair pointed at Janpier. "You don't count as a pack. You're a mere omega posing as a sigma. You think just because you have operated on your own and have accomplished a few minor deeds that you have the right to call yourself an alpha? You were always at the bottom of the pack, and you will always be at the bottom of the pack. What is this false talk of unity that you speak of? I have enjoyed one good laugh today; I implore you to bring forth another."

Florence cleared her throat. "We both know..."

Alistair spat on the floor before her feet once again. "I don't want...*her* to speak again, or this brief conversation is done."

Florence snarled, showing her emerald fangs.

Alistair took a step back. "It cannot be."

She beamed them once again. "Yes, it can. I tracked down the one lycan who could unite all our kind and killed him. He was hiding in the south, deep into Africanus territory. But I triumphed, which granted me the emerald eyes and canines of the True Alpha. I can do things that would make your father crawl out of his tomb. But above all, I can now grant sacred powers to all those in my pack, including quicker and painless transformations during the day and control over our beastly nature during said transformation. That old cripple was a fool. He only used his powers for him and his kin. I plan on using my powers for all lycan kind. Take the knee, and we will unite every single lycan on the continent. Imagine a world where we don't have to hide in the shadows like rodents. Imagine one where you can walk around in your free skin and enjoy the sunlight across your brow."

Janpier nodded his head fervently. He stretched his hand out. "We can mend burned bridges in whole new ways."

Alistair turned to his first wife, who was snarling. Then he looked to his brothers, who both had their fists clenched, "And what about the High Council? I mean, in such a world where the lycan is out in the open, who would need the High Council, correct? While we're at it, why don't we just eliminate most of the humans and the vamps?" He waved them off, "I have heard this talk from riff raff pups who have wandered into my territory in the past. The city is already mine. What need do I have to bow down to you? For ideals and glory?"

Florence clenched her fists, "It would be in your best interest to side with us now, to save yourself the trouble of being dragged down to your knees later."

Alistair chuckled. "I have an army at my fingertips. I have my pack, and I have the council in the palm of my hands. I can wipe you out with a single snap of my fingers. In fact, I have a little cleric excursion in progress as we speak. Could you imagine? There was an entire... well I wouldn't call it a city but an entire little village of free vamps living in the underground sewer system. Hidden away from sight. But they are being wiped up now, and if you push your luck—well... that goes without saying." Alistair revealed his rose quartz canines, "They may not be the fabled emeralds, but remember the ever-sweet rose bears sharp thorns underneath." He pushed past both Janpier and Florence, making way for himself and the group with him.

A few moments after they had left, Florence nodded her head slowly towards one of her pack members drinking in a tent nearby. Janpier sighed heavily, "Now what?"

She responded mildly, "I expected things to go like this, hence why I had the rest of the pack infiltrate his castle. By now they would have cleared him of his most powerful artifacts. It is only a warning blow, a reminder that no one is invulnerable. Furthermore, I took the liberty of sending a few new recruits to visit his smelting facilities and shut those down as well. People like that only understand one thing: the pocket approach. You hit them in their pockets, and they will do whatever it is they need to fill them."

"The final plan comes tonight, when we launch a full-scale attack on his safe house, the place he is most likely to reside in after today's theft. Naturally like a fool, he extended his resources by sending a large portion of the cleric army to eradicate the vampires and their blood knights. My shrewdness should be of no surprise, brother. I have foreseen victory long before my claws re-emerged upon this soil." Janpier gazed at his older sister for a few moments. *Just as diabolical and conniving as ever. But, as always... effective.* He shuddered at the thought of any man who would choose to lay with her after knowing her nature.

Their pack swarmed the safe house of Alistair Crumble. It was a grey castle with wards against vampires, but nothing to stop a flurry of lycan. Florence was in front in full wolf form. Her emerald fangs glowed bright green. Her howl was blood-curdling. It echoed throughout the snow filled region, making it seem as if they had twice their numbers. This was not a surprise attack. She wanted Alistair to believe there was no chance at survival if he fought.

With the stolen artifacts, she had managed to pay off several members of the High Council, as well as high ranking officials in the Cleric's Order. The knowledge that Alistair wasn't very well-liked played to her advantage. When they had arrived, most of his human guards fled at the sight of them. Janpier inhaled the cold air, allowing it to fill his large lungs. He gazed at the pine trees filled with ravens. *They smell it... the distinct scent of death.* Wearing legendary armor for the first time in wolf form, he howled to the moon. His eyes glowed green like his pack leaders. His legs shook from excitement as the extra speed and strength coursed through his veins. The pack waited on all fours for the signal to approach. In a situation like this where one wolf pack was backed into a corner, there was always dissent. Some would choose to run while some would choose to fight.

But Florence was a tactician of the utmost degree. Her prey was never left with an option. The Crumble Pack would run, but they wouldn't get far.

The first wolf opened the gate, dashing forward. It was one of Crumbles cousins, followed by a second, then a third. Florence let out a high-pitched howl, indicating for her pack to attack. They descended upon their prey as any pack of beasts should. Within minutes, Janpier had caught up with the first member of the Crumble pack. They were fast, but not nearly fast enough for the enhanced speed of the Florentine Pack. With a swipe of his arm he clipped the leg of the first lycan, causing him to stumble. Their orders were not to let a single one live to see the morning sun.

Alistair's scent caught Janpier's attention just as he was about to pounce on the wounded cousin. Seeing several other members of his pack arrive, he left the wounded cousin to them. With every muscle in his arms and legs working to maximum efficiency, he bolted towards Alistair and his first wife, who could be seen slinking through the gate in the opposite direction from the rest of this pack. *A poor excuse for a man is a poor excuse for a pack leader. Using his family as a diversion is no sign of true leadership.* The sparkling belt of enchantment seemed to beckon him. While charging forward, he was joined by his sister and her mate, who had also picked up on the scent.

Janpier barreled into Alistair as his sister pounced on the neck of his first wife. Florence's mate simply circled the group, ensuring victory. Alistair's fate was sealed. He assumed a crouched position as he approached Janpier on all fours. Janpier snarled, standing up on his two feet and howling at the moon. The howl called the other lycans to do the same.

His most hated enemy now had his bare stomach turned towards him. *What a repulsive sight. To think that he would grovel like a mere pup. Could he possibly expect mercy after all the agony he has caused me? After all the hate?* He placed his front paw on the stomach of his foe, applying severe pressure. As he leaned in, he looked into the groveling eyes of Alistair Crumble. With one swipe of his other paw, he slit the throat of the once wealthiest aristocrat on the continent. He turned to his sister to see she had ripped out the heart of her adversary and was about to consume it. Then he noticed her mate growling as he approached Janpier on two feet in lycan form. With his arms raised, he jumped on Janpier, who dodged the attack while transforming to lycan form.

As the two locked claws, their eyes met. This was a battle to decide who would be Florence's second in command. Traditionally in any pack it would go to the Alpha male and female pairing, but because Janpier had made claim to territory in the city, he was seen as a sigma who take over leadership at any moment. All the things he was taught as a young pup came rushing back to him. *I must make him submit, if I kill him then Florence will be forced to avenge her fallen mate. But if I lose, I will be relegated to the bottom of the pack... a mere omega.*

While maintaining eye contact, Janpier kicked him in the stomach, denting his armor. He dashed backwards, granting himself some space to think. This was a well-seasoned lycan who was slightly larger, but not faster. He focused his lycan energy into a ball of pure green aura that surrounded both his claws. With his enhanced claws, he pushed forward onto his sister's mate, who had chosen to enhance his jaw. With a front flip, Janpier landed on his opponent, whose teeth grazed his neck, breaking the skin. This was followed by tossing Janpier into a pine tree, snapping it in two. Breathing heavily, he arose to his feet. As the wound regenerated, he gazed at his unscathed opponent. *This foe will not falter unless it is with one blow.* With all of his energy focused on his left claw, he managed to extend them into one sharp blade. Florence howled her approval while her mate took a step backwards.

Janpier's opponent diverted his energy across his entire body, allowing him further protection from damage. Growing larger, he charged towards Janpier who now stood in a defensive position. The wild unruly movements of the other lycan strained his eyes, but he kept steady waiting for the right moment to strike. His sister's mate latched himself onto Janpier's arm, ripping flesh as it tore through his armor like parchment.

But to her mate's detriment, Janpier's enhanced claw was already lodged inside his chest, inches away from his heart. A twist caused him to bellow out in pain. The mate lowered his head and whimpered softly. It was over.

KISS OF DEATH

She held her bleeding stomach with one hand while carrying her halberd in the other. As she struggled to breathe, she leaned against one of the many wooden structures that lined the vampire community. While glancing down, her eyes intensified. *Why isn't it healing? Curse that Oko-Iku. Of all the clerics I had to run into, my luck would bring me to him.* As her eyesight started to fade, she gazed out into the distance. The vampire community that was Sovereign City had one entrance and exit that she knew of—a failure of a design if there ever was one. The exit was blocked by a group of high-ranking clerics each dressed in their white-and-blue armor with a cross in the center. To make matters worse they had brought one of the sunbeam cannons from the arena.

Zurie slammed her fist against the wall. "This isn't good." Struggling to rise, she made her way towards the exit. *If Oko-Iku catches up to me in this condition, I will certainly meet my demise.* While inching her way towards freedom, she was met with a flurry of vamps running from the clerics. Some were being wiped out quickly, while others were tortured for information on the Red Hand. So far, she was lucky enough not to encounter anyone else on her path. The few vamps that fought back had had their hands and legs nailed to buildings.

This was a massacre. *Can the difference in artifacts truly make that much of a difference? A foolish question if there ever was one. These clerics, with their superior weapons and armor mixed with their training, wipe the floor with the average vampire.* But she knew deep down that it was more than that. The average vamp, through decades and for some even centuries of servitude, had become cowardly and submissive. Their once-inherent virility had dwindled to mere specks, especially since the death of their Vamp Lord. Without a clear leader the vampires and blood knights are nothing more than specks at the bottom of a clerics boot. Breathing heavily, Zurie dropped to the floor a few buildings from the exit. Blood continued to leak from her wound. *Curses, I can't meet the second death yet. I have too many names to cross off my list. But above all... I will live to see the day when my people are free to make decisions for themselves. Where we are no longer forced to live a life of servitude under the might of an oppressive force. I have a new goal now. A new criterion for existence, one that under this night of demise I will see take seed. Every ounce of resistance we have mustered has been torn down. Every glimmer of hope wiped out. But still we will rise. I will make sure of it.*

A blinding light flashed, followed by a beam of concentrated energy. The beam shone past Zurie, sweltering the ground beside her. It came within inches of introducing her to the second death. The seared bodies of her fellow blood knights caused her to stand up fervently. *We will not be eliminated like roaches, scattered. If we're going to die, then we should die with one last charge.* She bit her tongue, causing blood to leak from her lips.

After spitting on the ground before her, she spoke the words to summon her most troublesome of serpents: "I need your assistance, one who speaks when none can hear. One who hears when none can speak." As if made from the soil itself, a large rattlesnake spewed from the ground. It coiled into a ball and lashed out at her, causing her to grab it by the neck before it could strike her. The snake rattled its tail rhythmically, causing words to flash across her vision. *You've summoned me for what purpose?*

With her hands firmly latched onto the head of the snake she focused her thoughts. *I need you to connect me to every vampire, blood knight, and Red Hand that still draws breath. Are you capable of doing such a thing?*

The rattlesnake shook its tail violently. *Of course. The real question is whether you can handle such a task?*

She glanced down at her oozing wound and nodded.

As she mind-melded with the rattlesnake, a sharp, piercing sensation entered her ears as the loud rattling of the serpent caused her ears to bleed. As she sat there in meditative stance, bleeding out onto the floor, she could feel the rattlesnake wrap itself around her stomach, closing the wound. Her mind drifted to a land far South filled with all kinds of strange beasts. A land where rules and regulations were often a second thought, and life was constantly on the brink of its existence. A world where a cunning and cerebral entity could find freedom bound only by their own hand. The deserts were vast while the rivers thundered, but it was a land that contained hope.

Just as the vision was about to end, the rattlesnake transmitted the words that would spark an entire generation of vampires to rally against their oppressors. Words to finally unite the remaining creatures of the night and provide them with the courage they so desperately needed to break through the barricade.

Africanus, the last salvation.

With scales covering her festering wound, Zurie stood in front of the sunbeam cannon. Her hand wrapped around her cursed halberd while she caressed the egg of her raptor. She gazed, smirking, into the eyes of the clerics that stood before her. Their faces were stern and resolute, but their hearts filled with fear. It didn't take heightened senses to know that they were vastly outnumbered, outpowered, and above all outwilled.

It was Iku-Oko who stood to lead this company of men. The dark purple skulls of death floated around his body, whispering blasphemous things. His once-white cloak now screamed the demise of all who stood before him. Instead of a golden apple in his right hand, he now held a skull. This was the reaper in his full form: the one who has come to take the lives of all those who defy him. He raised his scythe into the air. "On this night, history will be made. We are all that stand between our glorious capital city and these demonic creatures of the night. The vampire scum shall not pass! I urge every one of you to scream out the profanities that you have been conditioned to whisper in the comforts of your own company. Scream them loud and clear for all to hear, and charge my weapon. I shall redirect the karmic energy so that you are safe." Immediately the crowd of more than four hundred clerics began shouting things so vile and gruesome, they would make one's grandmother ill.

As the air around them became heavier, Zurie realized that this attack was not to be taken lightly. She raised her halberd and shouted to launch their attack. But it was too late. Iku-Oko's soul, dressed in a black cloak and wielding his scythe, appeared over the heads of over four hundred random vampires.

A menacing grin appeared across Iku-Oko's face as he turned with both arms raised high into the air. Purple aura surrounded his body in a flurry of a storm. It then covered his body adding further protection from harm.

Zurie screamed, "No, this cannot be. I won't let you." She charged towards him but was held back by one of her boa constrictors. She glanced back to see the vampires who had his soul above their heads struggling to hold onto their own. They kicked and clawed, but to no avail. By the time Iku-Oko lowered his hands to the ground, his soul image had removed the soul of each marked vampire. Their bodies collapsed. Iku-Oko's soul image took its scythe and slit the throat of each vampire that had their soul removed, causing a multitude of colored orbs to escape. The orbs flew towards Iku-Oko's scythe and into the mouths of the skulls.

The company of clerics cheered and bellowed a deafening war cry.

Zurie could feel her knees quiver. *His weapon drains the essence of all those that fall to his blade, temporarily granting him newfound abilities.* She glanced at her cursed halberd. *But if his cursed weapon is anything like my own, he will be drained of his power quickly. Someone needs to make him waste his aura while dodging his attacks. Someone... like me.*

Her arms tensed up as she pointed her halberd in his direction. "Iku-Oko, you're all that stands in the way of my liberation. You will fall on this eve."

With purple aura escaping his eyes and mouth, the deathly figure that was Iku-Oko spoke. "What happened to Catherine? I found her body in the sewers being eaten by the rats."

Zurie lowered her head. "She...she chose to take her own life, rather than become a creature of the night."

"A worthy end for a worthy woman. But to be left amongst the piss and the shit? She deserved better. How fortunate for you that I must offer you a similar option. This uprising will end here, and you lot will go back to your duties, or you will suffer the consequences ten times over."

Zurie clenched her teeth as she removed her armor to reveal the bandages that Oko-Iku had given her many moons ago. "Death will come for you on this evening," she said. As she removed the seemingly normal grey bandages, they dropped to the ground, creating large craters.

While both adversaries took their battle stances, it was an errant vampire who made the first move, launching himself upon Iku-Oko, only to be consumed by the dark aura.

Zurie stepped forward with her halberd aimed for the heart. Blocking the attack with ease, he leaned in forward and slammed his forehead into hers, cracking the bone. Dazed, she stumbled backwards as serpents sprung forth from her palm. While cleaving the serpents, Iku-Oko pushed forward, enhanced by the souls of countless vampires. Upon gathering her senses, Zurie diverted her opponent's attention with a massive boa constrictor that surrounded Iku-Oko. She heard bones cracking as he let out a low sigh. Dodging the errant blows of random fighting clerics, she jumped into the air to deal a killing blow onto the former Orisha known as the Dark Horse.

Within inches of meeting his demise, a skeleton crawled from Iku-Oko's mouth blocking the attack and throwing Zurie into the distance. She landed on a fighting vampire, snapping his neck instantly. The skeleton grew skin and clothes to become Iku-Oko in full form. Frowning, he twirled his scythe around, eviscerating the bowels of the vamps he passed on his way to her. Dark purple aura surrounded him in a tornado that shot towards her.

Zurie managed to dodge the deadly attack at the last moment, only to be swept by an upper cut to the jaw. Blood leaked from her dislocated jaw. Iku-Oko gazed into her eyes as he gripped her pulsating face. Squeezing tight, he spoke. "I am death."

With a flash of light, two blades swung down to sever Iku-Oku's arms. He bellowed in agony as he backed off. With eyes of thunder he redirected his attention to a new adversary.

The index finger struck an awkward pose before turning to Zurie. His body was riddled with severe wounds. It was a miracle that he managed to stay conscious, "It seems I will meet my end here. But at the very least, I must aid you in your endeavors. I want you to reach into my right pocket. If Africanus is your destination, then you are the rightful carrier.

Zurie reached into his pocket only to see his head severed with one single strike. Iku-Oko had his scythe in his teeth while bones began to grow from the stubs. She managed to slip the contents into the mouth of one of her serpents. Upon regenerating his left arm, Iku-Oko dashed forward, leaving a trail of dark purple aura. He raised his scythe above his head.

Zurie sprinted forward with her halberd aimed for the neck. *I only have one opportunity. I cannot miss my chance to glow. If he dodges left, victory... if he dodges right...* Once within range she threw her weapon at Iku-Oko, causing him to dodge to the left just as she thrust her entire body there. With both hands wrapped around his head, she placed her lips on his, filling him with all the toxins she could muster. His veins protruded, purple against the darkness of his skin. His body was paralyzed in excruciating agony as she gave him a last parting kiss.

Stumbling to her feet, she managed to speak, "No... I am death."

The End

We should not fear death, for it comes for us all. We should fear a life not lived—for not everyone gets to be alive. – Negus Lamont

AUTHOR BIO

My mind is a chaotic place to dwell. The dark thoughts that clamor for freedom spill out onto the pages of art. You have entered the mind of a bipolar author. Many have inquired as to why I bother to write in the first place. Some say it is a dying art form, while others claim it is a waste of time if I want to become successful. Truth be told, I write because that is what I have been called to do. Mental illness is a topic that still has a stigma attached to it, and I wish to aid in the removal of said stigma. My novel The Unworthy Blood Knight from A Tale of Vampires, Clerics, and Aristocrats is my next step towards that. Diving into the depths of one's abyss is the best way to heal for all those involved. It is my greatest wish that you continue with me on this journey. There is more wisdom to be revealed and more healing to be done.

Visit my personal website and sign up to my e-mail list to receive entertaining/ inspirational short stories, epic e-books, and exclusive illustrations.

E-mail List Signup
https://neguslamont.com/lies-of-the-abyss/

E-mail: neguslamont@gmail.com

OTHER WORK + REVIEW

If you made it this far, I hope you had a wonderful experience. It is my greatest joy to bring entertainment and knowledge to those who desire it. It would mean the world to me if you left an honest review of my novel *The Unworthy Blood Knight* on Amazon. Reviews help me as the author create better content for you the reader.

Additionally, feel free to check out my other work in the same series. All available on Amazon and other major retailers.

1. The Undisputed Blood Knight – A prequel which focuses on a young Althalos, and the rise of Lord Salem and The Vamp Lord. This novelette is action packed and fast paced. The novelette is free with an e-mail sign up. Follow the link to receive.

    https://neguslamont.com/lies-of-the-abyss/

2. The Unwelcome Blood Knight – Is the sequel to this novel which follows Zurie Valentine on her journey throughout Africanus. A hostile continent ruled by a deified/ascended family known as the Orisha. Continue to enthrall yourself in a story about death, treachery, magic and mayhem while deepening your connection with Zurie as she leads an entire army. It will be released Spring 2020.

www.ingramcontent.com/pod-product-compliance
Lightning Source LLC
Chambersburg PA
CBHW030426120726

47903CB00003B/827